PRAISE FOR M

BECAUSE *ji*

"I thoroughly, thoroughly enjoyed this book. I found it to be entertaining, informative and totally engrossing. I laughed, I cried, I marvelled at Marni's tenacity and undeniable strength of character and her commendable sense of loyalty. Reading this book, at times, scared the hell out of me - her excellent writing ability and choice of words gave me a sense of being there on that antique submarine chaser, Sondra, and experiencing all the trauma and disappointment. Not to mention the party times! I must add that I often hate telling people that I will critique their writing for fear of not liking it and feeling an overwhelming sense of disappointment. In this case, it was quite the opposite..........well done Marni!"

—Don Douglas

"I did not want this story to end. Not only is this book a beautifully written tale of exciting adventure, it touches on the complexity of relationships in a sophisticated and romantic way. Through the telling of her tale, Marni not only describes her escapades and romances, but she guides the reader through her journey of self-discovery—a wonderful combination for a great read. I know nothing of life at sea, and neither did Marni, but she had the drive to take the risk and learned it all. Her writing is both subtle and poignant; the strength and beauty of her characters and their tales are mesmerizing. This book will have you laughing and crying many times."

—Elizabeth H. Tilley

"*Because We Could* is one of the most interesting and up books I have read in a long time. Interesting, not only because of the story itself, but also because of the author's use of a variety of forms of writing. She has combined poetry, vignettes, play format and photos within the body of her work—all of which has greatly enhanced the reader's proximity to the characters and involvement in the action. Up, because it is fun and fast moving and does not rely on sensationalism or horror to keep us glued to the plot. I imagine that this novel would please just about anyone that dares to take the adventure with Marni."

—Chris Davidson

BECAUSE *We Could*

A Memoir
by
Marni Craig

*"Some years ago—never mind how long precisely—
having little or no money in my purse, and nothing
particular to interest me on shore, I thought I would sail
about a little and see the watery part of the world."*

−H. MELVILLE (Moby Dick)

RIVERHEAD FREE LIBRARY
330 COURT STREET
RIVERHEAD NY 11901

Copyright 2014 by Marni Craig

All rights reserved. No part of this publication may be reproduced or transmitted in any form or by any means, electronic or mechanical, including photocopy, recording, or any information storage and retrieval system, without permission in writing from the copyright owner.

Edition 3.3

ISBN 978-0-9936819-0-5

DEDICATION

For David Richard Keller
aka
"Crazy David"

.

ACKNOWLEDGMENTS

. . . to Fené Cartlidge and E. Ferrell—thank you for gently guiding me through the experience of learning to let go—to sit back with a glass of wine and actually enjoy watching someone rip apart your precious novel. Your devotion, insight and artistic talent helped me transform the magic of *Sondra's* and my journey into Canadian folklore.

. . . to my nautical editors who took me back over the waves of time to the open ocean with its many terms and rules that I had forgotten. A special thanks to Frazer McKee, Spud Roscoe and Marc-André Morin—WWII Naval Historians who connected me with the history of *Sondra's* sisters, The Fairmile submarine chasers.

. . . to Kate Greenaway, my copy editor, who did not question the word *foretaste* but nailed me on so many others.

. . . to my steamy inspiration (you know who you are).

. . . to my friends and family members that suffered through initial chapters, offering up inspirational thoughts that kept me going when the going got rough—and it did.

. . . to the many cafés from Panama to Canada to Europe to California—where, on comfy couches, I was served coffee with a side order of shine, noise and colorful hubbub that allowed me to focus inward.

. . . and finally to you, my readers, for taking this adventure with me through twenty-foot seas and twenty-foot love affairs—back to that unique era, the 70's, where we did more than ever before or since, because we could.

Thank you all!

CONTENTS

1

THE END ~ THE END ~ THE END

Key West Harbor, Florida
June, 1980

*"Life expands or contracts in
direct proportion to one's courage."*
-ANAÏS NIN

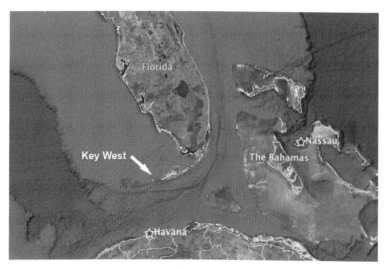

Key West, Florida

IT was the last time I would ever see the light of a Key West dawn through my galley's open porthole. Like a searchlight, it crept slowly across the round cherry wood captain's table illuminating used tissues and my beat-up thermal coffee mug. The rays reached the table's edge and fell over onto the significant props in this suspended drama. I knew David's eyes would likely follow the same path when he woke up. I guessed that he would be only mildly surprised (and perhaps annoyed) to see the two small mildewed duffle bags between my feet. He would be certain the bags contained none of the things important to me—no glittering azure drums, no diving gear or fishing rod, no piece of my beloved floating home.

And no David.

Leaving him had become routine, but in the past, it was simply my knapsack and a break from his hard-ass ways with a sanctioned fling. Lured by longings for our enthralling lifestyle, I had always returned. This time was different. I was running to avoid irreparable tragedy. I wouldn't be back.

I reflected on how much I'd changed during my five years with David—morphing from a fleshy, insecure, naïve girl of twenty-five to a buff, sure-footed woman and damn good first mate, engineer and registered owner of a 112-foot wooden warship. I'd adopted the truism that every turn in one's life abounds with opportunities and that just about anything we aspire to is possible. I was proud of what I'd become and I had my vessel *Sondra* to thank for it. Everything about this boat was serendipitous, even to the end.

It started with David, one of Canada's most creative and successful young entrepreneurs and media-favorite party boy, receiving me in his private office and asking me out on a date. I hooked up with David for what he offered—adventure, the good life—and I got so much more than I anticipated. Nothing about the final departure was going to be easy. This lifestyle and I had become one, each defining the other along the way.

Listening to the water slapping softly against the hull, I brought my weary eyes into focus in the break of day's light and began to absorb what I was giving up.

Those rare, red mahogany walls studded with copper rivets: It had taken me a year of tenacity in confined conditions to torch and scrape the layers of stubborn military paint from the entire interior of this vintage submarine chaser. During those months, David was often heard saying, "She has the patience of Job." Now, he was more likely to be heard saying, "She has the tenacity of a goat!"

The galley, my exclusive domain: I decapitated and gutted goliath groupers as long as my torso, pounded conch into submission and whipped up my famous Canadian Bloody Caesars.

The big brass portholes which time had covered in verdigris: Over my years on board, they had kept out North Atlantic winter squalls, let in tropical breezes, and vented alluring rock n' roll riding on whiffs of marijuana and exotic cooking.

The old, black-iron Franklin stove: I had so many fond memories of winter evenings back in raw-cold Nova Scotia, David and I snuggled up on our makeshift bed after a hard day of renovating, dreaming of what lay ahead. We had no clue. Our first fire-cozy romance giving way to panic as we realized our creosote-soaked firewood had over-heated the woodstove to a red-hot hazard. Suddenly our 112-foot ship looked more like 112 feet of kindling, sending us rushing for towels soaked in icy seawater. It was just one of the many times the story had almost ended before it began.

The companionway in the middle of the room: I couldn't help but grin at the thought of the hundreds of times I'd heard, "Holy Fuck!" and "Wow Man!" and "Oh My God!" coming from guests as they cautiously backed down those tricky angled

3

stairs with their skinny steps, wide eyes taking in the living quarters of our hippie conversion. How jazzed I felt when I mastered speedy front-facing descents and how pleased I was with myself when, at David's insistence, I could finally do ten chin-ups off the back of one of the steps.

I turned in my chair to look through the open bulkhead door that led into the main living area. How many memories I had made in this room! I gazed at the spare propellers and thought of our first open-ocean crossing, nasty twenty-foot seas and me on my hands and knees in the doorway trying not to throw up. Next to the props was the patched torpedo hole. Hard to believe our *Sondra* was once a fighter for the Canadian Navy. Under our watch, half the salon had become a dance floor with an impressive array of instruments: David's Hammond B3 organ, full Ludwig drum set, an acoustic guitar, a sound system taller than I was and a basket heaped with rhythm toys. My mind drifted back to my favorite night on this party boat, the get-together for paying guests on our first commercial disaster "The Bum's Cruise to the Bahamas." The boat rocked with live reggae and we danced between the two sets of woofers and tweeters that were powerful enough to rustle the girls' geometric-patterned skirts. It was a hilarious pairing of Canadians and Bahamians—white chicks trying to follow the lead of black Gumby guys.

No matter what my future life would bring—be it a new career, a new boyfriend, going back to university, or some other yet unthought-of iteration—the standard of "spectacular" had been set. Although a tall order for my destiny, I wasn't intimidated by this thought. After all, I'd already been part of a formula car racing team and a crewmember on this ocean-going vessel. *Bring it on, Life.*

The ship began to yaw through slack tide, and I shifted to wondering how long David might have been plotting the changes that had driven me to pack my things. It probably started with the blow to his ego from empty pockets. He never was able to accept not being in the limelight as "Crazy David, the 70's T-shirt King of Canada" and not having wads of forgotten money scattered throughout his wardrobe.

Or maybe it started when the Key West Cubans came

sniffing around the boat a few months ago. He loved it when they chauffeured him off alone in their tinted-glass black cars to the flamingo pink mid-range hotels. Funny how it never dawned on those machismos that the bikini-clad blonde they left behind wasn't just eye candy but the boat's registered owner. In the end, as I'd always suspected, it made no difference anyway. David with his grandiose plans would stay with *Sondra,* and I would leave with the responsibilities of ownership.

I began mumbling out loud. Anger and despair were in my voice and my eyes welled up again. "How the hell did this happen, David? Weeks ago, when we pulled up anchor, happiness was everywhere. Even our frickin' hair was happy! Just the two of us and our sweet cat Rhett and *Sondra* cruising from Key West through the Bahamas. So slowly. All of our favorite spots. Making love in the moonlight. We had it all—a beautiful movable home, three months' holidays every year, a good lifestyle in the Caribbean—what more could you want?"

It had been years since I'd had the feeling of being powerless. His determination to lead us into danger, with his deaf ears and often insulting tongue, left me no option but to pack up and head back to Canada. This was the end.

Me in Nassau

2

RUNNING

Key West to Toronto
June, 1980

"At the end of a long, long day, there is not much more to say
than, 'Love, so glad I met you.'"
-ROYAL WOOD

SLUMPING in my chair, I was waiting for David to wake up. Clad only in white Fruit of the Looms, he ducked his sinewy, lanky frame through the bulkhead into the galley area. His disheveled, ZZ Top mane and beard covered most of his crimson, pockmarked face. He looked hung over, exhausted, older than his thirty-five years. Stopping short on his path to coffee, I could see he was taking in the scene surrounding me, especially my bags.

We locked eyes for a long, quiet moment, the strength of our separate decisions drawing us apart into separate futures. I searched his face, hoping it might unwittingly disclose some indication of hope. It showed nothing. Without leaving his gaze, I broke the silence. "Take me to the bus." My tone was foreign, even to me, resigned and final.

"Why are you doing this?" he asked, but we both knew any discussion would be superfluous. I answered by turning away from him, and stood up to ascend the companionway to the deck.

On my way to the dinghy, I passed the open hatch to the engine room. It had become my station, and I was leaving it. I paused in the lingering diesel fumes, remembering that even at rest, that space of power would always exude its familiar traits of anxiety, fear and qualms, and that I had learned to dominate these traits.

Turning my head, I shouted over my shoulder, "This is *my* station! Do you hear me? MY engine room!" *Sondra* echoed my claim metallically and my voice disappeared into the darkness. Descending the iron ladder onto the suspended loading platform, the brilliant black letters I'd painted and re-painted on the back of the ship were right in my face. *SONDRA II.* A feeling of something akin to stage fright came over me. I put my hands on the letters and whispered, "This is it, my beautiful Lady, the final goodbye. Thank you for the magnificent ride."

We cast off the dinghy and crossed the turbulent main channel. It reeked of fish oil and roiled with enormous tarpons fed by shrimp heads from the nearby packaging factory. Silence traveled with us like a passenger, sad and final. At Key West's public dock, we tied off in a routine we had performed hundreds of times and walked four blocks through liquid heat to the bus stop. The long distance coach revved up. I watched David from my window seat as he disappeared down the sidewalk with his bouncy ball-of-the-foot step pulling our red island-wagon, now empty. His unkempt image looked clownish, costumed in a faded T-shirt, thigh-length cutoffs and black Converses topped by skinny brown socks. His windswept beard stuck out a foot over both shoulders, the whole ensemble crowned by his signature pirate scarf attempting to contain what ginger hair the ponytail missed. Was this really the three-piece-suit businessman I'd fallen in love with? Not anymore.

Incubated in smoky air, strangers' coughs and overzealous air conditioning, I put my head back against the bus-blue seat to contemplate day one of my intercontinental journey. Closing my aching eyes, I tried to recall if, in the awkward last moments, we'd even kissed goodbye. Not likely. He never liked kissing, or anything else physically romantic for that matter. There was no glamour in the departure. My exhausted mind slipped into blame mode, attempting to justify my actions with a checklist of objections: his attitude (holier than thou), his stubbornness (impenetrable), his demeanor (failed mogul), the sex (no foreplay). Although I knew what had lured me back over the years, I never really understood the fact that I actually returned to David. I always told myself I came back for life in the tropics, living on the boat, the music, and my job, but I was finally ready to trust myself to move on, even if all unknowns would be dull by comparison. Facing the future, I was afraid of being lonely or, worse, finding myself dependent on my parents while trying to get back on my feet. I certainly never envisioned something like this being the final chapter, but I was left with no choice.

"You bastard," I muttered one last time. "You threw it all away."

We motored past welcoming signs as we crossed the borders of Orange Florida, Peach Georgia, Bluegrass Kentucky—all their marketing efforts trivial at best. I drifted in and out of reflecting. What was it about my make-up that made me plunge out of my life and into a man's reckless dream of adventure? And now, why was I really leaving what many considered an enviable existence in the Caribbean to return to Toronto, broke, jobless and headed for winter? Couldn't I have fixed everything, talked some sense into him, pried him away from his schemes? No, I was done and had been for a long time. Fighting was just the push I needed to make a final breakaway. I was familiar with the oppressive behavior David had slipped into and was convinced it wasn't going to change. I'd lived under that wretched veil of self-deception for too long. It had taken me fifteen years to rid myself of adolescent insecurity and childishness. I wasn't about to surrender and become a casualty again.

The second day on the bus, while sipping on lousy 7/11 coffee, I realized that a night's sleep had replaced the bitterness with reminiscence. I wondered how five years could have passed by so fast yet end up holding more stories than we ever dreamed possible. We'd both changed and matured immensely, influencing and encouraging each other along the way. And what a brilliant bond we'd developed with *Sondra, Sondra* who had shaped us into the seafarers she expected!

My mind drifted back to the first day that I met David. I sighed as I envisioned us as a new couple falling in love. It had been so easy for him to sweep me off my feet. Although he wasn't handsome, somehow the overall package charmed. Many times, I'd observed a sweeping array of humanity fall victim to his charisma, and I was no exception. The first moments came back to me so vividly. As though remembering in the third person, I saw myself standing next to Len, my continually broke Formula Atlantic racecar-driving boyfriend, face to face with David. He was in his fabulously successful silk screening office with his empire of retail wear, while we had only our finish line fantasies of racecar T-shirts and elusive gold trophy victories. How could we ever have imagined we could sell enough shirts to fund those dreams? I smiled as I recalled our ledgerless innocence. I never admitted to David that we were nothing whatsoever in the Formula series world. To be in the winner's circle alongside the likes of Gilles Villeneuve would have taken more than a truckload of T-shirts. Len had the talent but he was one of Reality 101's flunkouts. I allowed myself to be conned into his Formula Fashion plan because I was angling to meet Crazy David! Rich, famous, infamous, draft dodging, party animal, business legend and hustler extraordinaire—he was a celebrity.

When Len and I first sauntered into the old Crazy David factory on the corner of Richmond and Peter, my artist's eye was thrilled by the patchwork of the company's wares. Samples of silkscreened shirts were stapled to the high wooden walls of the think tank/printing plant/warehouse. All the famous prints were there: Dopey shooting up, Minnie and Donald getting it on, Bob Marley smoking, Marilyn, Dylan, Canadian beer company logos—David was the daring king of politics and sarcasm, all created with much artistic flair. The Toronto hippies had made his fashion incredibly popular, but it was the papers that had made him famous by reporting on the lawsuits that were chasing every design. David really was quintessentially 70's, a voice for all of us, our counter-culture hero.

His secretary (imagine him having one of those) pointed to a door around the corner. "Just knock," she said without lifting her enormous Afro. I looked over to the door, which was covered in a life-sized poster of Frank Zappa sitting on the john. Where to put my knuckles? From the other side of my tenuous tap, we were beckoned in. What a sight David was to my unworldly eyes. The constant media coverage had familiarized me with his outrageous yet nurtured hair/beard combo, but not with his commanding demeanor and wiry frame elevated to 6'6" by leather platform disco shoes. The vested brown tweed suit he wore was tailored to perfection. I'd never seen a hippie in a tailored suit! I was grateful that I'd worn my teal blue suede ensemble and heels.

I was so busy gawking that I tripped up the uneven last

of three steps, a truly awkward entrance. But the charm of his perfect welcoming smile and his proper Boston accent soon smoothed over my embarrassment, and we got down to the business of T-shirts and racecars. He humored us with polite, patient attentiveness. Once finished, he invited us to join him for a coffee at the greasy spoon next door. While sipping, I remember watching him over my cup. Strange that, even now, I can't recall the color of his eyes.

Two weeks later I returned to David's office from the racetrack, alone, with the barely dented pile of consigned shirts and his meager share of the few we had sold. I was disappointed to see that he was not there. As I was leaving, the assistant off-handedly stated, "David wants you to call him when you get rid of your boyfriend."

My thoughts went into defense mode. *No way, I never call men, even if they are millionaires. And, everyone in town knows Crazy David has at least a dozen girlfriends.*

He probably never received my flamboyant reply: "You tell David to call me when he gets bored with his harem." Pride aside, I walked out of there feeling like Grace Slick. Imagine, a rich and famous guy wanting to date me!

Temptation to call him constantly gnawed at me for a couple of months. Getting in over my head in business finally gave me an excuse. I thought David would be the perfect advisor. He quickly offered to pick me up for an afternoon of beer and counseling. As I stood in the August sun in front of my High Park duplex, I was like a kid waiting for Christmas morning. Me and Crazy David. I was still trying to convince myself that this was strictly business. I had turned to David for help because I'd finally tired of the ridiculous money pit that was a formula racecar and its unemployed driver. I'd been wheeling and dealing my way through sixteen-hour days in a ménage of real estate, retail and renovation—all pretty much to finance Len's laissez faire approach to life. I didn't consciously realize it, but I'd had enough.

I tried to imagine what questions David might ask me so that I could have clever responses ready. That exercise turned out to be a waste of time because what I'd thought was going to be a simple brain storming session turned out to be something far, far beyond my wildest fantasies.

I heard his windowless brown jeep coming a block away, the air saturated with Hendrix blasting out from the oversized speakers in the rear. Hair and beard had parted to their roots and blew like Gatsby scarf-ends behind him. I distinctly remember the T-shirt he was wearing, too: **Don't Switch Dicks in the Middle of a Screw, Vote Nixon in '72.** That, combined with his grin, immediately ignited my smile.

David barely gave me time to buckle up before hitting me with the original pick-up line, "When do you have to be back home?" How presumptuous! He knew I was still with Len. I bet it was sheer comedy watching me muster up my courage for the response I couldn't resist.

I put some bravado in my voice and said, "Be back home when I feel like being back home."

"Good, because I want you to spend three days with me. That way, when you leave, you'll have a good idea of what living with me would be like."

Oh shit. I'm sure he took a bit of pleasure in seeing that I was doing my damnedest to look as if this happened to me all the time. I was rapidly running through possible responses in my mind but I had no training for this position! I also knew there was the possibility I might've been jumping to conclusions and I didn't want to embarrass myself with an equally presumptuous reply. How I felt about Len was left quietly vibrating between the lines. Nothing in my past had prepared me for the role of desirable woman. I was more familiar with my persona as a nondescript working class girl. But David had caught me at a strange time—a time when I had a tiny suspicion that I could be somebody, a real somebody.

I followed him into the afternoon dimness of The Gasworks pub, anxious to begin our meeting and avoid his proposal. Instead of asking about my problems, he started talking about how he was tired of business and how he planned to dump the T-shirts, buy a boat, and sail around the world. *With me. Me?* At that point, I thought he was pulling my chain and giggled nervously, further baffled as to what I should say. He snuffed the silence to confess, in rather trite but direct fashion, that he'd fallen in love the moment he'd laid eyes on me.

The timely second Heineken dropped into my hands and I stalled again, strategically peeling away the damp label as I tried to absorb what he'd said. How did I say yes? Words, tone, gestures, expressions had faded with time. I remember only the intoxicating feeling of yes—*Yes!*

Then there was the night that followed. My hand in his, he whisked my proud small frame through his kingdom where people literally bowed to welcome us. He was a good listener and a marvelous storyteller—intriguing, generous and, of course, fun. Who wouldn't have wanted to hop on his fantasy train? Nothing about fantasy seems reckless or dangerous at *that* age.

Finally we ended up back at his pad, right smack in the middle of downtown Toronto's action. It certainly was not what I had expected of a rich mover and shaker. It was Victorian-era, old fashioned with a general air of neglect: tattered stair carpets, scuffed pine floors discernibly slanting towards the street, grimy walls, windows layered with street dust. It did manage to look like a rock studio though, a musician's fantasy—an organ, guitars, vending machine sized speakers, a pro pool table, brown leather wingback chairs, and a dance floor! I don't know what I had expected, but I do know what I saw was far from it. As the bag of ice clinked into the sink over the six-pack of Heinekens, I couldn't help but think, *This might be my next home?*

David popped the caps off a couple of beers and pulled a joint out of his shirt pocket. I followed him to the organ, where we sat together on the bench and toked up. When he began to play, his talent astonished me. I couldn't help but swirl around the dance floor to the music, my long skirt fluttering through the air. Being the playboy that he was, of course he chose to end the serenade with "Tonight's The Night." He finished in a flourish, then stood and wordlessly disappeared to the upper level. I was alone for what seemed like a long time, sitting yoga style on the floor at the bottom of those tall stairs, knowing they led to the bed. I was mellowed out on beer and pot, and I could taste the future. Then, there he was, naked and tawny from head to toe, coming down the stairs to get me. He bent down, effortlessly picked me up in his arms and carried me up the creaking, winding stairway, laying me gently on the bed. Quickly, he removed my clothes, taking in every inch of my soft, curvy body. Our lovemaking was urgent, full of conviction. He was enamored with me, and I was absolutely lost in the whole idea of being in bed with "Crazy David."

Five years later, on a bus carrying me away from that man I had rushed toward so madly, the lovemaking seemed less predictable and more impetuous, but the romance was undeniable, even in retrospect. That night, I had crossed into a realm full of possibilities that I'd only read about in novels. And as though it were fiction, I'd blocked out the inevitable consequences of such a love. Somewhere along the line from this wonderful beginning through years of remarkable experiences together, those consequences started developing; and somewhere along that same line, I lost the ability to block them out. Sadly, David didn't seem to even notice them. Our endeavor with *Sondra* changed him dramatically. He no longer had a tangible direction, no blustering identity. Fame and fortune had not only abandoned him but also seemed unattainable. He had become a different person, someone I didn't like anymore, and I was tired of waiting for the former version to return—didn't even believe it was possible.

I tried to imagine what I would be like at thirty if I'd not met David. Thanks to him, I was a competent deckhand and a nautical engineer. I now knew and accepted that I was a natural beauty and I was no longer ashamed of my sensuality. I was strong, both physically and emotionally, and after my years at sea, I'd seen proof that I was absolutely fearless. Most importantly, I'd come to enjoy my mind—its intelligence, humor and creativity, and I knew a lot of other people did as well. Like the day I decided to drop into his life, I could just as easily drop into a new life that would undoubtedly be full of adventures too. Everything would be okay. Everything was fine.

Ready for a new start on the old turf, I stepped off the bus only a couple of blocks east of where the whole saga had started between David and me in the spring of 1975. Toronto the Good.

I headed north past old digs to drop anchor in a familiar port-of-call, where old friends met me on the same roach-burned couch. And through the smoke in my lungs, I declared, "I am sooooooo over that guy!" As if on cue, the classic stoner anthem encouraged me to remember that if I wanted to be free, I should be free.

Linda donned the huge headphones and began grooving and singing along. For a joke, Petie turned off the speakers and we all burst out laughing as Linda, oblivious, continued singing a cappella, loud and off key. I got up, sat on her lap, wrapped my arms around her neck and joined in, letting my friends know that I got the Cat Man's message and that my eyes were wide open to the many choices out there for me.

David and I in Jamaica, 1975

T-shirts do the talking

TORONTO (CP)—Let your T-shirt do the talking but it may mean you are on an ego trip and so poor at communicating you've got to use slogans that put a message across, according to a Toronto psyciatrist.

Dr. Mary Ewan said in a recent interview on why people wear slogan-laden T-shirts that "we don't know how to talk to people or make amusing remarks so we let the slogans speak for themselves."

"There is also the impact of the messages," she said. "Some are anti-social and people wearing them are trying to shock society."

But the mania for crazy T-shirts that started seven years ago shows no sign of letting up.
What's behind the craze..

"Ego", says Crazy David Keller, whose Toronto factory churns out as many as 80,000 T-shirts a week for distribution in 40 countries.
T-shirts have made Keller, 30, a millionaire.

"There's no end to the mania," he says. "It's out of control. We''re making specialized T-shirts for unions, companies, everybody, you name it."

Toronto Star, 1976

17

3

THE THREE-DAY DATE ROCKS ON

Toronto
Early September, 1975

"Some people are settling down, some people are settling and some people refuse to settle for anything less than butterflies."
-SEX IN THE CITY

YONGE Street woke me, coming to life with delivery truck doors slamming and horns honking. *Where was I? What happened last night?* I was curled up in David's arms; his long mane under my shoulder, his soft beard against my cheek. Needless to say, I was completely pleased with myself. Taking in his smell, brackish and musky, I pulled my arm tight over his chest to see if he was awake and to let him know that I was happy to be there. He gave me a quick kiss on the forehead, freed himself from our entanglement and bounced out of bed into last night's jeans. I studied his perfect, sculpted body, the warm honey-colored hair covering his torso.

Tossing my clothes at me, "Come on, let's go get some coffee."

Tying my sari skirt, I couldn't help but think that, although thrilling and urgent, the sex was a little underwhelming. There was absolutely no foreplay—a bigger letdown than normal given David's playboy notoriety.

Attired in boot-legged jeans, a "Dark Side of the Moon" T, jean jacket and his lace-up brown heeled shoes, all of which I came to know as his *look*, he grabbed my hand and down the dark stairs we dashed as if there were some urgency. Flinging the back door open, we charged out into the courtyard, now empty of other tenants' cars, and squinted against the bright fall sunshine.

"Wow, it smells like a urinal back here, David!"

"Well, it kind of is. The pub-crawlers use it as a secluded place to toke up and usually end up... I call it Piss Alley," he shrugged, "My backyard."

I scurried alongside David's long legs as we made our

way to McDonald's and back for the fastest coffee in town. Together, side-by-side on the organ bench, I ran my fingers around the gilded Hammond logo, and he ran his fingers up and down the yellowed ivory keys. He told me this was a special brand of B3 organs because it featured glass valves that glowed when played. These valves were what produced the big fat sound distinctive to a B3. The Leslie, a four foot speaker historically and popularly associated with a Hammond, changed the sound of the music by passing it through its rotating mechanism causing the sound to move closer to, or farther away from, a listener's ears. Hence, the wonderful warm vibrato that was pure rock and roll.

With voice enough for the Allman Brothers, David sang in 60's Southern style as he played…

> *"If she's bad he can't see it*
> *She can do no wrong*
> *Turn his back on his best friend*
> *If he put her down"*

I told him I loved that song. Who didn't? And that my favorite part had always been when the guitar came in after "he put her down" with those few high picked notes. Feeling cocky, I asked him if *he* would see it if I was "bad?"

He answered with,

> *"He'd give up all his comfort*
> *Sleep out in the rain*
> *If she said that's the way it ought to be"*

I watched his long freckled fingers move with agility over the two levels of keys as his shoes tapped lightly across the foot pedals. The music drew the curtain of glamour back, ridding him of his practiced smile and fame-peppered emotion. He sat liquid and calm and moved in a way similar to Stevie Wonder— eyes closed, head tilting down and then up when the words required emphasis.

He stopped singing and softly played on while, without looking up, matter-of-factly told me, "I played lead guitar on

Percy Sledge's original recording."

Disbelief made me grab his chin and turn his face towards mine. "What did you just say?"

"Yeah." Playing one of his aces, he added, "I was a session musician at a studio in Birmingham in my late teens. When Sledge showed up to record, I'd just finished playing for another group and got called into his session to replace a no-show."

"No kidding?!" *Well, Hmm, you may not be too hot in the sack, but you've got some credits heavy on the other side of the ol' scale. Besides, I can fix the lovin' thing.*

Unexpectedly he swung one spidery leg up and over my head, straddling the bench to face me. I didn't know him well yet but well enough to know from his expression that another ambitious question was on its way.

"Do you believe in variety in life?" Long pause. "I believe that it *is* life."

"Variety?"

"Freedom—within a relationship. But with total honesty and trust."

I turned my head away. I'd heard of this in the form of a game called "Key Swapping," but never imagined myself letting it be part of my personal life. I'd experienced infidelity but there was never any honesty attached to it and it usually sent trust flying out the window. I'd also seen that this sort of thing never worked out in movies and I still pretty much believed what I saw on the big screen. I looked back at him for some guidance.

"Don't worry. It's just dogma making you think that it's not okay. Relax. We'll just take it one day at a time."

During the Victorian era, there were actually courses in dogma and morals. Those lucky women. I wasn't looking forward to a hands-on learning experience, but I was intrigued by the novel proposition of equality. Little did we know about how that was going to shake down.

And so, on that note, the "Three Day Date" rocked on.

An old photo I found online of David back in
his recording days in Alabama at
www.garagehangover.com.

Everything so far was over-the-top enthralling, ego boosting, and perfectly fun, but it was David's unique intellect that ultimately won me over and made me take him seriously. The clincher was his crash course in marketing down at the Canadian National Exhibition. The EX, as it was called, was North America's fifth largest fair. We jumped into his unmarked work truck and headed down to the historical fairgrounds just before closing time. I loved the EX—the ultimate scene of thrills and shrills, games of chance and jumbo teddies, shared candy floss, love, and miles of smiles lighting up the shore of Lake Ontario.

Arriving at the east-end gate, I sat shotgun with a caricature image of the man sitting next to me proudly stretched across my chest. The two young gatekeepers, both wearing gratuitous "Crazy David" T-shirts that matched mine, approached our generic white vehicle to check for a pass. None materialized, but David's famous face brought to life by their flashlight did the trick.

"Hey, maaaaan. How's it goin'?" High fives and grins

five fingers wide. Up went the gate.

Sensing mischief, I asked, "What the heck was that all about?"

"The top administrators of the CNE have banned me from the property with an APB posted at every entrance."

"Oh? And why would that be, Jessie James?"

"Because I have small T-shirt racks all over the grounds and they have no signed contracts. No contract signed…no commission paid. They're a bunch of thieves and I refuse to do business with them."

My eyes took in the scheme as we drove from booth to booth. He'd borrowed a tiny area from scores of contracted vendors in return for a fair percentage of sales-space just big enough for a double rack of spit-through T-shirts that were selling for a buck. Spit-throughs. I'd never heard that word before, but these Pakistani imports were made of cotton so thin that it resembled cheesecloth you probably could spit through. The varied display of colorful mainstream-shocking art was selling like paper acid at a Grateful Dead show. As we drove from rack to rack around the fair, gathering one-dollar bills, I saw David's reputed genius at work.

Pakistani *Spit-through* T-Shirt

The *pièce de résistance* for me and thousands of others (including every newspaper reporter covering the closing events of that year's EX) was his final ingenious and humorous nose thumb to "The Powers That Be." In the last wee hours of the night, he had an army of teens running around the grounds with rolls of little red heart stickers featuring his famous logo-face with "**Crazy David Loves You**" written under it. They were sticking them to anything and everything, inanimate and animate. His presence was everywhere—the ride seats, the executive's cars, the washroom stalls, cheeks of smiling faces and bouncing pushed-up breasts. In the same way he had lovingly branded me with his T-shirt, he was expanding his empire with hearts, thousands of them!

Okay—branded, bedded, and be-dazzled, I was in. I wanted to walk on the edge with this guy. See life through his eyes. Be like him.

The third and last day together was somewhat daunting. I didn't have a clue where to begin with the spur of the moment task he'd assigned me that morning as he tore out of the door for an unscheduled meeting.

The parting words hollered over his shoulder were, "Any bank will do it."

It never entered my head to call a cab. To me, that luxury was reserved for the rich or those on welfare. Instead I lugged four oversized paper shopping bags down the back stairs, through the stinky courtyard and around the corner onto Yonge Street. The bags were heavy and awkward, packed with dollar bills hidden under T-shirts, the handles making grooves in my fingers, but I was determined to walk until I hit a bank.

"Hello. I have some small bills I would like to exchange for larger bills."

"Okay, just pass them to me under the glass please."

"I can't. There are too many of them."

"Well, how many are we talking about?"

I felt compelled to stage whisper, "Four jumbo shopping bags full of little bills," and then I hand signed ten fingers three times and watched as she lip-read the "K" that completed my pantomime of $30,000 and which I punctuated with a shrug.

The dumbstruck teller immediately called the manager. I

was shut in a room with a woman cursed with that bitchy "tsking" personality that I recognized from Western U girls. I wondered what she thought as she checked me out; a young woman draped in a tablecloth with my T-shirt of the day featuring a marijuana leaf and clutching four old shopping bags stuffed with cash. She was delegated to turn, flip and count. At that point, nervousness was replaced by severe hunger brought on by my two-day crash diet. I was also bored. I couldn't even tell the navy-suited professional across the desk the great story about where the loot had come from. She gave no hint as to what she thought either but I figured she didn't suspect drug money. Who pays for drugs in one-dollar bills?

The business completed, I left her with the four shirts as a tip and, having stared at her gaudy wedding ring combo, wondered if she would ever give her partner the black shirt that said "**Husband of Bitch Bitch Bitch**."

I held back the urge to skip through the bank, but couldn't suppress a loud humming of James Brown's "I Feel Good." Out the revolving doors and through the noon-hour foot traffic, I made my way to the curb to flag down a cab. I, Ms. Marni Craig, was rich. I had $30K in hundreds stuffed in my bra, panties and coat pockets, and I was in looove!

When David drove me back home at the end of our date odyssey, I left the jeep with my accepted title, "Crazy David's New Girlfriend," along with some simple ground rules—variety and trust.

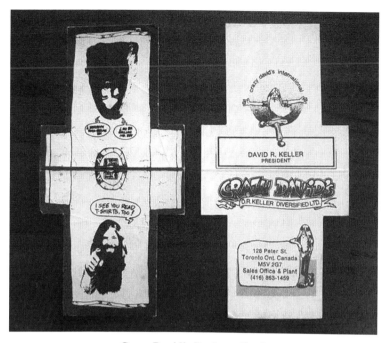

Crazy David's Business Card

"I SEE YOU READ T-SHIRTS, TOO!"

(upside down)
"ARE YOU PUTTING ME ON?"

"ME FAITES VOUS MARCHER?"

4

MY BACKYARD

Toronto
Spring, 1976

"Variety is Life."
-DAVID R. KELLER aka CRAZY DAVID

"**VARIETY** is Life." Variety is *not* the spice of—simply, Variety *is*. David probably never dreamed that such an aphorism would come back to bite him.

For the first six months of our otherwise congenial relationship, David indulged his appetite for flings at every opportunity. Why wouldn't he, when I, the trusting, submissive girlfriend, had sanctioned his freedom? I wanted to rid myself of dogma—something David pompously reminded me I was inflicted with whenever he wanted to step out. On rare occasions I even joined in (another exercise designed to overcome rigidity), thus further confusing the issue because those *ménages à trois* usually went well and were actually fun. I blamed that on champagne and grass because the next morning it seldom seemed like fun when a stranger was in the other arm of your boyfriend.

Try as I might to be rid of my attitudes, I couldn't shake the feeling that the truth of our relationship was demeaning. It came down to the simple fact that everyone knew what he was up to and what I wasn't up to, thus triggering and re-triggering my irritation.

It was evening rush hour in Toronto and I'd picked David up at the airport. The agenda was to grab a quick bite somewhere, then head home to pack for our much-anticipated trip to Nova Scotia the next morning. There, we'd inspect a motor sailor, the first potential boat for our future life. We were both exhausted and quiet. I felt compelled to make small talk because the silence was making me anxious. Even though more pressing things were on my mind, I opted for asking him how his trip was.

"It was great, Marge." He insisted on calling me that (along with "Flarge"). He said I looked and acted like a squishy version of the girl next door. In his opinion, these names were perfect but I loathed them. "Business was good! Last night I checked out a brothel recommended by a client. The blues pianist was great but I didn't find a woman that interested me."

"Asshole," I muttered under my breath. The honesty reminded me that my own Variety Life had become a reality in his absence. Even after six months of romantic indulgences on his part, I had no idea how the hell to tell him about my fling. The rest of the ride home was pretty quiet and I decided not to spill the beans until later, whenever later was. Turned out, the unscheduled moment would take on a life of its own.

At home, I sprawled on our bed, not having slept since taking him to the airport the morning before. I should have been packing for Halifax, but after last night's adventure, I could barely move.

The phone rang. David answered and, with a surprised, proprietary look on his face, passed the receiver over while mouthing in an exaggerated fashion, "It's for you, and it's a guy." Too bad for me that texting hadn't been invented. Or cell phones. If only he'd written a letter!

My heart raced. I started begging the heavens for divine intervention. *Please God don't let it be him. Please God let it be him. And oh God, make David disappear.*

Sitting up, instantly dry-mouthed, I quietly cleared my throat. Head down at the phone, face half hidden behind my hand, I spoke softly, "Hello."

"Marni?" It was him!

"Yes, it's me." *Oh shit, what timing. This couldn't be worse. How the hell can I have a conversation with this hunk while David is standing there?* And I ached to talk to him, to hear his voice again, to know what he wanted. Without looking up, I tried waving David out of the room but he wasn't going anywhere.

"It's Burton."

"Yes. I know."

"Are you, um, okay?"

It was tough to play it cool with the King of Cool and

ignore Crazy King David at the same time. My voice sounded high and airy. "I'm good. You?"

"Who answered the phone?"

"Nobody."

There was a pause. "I called to see if you wanted to come with me to the next couple of gigs." His tone was so up. So confident. The way mine should've been.

My volume rose. "You want what?!?!"

"I want to see you again. Now. A lot."

I answered with a silence.

"Are you still there, Marni?"

"I can't do that. I really cannot do that."

"Why?" I could hear both surprise and disappointment in his voice.

"I have other plans—plans I can't change." This killed me. "Listen, I have to go." And in a whisper so David wouldn't hear, "I am so, so sorry."

I assume Burton's silence had something to do with his lack of familiarity with being shot down. "So. I guess it's good-bye then," he said, in the tone people usually use to say, "Have a good life".

"Yeah."

He hung up. Not in a million years had I expected a rock star to fall for me. And, he was what we girls put in the category "Drop Dead Fucking Gorgeous." Although Canadian, he looked Egyptian-exotic, like Omar Sharif, with thick almost black curly hair and a full chevron moustache that covered his upper lip. Even his nose was a bit Arabic in shape and there was one of those sexy dents in the chin. When he smiled, which was often, his moist white teeth and laugh lines at the edges of his spangled brown eyes collectively drew you in like a full moon. And that body!

When I went after him at the bar the previous night, I only knew of one song he'd made famous and that was because my girlfriend told me he was a singer in the band that made "American Woman" a hit. If I knew The Guess Who had outsold the Beatles in the early 70's, I'm sure I would've lost my nerve, beer fortified or not. But, the fame I did know about, combined with his good looks, was just what I needed to get my job done—to even the score with David and put me in the Variety Club on my own terms. I'd used Burton, thinking he'd never know, let alone give a damn. And then to find out he had feelings for me! What a mess.

With my head still down, I held the receiver out to David like a kid giving back stolen candy. "Who was that?" He tried to sound casual but didn't even come close. Although I'd agonized over how I would tell him about the night before (so many versions), the phone call was decidedly not the way any of them started. And, while they say that all things eventually pass, I didn't have enough experience in that area to believe it. That wisdom might have given me courage, but I was so nervous I felt ill. Finally I just blurted it out, hoping for the best.

"Burton Cummings."

Like a chicken he thrust his neck forward, eyes bulging, and asked with substantial disbelief, "Of The Guess Who?"

Something told me it was time to get the hell out of the bedroom, a room that seemed, all on its own, to be heading towards the tragic ending of a self-written Film Noir. I quickly walked past David down to the living room.

He was on my heels like a piece of street gum asking, "Why was he calling *you*?" I immediately wanted to throw back a *fuck* you!

I knew better. I was practicing not using the F-word anymore. David had emphasized that it sounded like red wine on a party dress—and nobody wants that. Instead, with arms gesturing Italian style and a Woody Allen stutter, I pleaded.

"David, you have to believe me when I tell you that I…I…I didn't set out last night to make a point or…or to get even. The plan was born in a beer glass—the third actually—as are many risky endeavors. Besides, you were away on business." And then, wanting to get through this, my speech went into Joan Rivers' rapid mode. "My girlfriend and I zipped to the bar across the street to catch The MacLean Brothers' comedy act, and we were just lucky to get an up-front table, and even luckier to find ourselves staring at Burton, who, (gulp for air) being a good friend of the brothers, had decided to join them on stage for some songs, and well, you know, some good ol' Canadian humor. (Another gulp.) Yeah, I know he's good looking but I swear, I had nooooo idea he was going to be there."

"So did he end up in *my* apartment? And—I hope—you didn't have sex with him in *my* bed."

The instinct to leave the room had been a good one, and I didn't miss that this was *his* apartment and *his* bed all of a sudden, and that really pissed me off. Slowed me right down.

Not giving weight to his exclusion, I continued, "He was teasing the audience, well the girls anyway, by opening his shirt. And the beer spoke through me to my friend, resulting in a bet that...I...could..."

"David, I had to know if I could have Variety too, and I figured it would take someone like him to show you how I felt...when you got some Variety. Just so you would know." Now I had his attention. "Well, they closed at 1:00. I knocked on the door to the green room. The MacLeans didn't remember meeting me, but it didn't matter because now it was all about my offer of after-hours at *your* pro pool table. I thought only the two brothers and Burton would follow me to *our* apartment, but it turned into an entourage of techies. I was like a stunned pied piper. With their stack of beer-cases, I knew my plot was working but that I'd seriously overlooked other scenarios! We'd already passed the point of no return and losing face was out of the question. I had to take them to the front...through the store...which they liked a lot! I had a heck of a time getting them out of the store. Actually, they bought a bunch of those T-shirts with Farrah in her red bathing suit and Supertramp, Keep On Truckin, Harley, and on and on they shopped!"

I watched David and felt very uneasy. I thought back to the night before with Burton. It had been a gift! No other way to see or describe it. He was a man known all over the world for his voice and creativity and to whom we'd flock by tens of thousands to enjoy and share with friends. Yet he'd been in my kitchen, at my shoulder, singing "These Eyes," a cappella. And then in my living room running his fingers up and down the B3 in a creative frenzy, banging out "No Sugar Tonight." And then...he made music with me. Just me.

Although I practically had to slap Burton to get him to notice me, once he did, something clicked. I could see it—those dark eyes stopped dancing and unexpectedly became fixed on mine. He saw something he wanted, needed, and it wasn't a quickie.

When I'd made that $50 bet with my girlfriend that I could touch his nipples, I had laughed up my confidence with the aid of the beer, but I hadn't thought beyond that moment. I knew if I could somehow put myself in his path, instinct would kick in and I'd know what to do next. I never really imagined how absolutely intoxicating being in that man's company would be.

My best move had come around four in the morning when, after painstaking hours of being ignored, I'd all but given up on even talking to Mr. Guess Who. It happened in the kitchen under the gaze of the cheeky cupboard dwelling mannequin. Her talking cloud that day said, "I'm hittin' the high seas boys!" She was usually a source of amusing conversation, but when Burton passed under her legs with a fresh pint, his head was down, probably so as not to have to deal with yet another chick fawning over him. We bumped shoulders on my way to the fridge. He wouldn't even make eye contact!

So, fed up with his attitude and figuring I had nothing to lose, I nailed him in the shoulder with a good poke using all four fingers. I'll never forget his expression when he looked up. And, not missing a beat, I immediately let him have it with what I didn't even know was in me.

"Who the hell are you anyway? You've been in my apartment for three hours. Now you're in my kitchen helping yourself to my fridge, and you don't even have the decency to introduce yourself." And then I just stared him down. Up close and personal. *Man, I would go to battle with Aphrodite for this Adonis.* I wanted to crawl into his smile. And that hair—any normal woman would just want to grab it and use it to steer his head. Not only did he exude sex appeal, but everything was working together to make him look like a joyful person. Someone who loves his life. Regardless, I held my ground and raised my brow to let him know I was waiting.

"What? No, you've got it all wrong. I wasn't ignoring you and I didn't mean to offend you. I thought the other guys had taken care of saying thanks and that you were cool."

"Hey. I only invited Blare and Gary, guys I knew, and look what I ended up with. I hope you're all having a good time?"

He smiled: "I'm really sorry… Burton Cummings."

And there I cut him off. "I know *who* you are but I don't know *you*—as in: *you're-in-my-house* know you."

He put his arm around my shoulder and led me to the stairs motioning me to sit with him away from the group. He began by asking me about myself, listening with undivided attention and making me feel at ease. He was clever, witty, incredibly interesting and funny. When talking about music, his whole being lit up. He told me how he'd been influenced by Little Richard, Fats, Richie Valens, Presley, and how, as a young musician, he'd done everything possible to be noticed—first by The Devons and then by The Guess Who. He never once bragged about how successful he really was. I later learned The Guess Who had been one of the very few bands to score a number of split 45 double-sided hits which put them right up there with Fats, Credence, Presley and, of course, The Beatles. Needn't mention that to David, though.

"David, it was really nice for me to see how much they respected and enjoyed my invitation. They loved the apartment and all of your toys. You know what it's like to be on the road. They played music and sang and laughed and sat in the window seats talking and watching the late-night Yonge Street crowd. They came to say thanks as if *I* were the rock star, and they came to *my* show. When they announced they were going out for breakfast… yeah I know it was a long party, but it didn't seem like it…and no, your brother never came downstairs. I don't think he even woke up." *Thank god for that!* Since Bruce and his girlfriend had moved in, the dynamics in the apartment had shifted drastically for the worse. No love lost there and he would not have been impressed with my late night collection of men. Being the Alabama redneck that he was, he'd probably have felt it was his job to defend his brother's territory and make fools out of both of us.

"Anyway, we went for breakfast, just the two of us, and probably because I didn't fall all over him at the apartment, he was really…" I searched for the right word, "intense, on me. After eating, we walked and talked and ended up back at my place."

"Oh, how very convenient that your house hasn't sold."
Yes, it was.

"Oh, David, let's not forget how convenient it was that you were out of town and occupied at, what was it? Oh yeah—a *Brothel!*" Loud emphasis on "brothel" and a sudden realization that for the first time I'd found some balls! "Are you starting to get it David? (my right index finger dared to wag). Only YOU know that I slept with (finger stopped wagging to indicate its universal number sign) ONE other person (both arms got into the act, circling an imaginary globe) NOT ALL of TORONTO who, thanks to the press, probably think that you're the reincarnated Casa-fuckin'-nova!" The balls I'd found were apparently made of brass, and sometimes there's just no substitution for that dress-staining word. I turned my back on him and resumed my seat on the sofa. This was either going to be an enormously triumphant moment, where I would approach equal status with this man, or he would send me packing. I really didn't know which way it would go, but I also knew I could likely retrieve at least one attractive option from the wings.

"So what did he want, on the telephone?" he asked, bringing the temperature down.

I began to experience an odd sensation. Suddenly this all seemed really personal. I wasn't infatuated with a rock star. This was a man I'd connected with. I had chosen him, taken him away from Planet David outside of David's context and made it about me. I didn't want to tell him why Burton called. I wanted this discussion to be over.

"He wanted me to go on tour with him for his next few dates. Said that he was smitten." I was reading between the lines rather liberally because Burton didn't exactly say that, but I felt it added appropriate stress when stress was needed.

David couldn't resist another snide one, "So, I guess you won the bet."

"I hope I won more than *that*," I threw back at him.

"So what are you going to do?"

My thoughts returned to Burton: talented, smart, sensitive, rich, leading a charmed life. Making love with him had been just the way my friends and I imagined it would be with a famous looker. Our encounter had been in my house, not because it was convenient, but because it was *mine*—a place to conduct *my* business. The eclectic artsy décor and attention to details, such as seductive downtempo music at the ready and yummy bedding, made it a pretty good love nest. I couldn't remember walking to breakfast. It seemed we just materialized on the bed. *My* bed.

I lay waiting for Burton, watching his every move as he stripped down for me. Then he told me to sit up and take off my sweater. Sitting beside me, he undid my lacy bra, removed it and gently pushed me back. Straddling my legs, he began kissing my neck, my lips, my breasts, my belly—taking his time and talking sweetly to me, his soft delicious voice falling all over my naked skin. Hot breath met goose bumps. As he worked my jeans off, I followed his head with my hands, grabbed his hair, and brought him between my legs. This man was willing to pleasure me in a way I hadn't been in months. My hips rose to his tongue. Then he segued back to my face, held it, looked at it and wildly kissed my lips again. There were feelings rolled up in this lovemaking. Again, I could see it in those eyes. And we laughed, also something I hadn't done for ages while making love.

Because David wasn't interested in this kind of sex, it didn't even feel like I was cheating. Unfortunately, a big part of the experience for me was the fulfilled desire to taste revenge on Burton's lips and later share the conquest with the girls.

Although stellar in bed, back then Burton was a novice superstar. Constantly inundated with devotion, on and off stage had melded into one for him and fame was something he donned like a pair of glasses in the morning. I'd experienced this in David's apartment when he behaved as though his celebrity decreed protocol surpassed common etiquette. It happened again in the little corner grocery store   while we were buying rolling papers for an after-sex toke. This was a blue-collar Italian neighborhood where nobody would know who the hell he was, but he seemed obliged to work it nonetheless. To him, the *world* was his audience and therefore always his obligation to 'be famous.' His peacock-like behavior put a wedge between us and for a few minutes, we both seemed lost.

I'd enjoyed my time with Burton immensely and his offer was certainly alluring, but I knew all too well from being with a much less-recognized man, that I would likely only be the arm candy and probably just the flavor of the week. I asked myself *How will I ever have an identity, a life of my own, if I'm the girlfriend of the lead singer of The Guess Who, one of the most famous bands on the globe?!* Luckily, even at that young age, I had an idea of what this might mean.

David hadn't sat down yet. Still waiting for my answer, he was letting me think. I weighed life with him and thought *It's not going to be easy; David is such a hardass sometimes. But, with the sale of the T-shirt business, fame won't be an issue and the life we've planned will be sure to offer up exciting unknowns. I've made a commitment to this man, and last night with another was just the Variety Club.*

In that moment, after all that had happened in the past couple of days, the path laid for David and me was still very clear to me, and the fact that I belonged on that path was also clear.

I stood, slipped my arms through David's, around his waist, and looked up at him with love in my smile, "Let's go upstairs and get the bags ready."

I had thought the scene was over when Burton left my house and again when I had reached resolution with David. Unbeknownst to me, the lights on that stage were still lit. Against all odds, Burton showed up at the same bar with the McLeans the next night. Over drinks with our mutual friends Peter and Linda, it was decided that afterhours should be at their friend David's well-appointed apartment. This time, there were just five of them and they headed to the back entrance with an around-the-block-hike where, from the back courtyard, they could access the bell to our second floor apartment. The bell was rung, shouts were shouted, pebbles were thrown at upper windows—nothing worked. We had left for Nova Scotia.

Linda commented, "Too bad, they're a lot of fun. I would've liked to shoot some pool." That's when Burton frowned.

"Who's the other part of *they*?"

He was putting two and two together, realizing that he was in *my* backyard. According to Linda, she added me into the formula by answering, "Oh, his girlfriend Marni. She's sweet. And you would've liked her." Then she blabbed on about us looking for a boat down east for sailing around the world. Afterwards, she told me she couldn't help but pick up the vibes in the strange looks that passed between the guests. Blair piped up, "Oh, we already know Marni. And Burton here, he knows her really well." And so the word was out that Marni Craig had officially earned her stripes in the infamous David Keller Variety Club.

David accepted all of this. Everyone who knew us eventually knew the story. The happening had changed both of us. People now actually looked at and talked to *me* when in his presence and, remarkably, David seemed to be losing his wanderlust. I was surprised and pleased that he'd kept his cool perfectly intact. So it was all good and getting better until the day when Burton's new release entitled "Your Backyard" came intruding like carbon monoxide out of the speakers and into our truck. As soon as his recognizable voice sang the first phrase, "I wrote you long love letters, Mama," we both tried to pretend we weren't paying attention. On he went with,

> *"...I sent 'em on day by day*
> *Need you now even more than I did before*
> *As I'm lookin', here's your Daddy comin'*
> *With a big ole shotgun too*
> *Lovin' situation look mighty poor"*

But when he hit the chorus with his commanding piano and these words, everything changed.

> *"So if'in you're really wonderin' what I'm*
> *doin' in your backyard*
> *I told you, Baby, I'd beat it home so soon*
> *But if you're really worryin' 'bout what I'm*
> *doin' in your backyard*
> *Come on out later, I'll show you by the light of*
> *the moon"*

It was pretty obvious to us both where Burton's

inspiration had come from. But it wasn't obvious to me what it was doing to David until the back of his hand connected with my left cheekbone. Hard. Then he yelled at me, "GET IN THE BACK OF THE TRUCK WOMAN! GET THE FUCK OUT OF MY SIGHT!"

In total shock, my heart pounding and every muscle tensed, I stared at him, and then beyond him over my shoulder to the mostly empty cargo space behind. Turning my gaze back to the road ahead, and to my own amazement, I talked over Burton and calmly said, "There's an axe back there. If I were you I'd stop the truck, right now, and let me out. *Now!*"

I would have used that axe. I was experiencing an unfamiliar level of anger—the blind rage before you really clobber someone. Strangely, although edgy, I also felt composed, the numbness that comes with shock. I wouldn't have killed him, but I would have done some damage—at least to the truck. He must have known this because he pulled over before I had to repeat myself. We both leapt out, me with a head start. I had such a rush of adrenalin, I was almost able to outrun his long legs. He finally grabbed my arm and whipped me around. Placing me in front of him, he locked his hands on my shoulders and his eyes on mine in an expression near fear.

"I'm so sorry, so sorry, so sorry." His delivery was surprisingly slow and quiet. "I've never hit a woman before. I don't know what got into me. Marni, please get back in the truck. I promise this will *never* happen again. My stupid ego just took over, Marni. Look at me. I love you!"

I was shaking and screaming for an explanation and crying all at once. It wasn't from pain. It was the fact that he dared to hit me for an idea that had been his in the first place. I had to make sure he understood that I could not live under the trepidation of violence.

I looked him square in the eyes, holding him there. "So are we finished with this then, David?"

"Yes. We're finished. You have my word," he answered morosely, nodding acquiescence with all the sincerity needed for us to be able to move on.

We returned to the truck and drove the next half hour in total silence. It was the kind of silence that comes when something profound has happened between partners and you each need personal time to process it. I always figured I would never understand why abused women went back. But in the moment of my own personal experience, I saw our love as a journey through unmapped territory and somehow knew beyond a doubt that violence was a place we'd never pass through again.

Turning off the highway onto the winding country road that would take us to Potter's Marina and the water taxi, David put his hand on mine and softly asked, "Are you okay?" I nodded. "You know you have a bruise. I'm sorry about that too."

"Don't worry, doors get in everyone's way at least once."

We unloaded into the old cedar strip, jumped in and sat back to enjoy the ride across Go Home Bay under the Milky Way. It was a holiday weekend—open house at David's rented island, mainly for the staff, but it could never have stopped at that. There was even a token number of unsuspecting hitchhikers kidnapped for the event. Tying up at the dock, I could smell the cottage party tradition of curried goat simmering in an oversized iron kettle above the open fire pit.

When I stepped onto the crowded dock, I donned an expression that I hoped would protect me, one that didn't give room for speculation, one flavored with a drop of humor that would distract like the cherry extract in cough syrup. It was an oddly strange feeling to walk past the onlookers and share my shiner with all those other eyes, eyes that weren't likely distracted by any cherry coating. But I was there with my new membership card for the Variety Club in my back pocket and Crazy David was walking behind me carrying my suitcase.

Burton Cummings

In 1978, Burton also recorded "When A Man Loves A Woman"

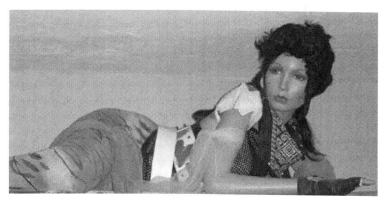

Bad Girl of the Cupboards

THE SEARCH IS ON

Halifax, Nova Scotia
Spring, 1976

"No idea is so outlandish that it should not be considered with a searching but at the same time with a steady eye."
-WINSTON CHURCHILL

WITH a clearer understanding of Variety and David's new mantra "Now I Get It!", we set out on our emprise to hunt down the perfect boat for our trip around the world. This was unprecedented glamour for me. Actually, flying anywhere fell into that category. Other than our trip to Jamaica a few months previously, I had pretty much been confined to the inside of Ontario's borders.

Now we were jetting off in a silver capsule of luxury to the eastern province of Nova Scotia while sipping on Bloody Caesars (Canada's famous eye-opener concoction of clam and tomato juices, vodka and the borrowed trimmings of a Bloody Mary). David was telling me how much I would enjoy Halifax and how artsy the harbor front was. He said it was unique for an old harbor, having been totally rebuilt about 60 years ago following the big explosion.

"What big explosion?"

"You've never read about that disaster?" He could see I was embarrassed so he just continued. "Two ships collided in the narrows of Halifax's harbor during the First World War. One of them was en route to France fully loaded with explosives. A fire resulted in a cataclysmic explosion that devastated the city. About 2,000 people were killed and another 10,000 were injured. Apparently, it was one-fifth the size of the Hiroshima bomb and it's still the world's largest accidental explosion caused by man. The blast nearly emptied out all of the harbour's water which triggered a 60-foot tsunami on the return." He was shaking his head at the thought of it.

"Oh my god! Did it happen during the day?" David nodded. "How can two big ships run into each other in broad daylight? That's unbelievable!" I tried to imagine what it must've been like for those Nova Scotians beginning their day, their ordinary day, and in an instant be filled with the terror that everyone they loved might be dead. An image came into my mind of thousands of people walking around ripped and burned, trying to make sense of what had just happened. I envisioned the tidal wave, full of rage, tossing annihilation and death. I returned to what I'd been looking at through the scratched Plexiglas window, the landscape of the ancient snow-capped Laurentians, cuddled by clouds, trustworthy in a way that Halifax harbor must have been when its people greeted that day at sunrise.

The stewardess, asking if we would like another drink, brought me back to life inside the cabin—orderly, hushed, and I couldn't help but think, bloodless. We reflected over our fresh drinks.

"Tell me about the boat we're going to look at."

Happy to have the subject changed, he replied with an air of pride, "It's a motorsailor."

"I don't understand what that means."

In his usual patient way of explaining things, he continued, "It's a cross between a sailboat and a motorboat. You have the quiet, inexpensive, guilt-free fun of sailing but with propulsion back-up when you need it, and much more deck space."

But the motorsailor didn't pan out; David decided that the engine was too old and the boat in need of too much repair. Disappointed, we hit The Lower Deck, a charming wooden ocean-side pub, for a Happy Hour cure and a discussion about what was next. Halfway into our second icy mug of Alexander Keith's, a casually dressed gentleman with a tell-tale seadog face asked if he could join us. Always anxious to meet new people, David and I simultaneously gestured to the empty stool beside me. He introduced himself as Captain Andy Thomas. David raised a finger to the bartender indicating one for our guest, who accepted with the kind of grace that comes with reputation and often being treated to a beer.

He seemed like the sort of man that would respond to being charmed so I swiveled my whole body toward him and asked, "So, Captain Andy Thomas, just what are you the captain of?"

With capable forearms on the bar, the Captain turned his grinning face to us. *"The Bluenose."*

He got it from both of us—*"The Bluenose!"*

"Ha! What fun!" I blurted out. Thanks to my grandfather, this was one piece of Canadian history I did know about. The famous *Bluenose* racing schooner was always my favorite engraving of all those on our coins.

The Captain, taking a sip of his cold beer, continued, "This replica of the original, which sank in 1946, is an ambassador for the province. We sail her out of Lunenburg every summer to ports all over the world. And by the way, please call me Andy. When we finish up our beers, I'll take you on board for a tour if you'd like." I wanted to hug him. This would be the highlight of the trip.

Andy showed us every inch of that sleek 160-foot piece of floating art. He explained that under full sail, she had 11,150 square feet of sail area. It took six officers, fifteen deckhands and a chief cook to sail her. At the end of the tour, Andy invited us to join him in his private quarters for a whiskey. Placing the shots on the small table that looked like an oversized tray, he produced a folder of yellowed newspaper clippings and photos.

The Bluenose I (1921 – 1946)

"During a 17 year period of racing, no challenger, American or Canadian, could wrest the International Fishermen's Trophy from her. It is notable that she was no mere racing ship, but also a general fishing craft that was worked hard throughout her lifetime."

"Bluenose and her captain, Angus J. Walters of Lunenburg, were inducted into the Canadian Sports Hall of Fame in 1955, making her the first and only non-human CSHF inductee."

Over the course of the evening, David explained to Andy why we'd come to Halifax and what he was looking for in a boat (just about anything seaworthy that was a good deal). The Captain promised to ask around and to keep his eyes open for something. We parted with sincere down-east embraces and handshakes. Somehow we all knew we would meet again soon.

Back in Toronto about a month later, David charged up the back stairs swinging a six-pack. He was as animated as his caricature—big feet outrunning his long thin legs outrunning his beard and hair. Suspecting the news that had fired him up had something to do with a boat, I was happy for the coincidence of having a party-worthy meal on the stove. I'd been preparing Indian cuisine, our favorite. With cold clinking 'Heinies' under one arm and my neck under the other, he escorted me to the leather love seat in the living room. The lanky lubber took his time telling me what was up.

Finally, small talk and half a beer later, "Guess who called?"

With David, it could have been anyone from the King of Switzerland to the President of Pakistan to any of his six ex-wives (not all legally bound). Of course I couldn't resist giving him a taste of his own medicine by taking a long haul from my bottle while trying to think of a smart-ass response. Patience expired, he blurted out, "Andy Thomas! He has found a boat for us that he thinks is just what we're looking for."

"Tellmetellmetellme!"

"Well, you're not going to believe it, but it is a 112-foot subchaser from World War II."

I tried to conjure up an image of this. The sub part kept... "He thinks we want to buy a submarine?"

With a slight laugh, "Noooo. It's not a submarine. It's a submarine chaser. A fast gunboat built in the 40's for hunting down U Boats."

"U Boats? Gunboat?"

"German subs, and it's not a gunboat now. It's all mahogany and could be converted into an amazing luxury yacht. She has new engines, and Andy said this guy named Slater, who lives near him in the little village of Mahone Bay, bought it at auction years ago and just parked it at the end of a pier behind his military surplus business. Never moved the thing once, and apparently he's ready to sell."

"How much?" I ventured to ask, not that it was any of my business.

"Fifty grand and it needs work."

I assumed this figure wouldn't even come close to pushing him into the red. David's enthusiastic mood was contagious, overwhelming me with emotion. I actually teared up.

"So when are we going—to see it?"

Over the exotic feast of tandoori chicken, curried vegetables and basmati rice topped by a dessert of daydreams, it was decided that we should return to Nova Scotia immediately, meet Slater, and check out his subchaser. I was ecstatic. Sleep being out of the question, we hit my favorite bar, The El Mocambo (most famous for surprising its patrons one night with an unscheduled Stones live recording session). At closing time, we headed to Toronto's best after-hours club where David didn't even have to say, "Joe sent me." Mingling with the other creative minds, we celebrated in the unexpected company of Gordon Lightfoot and his guitar. We cuddled up on one of the old stained couches, ordered coffee and brandies and luxuriated in Gordie's smooth ballads and the excitement of what lay ahead.

Early the next morning, we were en route once again to Halifax sipping on a generous portion of hair of the dog. Also helping us with our hangovers was the air of certainty traveling with us. The mere description of this boat, with Andy Thomas's endorsement, had us primed.

Up until the moment I actually stood before the boat, I'd envisioned myself the Patrona of a gorgeous long yacht, something like an enlarged, luxury version of one of David's collection of Shepherds—those sexy piano-top-polished inboard mahogany pleasure boats circa the late 30's. Something you would imagine Hudson and Taylor cruising around in, Liz's white silk scarf framing her coif and billowing out behind her.

Standing in front of Slater's ex-gunboat and meeting *Sondra II* for the first time, my fantasy of opulence turned into incredulous disappointment. My mind's eye view of her length was off. She was much longer. That was good I supposed, but what a picture of neglect! Her dull grey paint hung like peeling sunburned skin. The remnant of her wooden sheath at the water line was sparse, twisted and ugly. There were no staterooms above the deck, just a small lookout room in the middle with lots of tarnished brass portholes. An enormous, dull black metal smokestack spotted with rusty holes looked like it had been a target practice for the Germans.

I looked over at David who was flanked by Slater and his son Fred. The Father was an outdoor-handsome sixtyish with Italian style, age-tinted hair. His clean, pressed and coordinated look gave the impression that he was well cared for by the wife. His smile was that of a salesman and his manner frictionless. The son, a dark haired version of his dad at 35, sported a vaguely inbred manner. He looked out of place in ironed army fatigues and tightly-laced spit-shined war boots. Unlike his dad, Fred sort of jittered through life, moving about with the kinetic static of a crack-head. He didn't date and lived with his folks.

"Special guy, that Fred," the locals would say.

The men strutted down the pier and boarded the ship ascending at a 60-degree slope due to the dramatic eight-foot flood tides of Mahone Bay. Embarrassed by my small fear of heights, I waited until no one was looking before scurrying on all fours up the long plank suspended over a mass of jellyfish. The deck's wood resembled the floor of an abandoned dance pavilion rather than a Steinway. We headed down below by way of a large-stepped ladder, which Slater referred to as a companionway.

It was dark. Airborne spores of fungi thriving from years of neglect instantly assailed our olfactory system. Visible dry rot had comfortably taken up tenancy in most beams, ironic because the beams were also blanketed with cottony mildew. The room we were standing in, about sixteen feet across by twenty feet long, showed evidence of being the galley—a large galvanized sink stood solo. I couldn't help but wonder what kind of grub had been served up on a gunboat in the North Atlantic in the 40's. Moving over a foot-high wall into the main room, we entered what appeared to be the set for a horror film. Spider webs, mimicking what remained of the foul crew hammocks, clung to our faces; chairs and tables lay in pieces, piled like giant, faded Pick Up Sticks. *Sondra* moaned as the wake from a passing boat gently rocked her, sloshing the seawater sitting in her partially exposed bowels where floorboards had rotted away. No sign of staterooms down there either. David was busy randomly poking with his awl while asking Slater questions. The tool disappeared up to the handle many times into what outwardly held promise of being healthy wood. I was clearly thinking we had wasted another trip, knowing David would say the same thing about this boat that he had about the motorsailor: "Too old, too much work."

As I started to ascend the ladder for some fresh air, I was stunned to hear, "I'll take it!" Looking back down into the pit below, I witnessed David shaking Slater's hand in a gentlemen's deal sealer.

I stood alone on the deck, draped in spring drizzle, cold from my collision with disenchantment. I felt he had baited me on our first date with, "I'm going to buy a boat and sail around the world and I would like you to come with me." Based on his reputation and lifestyle, the image those words had conjured up months ago featured me in elegance, hobnobbing with the Cannes crowd. This old wooden piece of crap had not a toothpick of elegance, reeked of aseptic Navy functionality and looked like it was in no condition to go to the end of the bay, let alone around the world. I could only imagine that the appeal of this ship for David was the new engines promising speed and performance beyond his dreams—the typical man vision. My enthusiasm had fully abated.

6

DOWNSIZING DAVID

Toronto
Summer, 1976

"Everyone lives by selling something, whatever be his right to it."
-ROBERT LOUIS STEVENSON

THE concept of downsizing completely eluded David. Consequently, as the clock ticked closer to our scheduled relocation to Mahone Bay, I became more and more anxious about David's approach to minimizing his assets. I had liquidated everything I owned: plant store, duplex and car. I was cash-ready for our move, but David had pushed the date ahead three times. Six months had passed and I'd gone from lightheaded, to raring to go, to antsy as hell to get out of Toronto. My two 50-pound suitcases and newly acquired second hand Ludwig drums stood patiently waiting in the corner of the guest bedroom. One whole year after the downsizing exercise began, David announced he was all set and that we would be heading out in five days. This was incredible to me. He hadn't sold a damn thing, not even his business, for which some guys from Pakistan had offered over a million dollars.

"Too much responsibility attached to the deal," he'd said blandly.

Something about them wanting to use his face and name didn't set right in his mind. I didn't understand, but I knew enough to keep my thoughts to myself. *By the time we finish pumping money into the Sondra you'll be down to your last lousy dollar. Then you'll be begging for that responsibility and wishing you'd let them plaster your face everywhere from Toronto to Pakistan and back.* Although none of my business, it irked me.

There was also David's collection of boats to consider: *Sondra* left no room for other nautical dalliances. It included an old Chris-Craft docked in Toronto Harbour, re-named *Jaws* immediately after its namesake hit the big screen. The bow, freshly embellished with an angry open-mouthed shark's jaw, and the stern, branded with the huge letters **J A W S**, brought press photographers tripping over each other. Their articles were printed front page before the paint had even dried. Surely this treasure of emotional inspiration would have fetched a few bucks. Then there were the fine vintage mahogany Shepherd and Grew powerboats that somehow David never got around to liquidating either. He must've known that someday these acquisitions would be worth tens of thousands of dollars each. My stress devolved into nagging, which inevitably developed into a heated discussion about the boats. Consequently, they became *my* business and I was sent packing the next day to the storage unit in Gravenhurst to deal with them.

I tried to make arrangements for their sale, but fall had arrived and the market had gone dormant. In the end, David never saw a cent for any of his boats. At some point, he stopped making the storage payments; the boats were eventually confiscated and sold at auction. Although I was sucked into excitement by his future ideas of how we'd make another fortune using *Sondra,* and I truly believed in him, I still never got my head around walking away from money you had already worked hard for.

Seeing cash fly into the portholes of our new floating home with no more income and no cash from his assets made me think that this just might be the end to our easy lives. I was beginning to wonder out loud what on earth we were going to do for money once we reached Key West. This is when the schemes and dreams started popping out of David's head, usually after dinner over beers and joints.

Typically, he began with a story of some successful venture he had devised in the past, like the one in Alabama where he launched the best ever dance venue in Birmingham in his early 20's; an experience that taught him the value of grey-area marketing and produced his first fortune. I must admit that the hall sounded innovative and alluring. It featured a long, dark tube-like entry that emptied teens into the middle of the dance floor, where wildly moving search lights found their wide eyes, causing them to collapse on the floor, blinded and in fits of laughter. This, along with the ten-foot high, 360-degree overhead screen featuring never-before-seen psychedelic images and live music from the likes of Ike and Tina Turner blasting out, made it the talk of the South.

Another issue that affected David's efficiency in the downsizing exercise was his family. For years, they'd not only been employed by David, but had become dependent upon him for a wild high-end lifestyle beyond their dreams and means. If David was the main event in this circus, older brother Robert and his wife Anna were the cleanup brigade. Bruce, the youngest, was the ringleader. He was a wiry little bugger with a face full of lingering puberty who constantly protected his territory by 'pissing' on anything that came near it. His redneck tactics always caught me off guard. He made sure I was kept out of important decisions in the making and talked *at* me in a condescending tone the few times he blessed me with verbal attention. It exasperated Bruce to no end that I was going everywhere David went. Until our departure, our discord was discreet but it was in his nature to push the envelope towards open combat. Since I'd been looking forward to a romantic time at sea as a twosome, this family intrusion was not a welcome change. I hadn't even been asked for my opinion.

It was with financial and emotional tension that all five of us boarded the Winnebago for the big trip to Mahone Bay and the beginning of our new lives on board *Sondra*.

7

MAHONE BAY

Mahone Bay, Nova Scotia
September, 1977

"The nice part about living in a small town is that
when you don't know what you're doing, someone else does."
-UNKNOWN

**Mahone Bay's Motto—"Unio Silvae Marisque"
meaning "Union of Forest and Sea"**

THE Winnebago trip east from Ontario to Nova Scotia, spanning 1800 kilometers (1100 miles), was one continuous rolling party. We were all so excited to finally be underway that our differences lay dormant, and sleep never entered our minds. We planned to make the whole run on the Canadian side without crossing into the US, so no one saw any reason why we shouldn't put an ounce of grass in the Altered State compartment of our home-on-wheels.

The reason not to, which we didn't take into consideration, came in the form of a weigh station just after the Quebec border. We flew past it, oblivious, and continued on in that mode with a police car following us for at least an hour while we smoked up an evening storm of laughter, music, and munching out. When the cop finally pulled us over, it was like something out of the Cheech and Chong film *Up In Smoke*. Luckily the little Frenchman was shorter than the window and the escaping smell when David rolled it down must have gone up and over his head. Either that or, as we later joked, he was stoned himself. Thank god he didn't search our party central, but he did make us turn around and drive back to the weigh station. The rest of the evening was filled with re-enactments of our experience melded with the movie's script or, more accurately, its renowned non-script, using various exaggerated versions of the cop's Quebecois accent.

We finally rolled into Mahone Bay on a crisp Saturday morning. The little village of about seven hundred, which seemed to feature a church for every fifty inhabitants, was awake and bustling with chores and chatter. It was stunningly beautiful with its fall foliage, slate-blue harbor and rocky, tide-cut shoreline lined with pastel clapboard architecture. Being a vacationers' town, no one took particular notice of our rig or its contents until we parked at the small grocery store to pick up supplies.

Of course, our coming had been heralded in the coffee shop buzz. "Mind you, the fella that bought the *Sondra* is a hippie out'a Toronta," and he was "comin' to the Bay this weekend." The first local to lay eyes on David guessed instantly that he was the new owner everyone had been talking about. David had barely placed his foot on the pavement before the guy who spotted him spun on his heels seeking someone to share the coveted gossip with. This was hot news. The boat had been in the water at the end of Slater's pier for 20 years without moving an inch. It was even on the Mahone Bay post cards. "They ah heah and the guy driving the rig has hair down to his arse and a beard to match. As well, all red eh!" They spoke with a heavy Maritime accent, dropping their r's at the end of words that, in the beginning, was often indecipherable to our gang. "Park your car" would be "Pakh ya cah" and I was "Mahni."

David pulled the Winnie up alongside Fred's antique Army Jeep and we piled out once again. Warm smiles full of anticipation were on everyone's face. Introductions to Bruce, Robert and Anna were made and exuberant handshakes were exchanged. Slater sensed that the brothers couldn't wait another minute to see the boat, so with no further ado, he led them to the waterfront where they stopped at the top of the pier to take it all in. There she was—our new home—the *Sondra II*. Somehow, in the same way your hair can look great on the day you're getting it cut, *Sondra* managed to look regal this time. Morning light perhaps? Rose-colored sunglasses?

"Damn, Bro!" came flying out of Bruce's mouth as he headed the fast-stepping parade down the two-hundred-foot, gravel-topped jetty. Fred managed to pass him with a military style gait and, positioning himself at the bottom of the plank, doled out an even heartier round of hand locking, accompanied this time by mini bows. I half expected him to click his boots together and salute. Resembling beach crabs running from hole to hole, Robert and Anna followed Bruce as they began exploring every inch of what, in that moment, was a yacht to them. Giddiness, like a lightning flash, broke through the gloom that had been shrouding the ship for many years, and she glittered. But, as the dankness filled their nostrils and the chaos their eyes, the reality of what lay ahead started to set in. A coffee break suddenly seemed like a good idea.

Jim and Fred Slater were in highest form. Coffee was all ready to brew, and the peach muffins Mrs. Slater had baked that morning were waiting to top off the perfect "down-East welcome." We gathered in Slater's enormous warehouse and, while sitting on wooden ammunition boxes, began to get to know each other as neighbors.

"What a beautiful village," Anna said with her cute Guatemalan accent. Then she further exposed her background with, "Why are there three churches all close together on the waterfront over there?"

Fred took a sip from his mug, puffed himself up, put his free hand on his knee and then leaned into the explanation, speaking in a way that sounded like the words were passing through molasses—a contradiction to the way he moved. "Welllll, Anna, th town of Mahone Bay wahz, and still e-iz, th central meetin' place foah small communities in th area. Th reason why dese three chuuches ah so close togethah, on th watafront, has nevah really been detuhmined. Th oldest chuuch dates to eighteen eighty-seven. It's been said dat sailuhs knew dey wuh in a safe place when dey set sight upon dem. Dere ah a total of five chuuches in town, eh?" He sat back and smiled a square smile, resembling a ventriloquist's dummy.

I was restless on my box but Anna had one foot in heaven. "Where did Mahone Bay get its name?"

"It comes from th woud 'mahonne', a type of 16th century nautical vessel dat employed both a sailin' rig and oah foah propulsion."

David leaned back against a pile of mold-spotted canvas life jackets and stretched out his long legs. As was his habit, he checked for muffin crumbs by following the lines of his moustache with forefinger and thumb, opening his mouth part way through the action, and carrying down through his foot-long beard.

"I see that the German did quite a bit of work on the

Sondra before he had to quit. Too bad about his heart attack."

This is when Slater 'fessed up and told us the man he had referred for repair work probably wasn't that great a carpenter anyway. "Because his own designed and built catamahran sunk befoah it hit open watah." No one was quite sure how to take this news but it seemed like a good time to excuse ourselves so that 'the men' could take the afternoon to brainstorm and map out a plan for continuing the restoration.

"Something about that old man I don't trust," David threw out as we all walked down the pier.

The next morning we began our routines, which would last for weeks until the smoldering confrontation between the brothers and me finally became a blaze. Everyone was up for coffee at sunrise. While Anna and I cooked, the boys got things organized for the day's work. After the meal, we girls cleaned up the mess in the pan-sized sink of the bathtub-sized kitchen and then joined our fellow workers.

The first big task was to remove everything remaining below deck that was not wanted or was beyond repair and dispose of it. The German had only replaced support beams in the main quarters, so rotten floorboards, sailors' bunks and the remnants of the galley remained. Nothing could be burned near where we were working because of the multiple layers of caustic paint; the job of copious off-site hauling was allocated to Anna and me. We became experts at rolling wheel barrels down the plank no matter what the angle. Apparently there was a saying in the Navy, "If it don't move, paint it." I guessed that no one ever added that a couple of coats would have sufficed.

Meals became a natural daily highlight (second only to cocktails prior to dinner), and the cuisine constantly rose to new levels. Gathering and preparing took a good part of our day as well. Often seafood was featured, which we would buy from the traveling fishmonger. Some of it was so fresh it was still moving in the kitchen evoking my rendition of Annie Hall and fits of laughter.

Happy Hour soon became my best friend. It was the only refuge I could find in our tight quarters to numb the cruel macho antics that oozed out of the brothers like a cancer. Their offensive strategy consisted of exclusion, lots of snide comments, eye rolling, tsk-tsking and dirty sexual undertones from Bruce. Due to their limited repertoire, they began to look comical and not too bright to me, especially through my inebriated eyes. David was either oblivious to all of this or took my gaiety as a sign that all was well. I never knew for sure what he was thinking because he never participated, and crying on his shoulder was out of the question. Instead, while in a drunken pre-sleep, I began planning a much more permanent escape.

As the weeks went on, the work turned into drudgery and the weather turned into a coastal Canadian November. By nature I was not a quitter, but the bullying was making me bitter. Fleeing back to Ontario seemed like the solution to everyone's problems. I felt terribly distanced from David, who was totally absorbed in the project. So nothing was holding me back. Funding was the only obstacle in my way. I had come to Mahone Bay with the proceeds from the sale of my High Park duplex in the bank, but that had quickly morphed into screws and lumber with no sign of my name beside these expenses on the non-existent ledger. I'd paid my dues in blues, as Dylan would say, and consequently should have had a free ticket out of there. Unfortunately, hitch hiking was my only option.

My plan was to leave quietly after cleanup on a Monday morning without any downtrodden, defeated goodbyes. That morning came and started with the usual routine of coffee and breakfast which, at that stage of the game, was pretty sedate. I had stashed my suitcases in Slater's warehouse the day before and placed my goodbye letter under our pillow while making the bed. When I stepped out of the Winnebago, ready to take my leave, I was astonished by what I overheard from around the corner of the rig. Bruce and Robert were giving David an ultimatum, "Either she goes, or we go."

Further to my stunned ears, "Well then, I guess the three of you had better pack your bags." Before I could find retreat, the brothers walked past me on their way to begin packing.

Bruce couldn't resist one last snarky remark, "Are you happy, cunt?"

And I couldn't resist putting my face in his face-space and in the sweetest voice I could muster up, "No, prick—I'm *ecstatic!*" And I bit my tongue to keep from adding "*you fucking insecure redneck idiot!"*

We never saw or heard from them again.

Life changed the second they were out of sight, and there was no follow-up discussion between David and me. I snuck the bags back into the Winnebago and he never knew that I was minutes away from walking out of his life. Actually, my Captain seemed completely at ease with his decision. The privacy and quiet that ensued was sublime.

Soon after, we were able to move into the room located amidships at the base of the companionway. I had finished removing all of the old paint using stripper, a propane torch, a constantly sharpened scraper, lots of elbow grease and the patience of Michelangelo. The result was a glowing tropical mahogany that framed the room. The *pièce de résistance* of this work was the hundreds of wire-wheel buffed copper rivets that held the double planks together, lustrous in the way that only polished metal can be. All was preserved with two coats of rich Spar varnish.

This area was to be the new galley and home for the captain's table, but initially we used the dining space for a makeshift queen bed. The galley and its bar, the Franklin stove that burned morning and night, a small TV and the multi-pillowed bed/lounge area made our new home downright cozy. Not too long after that, the renovations in the living room quarters were completed and our collection of instruments was lowered down through the new oversized hatch on the foredeck—enough toys to create a bona fide band. The *Sondra II* now featured the quintessential ingredients of blues, rock and progressive. Leaving a generously-sized dance floor, we placed David's Oriental carpet, the leather sofa, wing-back chairs and a large antique coffee table below the hatch. David took to serenading me with tunes such as "Proud Mary," "You Sexy Thing," and "Hot Fun in the Summer Time" while I prepared dinners. We would talk and laugh about many things, in the calm space of our renewed friendship spiced with love. I had never been happier.

Temporary Living Quarters
Queen Bed/Lounge Area, Franklin Stove & TV

8

THE ANIMATE PROPELLERS

Vignette 1: Self Replication

"The goal of all inanimate objects
is to resist man and ultimately defeat him."
-RUSSELL BAKER

WHEN one first moves aboard a ship, one begins to become familiar with a collection of inanimates (propellers, generators, anchors, ropes), managing them as they are defined in the dictionary:

INANIMATE—*adj*: not endowed with life—i.e. no capacity for self-replication, growth, metabolism, or reaction to stimuli

I first gave thought to the propellers shortly before our cast-off date, when their siblings appeared unannounced from the bowels of Slater's wondrous cave of war oddities. Neither David nor I had ever seen the original pair attached to the shafts as they were well hidden under the stern, lying dormant for twenty years in the deep, dark waters of Mahone Bay, supposedly inanimate. It seemed to me that *Sondra's* props had replicated overnight. How beautiful those robust twins were as they glistened in the early-morning sun, contrasted against the washed-out pebbles of the pier. Thirty-three inches in diameter, these triple-bladed solid brass sculptures were honed for maximum, frictionless efficiency. We admired them with our steaming coffees in hand, later again in the mid-afternoon warmth with frosty beers in hand, and then again at sunset with sweet Cuba Libres.

The next morning we set out down the gangplank for the *tête-à-tête*. How were we going to get the spare propellers down the length of the pier, on board and lowered through the living room hatch to their allocated traveling spots against the wall? We made our way up the pier, coffees again in hand and plans in mind, only to discover that our brass beauties had transported themselves elsewhere. They were gone. We stopped and turned to look back at the boat to see if someone had put them on deck for us without saying anything. *That would've been nice. Those suckers are likely really, really heavy.* We continued up the pier to where we last saw them and discovered two drag paths through the pebbles leading to the water's edge.

There they were on the ocean bottom in four feet of water—nestled neatly among the splintered wooden floorboards of a faded old skiff, the whole scene framed by the circumference of the foundered get-away boat. We both cracked up at the absurdity of the situation and wondered how thieves could be that daft. "They must have been Newfies!" I wished I'd been a fly sitting on top of one of their probable baseball caps, watching as they struggled to lower the second prop to the floor of the boat. I could almost see it—the wood suddenly snapping, the sound loudly piercing the thin night air; boys dropping like criminals through the hangman's trap door as icy black water gushed up like oil through the hole.

David put his arm around my neck and we howled with laughter.

Getting those dead weights out of the water was quite a chore for David and the three volunteers he rounded up off the street, especially as their work was interspersed with reenactments ending in all of them doubling-over in hysterics. Our helpers disappeared once the propellers were back on the pier. Unfortunately, I then remembered the props did not belong there; they belonged on the boat. El Capitan, stroking his beard, began looking at them and then at me. I began looking at them and then at the distance from where they lay to the gangplank, which by then was at a 45-degree uphill angle due to the incoming tide. I could see where this was going.

"Nooooo way. You've gotta' be kidding me, right? I can't do that! I can't lift half of those things!"

I was pretty sure those babies weighed as much as I did. But David, extolling my fine new fitness and my workhorse mentality, manipulated me into doing it. Using my thighs as a shelf combined with all of my hundred and fifteen pound might, I held up my end of the one-sided bargain and my side of the prop, and shuffled backwards to the end of the task—twice!

Amazing what I could accomplish with a bit of praise ahead of the effort. Too bad it also couldn't have protected from the pancake-sized bruises that would peek out below my shorts for days. Oh well, they added color to the luncheon tale in the "Gossip Diner," and I believe that an element of respect from the sea-seasoned listeners floated up to mix with the mirth and smoke that filled the air.

No one knew then, or ever, who the culprits were, but I was convinced that the propellers were anything but inanimate. They had moved and were certainly capable of replicating.

Man Art

9

FINDING THE PERFECT BOAT

"*THE SONDRA II*"
Formerly "*FORT PITT*"
of the Royal Canadian Mounted Police
Formerly "*HMCS ML Q119*"
of His Majesty's Court

"Build me straight, O worthy Master!
Staunch and strong, a goodly vessel,
That shall laugh at all disaster,
And with wave and whirlwind wrestle!"
-HENRY WADSWORTH LONGFELLOW

Mahone Bay,
Nova Scotia,
Fall, 1977.

Dear Mom & Dad,

Today has been a really exciting day for me. The *Sondra II was officially registered in my name! Imagine—I now own a 112-foot warship! I'll let you hazard a guess at David's reasons for doing this (wink, wink) but regardless, his show of trust in me warmed my heart. I've enclosed a copy of the "Certificate of British Registry" with the latest addition typed on the back by the Custom House in Halifax, certifying that I am "the registered sole owner." Heck Dad, you even got honorable mention!*

Coincidentally, a few days ago one of the original crewmembers of Sondra, a Mr. Jim Dowell, stood at the bottom of the gangplank and asked for "my" permission to come aboard. What a great surprise. His stories held us in awe for hours. He told us he was the telegrapher on this very boat and that she was called HMCS ML 119 during the war—His Majesty's Canadian Ship, Motor Launch 119. She was one of only eighty-eight of these Canadian Allied warships ever built. They were sister ships to the American subchasers. We knew she was built in Port Carling by Carling Boat Works but could never figure out how the heck they moved such a big vessel from a land-locked lake in Ontario to open ocean in the 1940's. He

72

explained that this shipyard had established a branch operation in Honey Harbour on Georgian Bay, near Grandpa and Grandma's cottage, where ML 119's assembly was finished before launching. Then they delivered her through the Great Lakes to the Saint Lawrence. Never thought of that! I've enclosed a copy of a photo that Mr. Slater gave me of Sondra and her three sisters sitting in front of the branch before being conscripted for service.

Sondra and her 87 sisters became affectionately known as the Fairmiles. Apparently these ships were the most massive "kit boats" ever produced. The Fairmile Company designed and prepared all of the timber to specs in Britain and exported the works to every allied country during the war for assembly and outfitting for a total production cost of $80,000.

This figure was particularly startling to us because, as you know, we only paid $50,000 some 30 years later and, apparently, when she was sold to the RCMP after the war, she went for a scandalous $3500. No wonder the government is always in the red.

I thought it was cute when our visitor referred to them as "Sexy little warships." He said, "We had a good war in the Fairmiles, acting as flotillas, rescue vessels, mine sweepers, runners, and convoy escorts." He left us a small copy of a beautiful oil painting by an artist named Tim Brown that I think you would enjoy seeing. I guess it is kind of sexy looking. With those sleek lines, they were clearly designed for the hunt—the chase. This painting was done just before HM ML192 was blown out of the water killing all on board—an interesting part of the World War II history. Of course we couldn't resist asking Mr. Dowell how many subs they blew up.

He surprised us with, "No Canadian Fairmile actually attacked or sank any U-boats, but from Nova Scotia to Newfoundland and all the way down to the

Caribbean (when on loan to the U.S. Navy), we protected merchantmen from attack—which was, after all, the name of the game."

"Wow!" We chirped in unison.

And here's the firepower they never used:

- 12 depth charges
- 1 Hotchkiss 3 lb. gun for aft
    (a big, long sucker designed in 1886 for defense
    against fast vessels and later used against subs)
- 1 set of twin machine guns
- 1 or more Oerlikon cannons
- Grenades—"lots of grenades, for the deck"

Wow again! Based on the number of bunks we've torn out, I always figured the wartime crew would have numbered about a dozen. As you can see in the photo that Mr. Dowell took of his mates, I underestimated by half a dozen!

Mr. Dowell was both amused and pleased by the new look of his old ride: her hull shining white, her butterscotch deck looking fancy with green striped deck chairs, her new brass radar protecting and the interiors radiating the richness of the original mahogany. Then there was the pièce de résistance for him: the living area full of rock and roll instruments, comfy leather furniture and fresh flowers. He said that now the lower quarters made him think of the smell of a good Scotch—not the diesel, dirty socks and wet paint mix he remembered. It was with pride that I led this seasoned seaman around his old warship. All of the tension and discipline had been replaced with luxury and peace. It was a special afternoon for all of us, and an emotional moment when we said our goodbyes. The visit reinforced the good times he spoke of, and I knew he was gratified to see the loving restoration of this piece of his personal history.

Today, while we were signing the registry papers with Slater, he brought the history of Sondra up to date. Apparently the RCMP outfitted Fort Pitt (Sondra's police-boat name) with au courant engines and the radar that we inherited. She was put into service in their Marine Division to patrol the North Atlantic. A short time later, the cops retired her due to the Fairmile's rough performance in turbulent waters and the constant struggle the crew had with seasickness. Thank god, we are headed to the calmer waters of the Caribbean. Slater bought the boat at auction and tied her to the end of his pier where she bobbed in the waters of Mahone Bay until we came along. We didn't venture to ask what he'd paid and it's anybody's guess, because I understand that many were purchased for use at that time as cargo carriers and private yachts. Even Jack McClelland, the famous Toronto publisher, owned one!

She is presently named after Slater's daughter, Sondra, whom we've yet to meet. David has decided not to change this because it's bad luck and even considered shady—a sort of alarm that there's something to hide. But once I figure out the appropriate English honorific, I will be hanging that tag in front of my name. Maybe it's Dame or something like that, and I can be known as "Dame Marlaine of the Order of Fairmiles." That would be fun! Not to be confused though with Mom's occasional frustrated parental rant, "Damn you Susan Marlaine!" Ha Ha.

Well, the afternoon is fast disappearing and a thin chilly fog has rolled in and found its way to my private little spot behind the wheelhouse. And, I still have to go shopping. We're fresh out of Grenades!

Write soon—you know how much I love your letters.

Hugs and Hi to my brothers,
Marni

Custom House
Halifax, N.S.

I hereby certify that on this
5th day of January, 1978,
Susan Marlaine Craig, C/O
D.T. Craig, R.R.#4, Belleville
Ontario, School Teacher, is
registered sole owner of the
ship within described.

Col.14: David Richard Keller,
businessman, C/O Slaters Ships
Outfitters, Mahone Bay, N.S.,
appointed manager. Advice received
dated December 21, 1977.

NATIONAL REVENUE
REVENU NATIONAL **Canada**
CUSTOMS DIVISION — DOUANES

5 JAN 1978

REGISTER OF SHIPPING
REGISTRATEUR DES NAVIRES
LA HAVE, N.S. (N.-E.)

**Port Carling Boat Works Showing *Sondra* & Three Sisters
Ready To Go To War**

The Sexy Little War Ship—B&W of Oil Painting by Tim Brown

Crew Men on ML Q119. Photo by Jim Dowell

10

DOWN TO THE WIRE

Mahone Bay, Nova Scotia
August, 1978

"I watched a snail crawl along the edge of a straight razor. That's my dream; that's my nightmare. Crawling, slithering, along the edge of a straight razor…and surviving."

-KURTZ in *APOCALYPSE NOW*

AUGUST brought with it radiant, rainless days. With only two weeks remaining until our scheduled departure date, David and I were busy sweating out the last-minute details. When David's brothers were onboard I thought they were my worst problem, but now we had no crew, and that seemed a much bigger issue. As the calendar quickly turned, I began paying more attention to my acquired collection of books on surviving at sea. Curled up beside David under the eiderdown, the fire glowing in the Franklin stove, I would read the useful parts aloud to him by the light of a kerosene lantern. One night I hit the story that made a zealot out of me. I poked David to get his attention.

"Listen to this!" He took off his glasses, turned over the book he was reading, "Beat The Craps Tables," and gave me a nod of attention, something he would soon regret. I read quickly to him from the book jacket while my index finger hurried along under the lines, a story of true survival…how a father and his young family of three prepared for an Atlantic crossing in their forty-foot sailboat…rammed by a whale…sank in a matter of minutes… survived for thirty days…trapped drinking water in their lifeboat's roof tarp or extracted it from fish eyes…"

My head whipped in his direction, "David. When are you getting our lifeboat from Slater?"

Long pause. "Actually, there isn't one," he said, picking up his glasses and book, signaling end of attention.

"Whaddayamean there isn't one?" There *has* to be one! When they went out into the Atlantic to run after submarines in this thing, I'm sure they'd have had at least one onboard."

He answered with silence, which triggered an imploring

mode in me that would follow him around for days. The next
morning I began beseeching him with dazzling wake-up sex,
hints about my upcoming birthday, his favorite Indian dinner—
the works. All to no avail. My mind's eye was creating a lifeboat
mise-en-scène for David, the totality of which I was certain
would somehow make obvious the severity of this issue. The
theater props I was envisioning consisted of what seemed to be
the norm in any collection of survival items: a tarp, poetry by
Leonard Cohen, multi-purpose tool, first-aid kit, the cat's bed,
fishing supplies, the snare drum and sticks, a bottle of rum and of
course some tequila, limes to refresh and prevent scurvy, sewing
kit, a couple of blotters for the still days, waterproof container
for said tabs, matches in a jar as well as some weed and papers,
my very best Indian garam masala, candles for the romantic
dinner, bandanas, flashlight, flares, dehydrated food, bottles of
water, "Beat the Craps" book in case we ended up washing onto
the shores of Monaco, and a cocktail dress, nail polish and heels
for me. Early the next day, I began putting Plan B into action by
gathering and then laying many of these objects on the deck in
an approximated life-raft-sized oval, topping the whole scene off
with a cardboard sign in the middle that read, **EMERGENCY
LIFEBOAT LOCATION**.

All of this pushed David towards his wit's end. I was
already over my limit when my sailor friend, Dr. Dan, expressed
his shock to hear that the leather couch, wingbacks, spare props
and organ had not been secured to the boat. David had casually
mentioned that because *Sondra* was a ship and not in the same
category as the local's little sailboats, it was not necessary to
secure things onboard, and I'd bought it.

Walking home, Dan's words "Absolutely insane!"
rattled around in my head. Back at the pier, my mouth outran me
up the gangplank and delivered the new worry to David.
Consequently, this new issue ended up simply walking the plank.

That day, my mind was literally obsessed with my
concerns: life raft, securing, life raft, securing. I was so frantic
that I actually cried in front of David or, rather, while following
him. I couldn't do anything further about the raft, but I could
fasten the furniture to the salon floor. This was just a ploy
because, as we all know, most men hate to see women messing

with tools and usually come running to take charge and do the job for us.

I headed for the engine room to gather up what I needed along with a few things I didn't need to be sure it looked like I was going to do something monstrous. I had his precious electric drill, a saw, an angle grinder, extension cord, a bag of assorted brass screws, L-shaped brackets, an assortment of screw drivers, plumbing wrench, twine, hammer and huge nails that I made sure were visible. I fired up the small Honda generator, plugged in the extension cord and went below with my basket of tools. After only minutes of hammering and drilling into a leg of one of David's coveted leather wingbacks, his long hair filled the hatch. His upside down face, although somewhat veiled by his upside down beard, held a look of panic. When I put the drill down to grab the screwdriver and a screw, I waved.

David, now with a red forehead and bulging eyes shouted, "Marge! What are you doing?" I smiled sweetly. I knew the testosterone would kick in any minute and he would be down below *tout suite*, take over and finish the work for me.

The plan worked for the furniture, but Captain Stubborn refused to hear another word about the top-heavy antique treadle sewing machine, the two enormous spare propellers and the Hammond organ. So I acquiesced and decided to leave one other thing *unscrewed*—not a tactic I normally resorted to, but hey, desperate times require desperate measures, although they don't always work!

Two days later, David miraculously succumbed to my other more important concern. He and three strong boys clambered up the plank carrying a big, bathtub-sized, yellow, tattered cork donut that appeared to be of the same vintage as *Sondra*.

"Slater found this thing in the back of his warehouse under a bunch of ammo boxes." He was all beardy grins, sure he'd just done something to undo the curse and be assured of a good lay. I suspected Slater had had a glimpse of my mini stage.

After inspecting what looked like an oversized bedraggled buoy of some sort, I looked up at David. "What is this thing?" The volunteers, sensing a conflict, gave little bows and left.

"It's your birthday present. Just what you wanted," he said gesturing with both arms in a ta-da-like fashion.

"David," and articulating here, "there is no floor in it!"

"You asked for a life raft. You got a life raft. Official Canadian Navy Issue."

"You've got to be fucking kidding me."

No verbal defense. He simply walked past me and disappeared down the three steps into the wheelhouse and reappeared surprisingly quickly to the scene of the standoff with a stack of six small flat bags he was carrying like a Hilton room-service waiter. I'd not seen these before. Dropping them at my feet while staring me down, he said, "There you go. Official Canadian Navy Issue Survival Suits. With these, you don't need a floor. Problem solved." He briskly retreated to the engine room, leaving me to examine the contents of one of the bags. Holding the long, electric orange-yellow suit up to my jockey sized body, all I could do was let it slide out of my hands and shake my head.

The suit was a simple waterproof one-piece "Gumby Suit" made from neoprene fabric, accessed through a waterproof front zipper and accessorized with rubber seals at the neck, wrists and ankles.

"Shit, there's enough room in this for me plus the cat, his litter box and a fifty pound bag of kibble. With my skinny ankles and wrists, my clothes will be soaked in a heartbeat and my survival time maxed out at three minutes. They say death by freezing is a delightfully euphoric way to go. Damn good thing. And I can just see the obituary now…"

Susan Marlaine Craig died at sea today. Authorities are not sure whether she drowned in an attempt to swim to her pathetic lifeboat or whether she succumbed to hypothermia to prove a point. Suicide has not yet been ruled out. The Coast Guard did say they had a difficult time finding her icy and underappreciated corpse inside the XXL antique survival suit she was wearing when discovered. They also alluded to the fact that this could possibly have been worn as a ritual costume or as a last desperate act of irony. According to their report, she passed away with an angry grimace on her face.

As I stuffed the ridiculously large suit back into its comically tiny bag, I was filled with the wrath of a defeated boxer who knows she just got decked in an unfair match—a featherweight against Rocky. I still had fight left in me, but found myself alone in the ring. Every muscle was tense. I was super-fired with adrenalin. I knew that with this supposedly impressive display, David had decided to take a completely irresponsible position concerning our safety. In that moment (and for the first time), I absolutely detested him. I also knew that in that same moment, I had evolved yet again into someone stronger. The man I loved and trusted with my life had just left the scene dressed from head to toe in poor judgment knowing that his pockets were filled with my disappointment. And just like that, I no longer saw him as infallible or myself as his disciple. Under some circumstances, important circumstances, I was actually capable of making better decisions than David was.

All of my savings had gone towards fixing the boat. Throwing in the towel and walking away was not an option. My insane yet innate desire to follow through with my commitment to take that old boat from Nova Scotia to Key West prompted me to swallow my objections, redouble my efforts, and take the chance.

I began by tossing my pile of survival supplies off to one side, and with the power that rage pumped through my veins, I muscled the moldy old donut into its spot on the deck. From belowdecks, I retrieved a large grommeted piece of canvas, four overstuffed, neck-strangling life jackets and a waterproof duffle bag. Returning to the deck, I loaded the bag with the realistic survival items, placed it in the raft's bottomless pit and packed the lifejackets around it. Using my recently acquired skills in knotting, I lashed everything together, and to the raft. I finished by covering the works with the canvas and secured the raft itself to the ship. The final touch was to christen it *Marni's End* (with a bit of spit), while praying it wouldn't be.

I wasn't the only one with concerns. Rhett, our Garfield lookalike, shifted his stateroom to *Marni's End* for his afternoon nap. It wasn't long before he successfully petitioned his food and litter box to be relocated there as well. He had no plans to go down with the ship either.

By dusk of that day, I felt like something had been accomplished, although I wasn't sure exactly what. I poured myself a stiff, jumbo-sized rum and coke, dished out silence to David, and headed to the bunks in the stern where I could enjoy my cocktail in peace. My strong drink carried me off into a restless sleep and nightmare.

My hands are sweaty, but I don't understand because without the stars it's cold. I am dressed in a flowing satin-like nightie made of skin. I don't feel right at the helm. The wheel is slippery in my control.

I hear someone yell from behind me, "All Aboard!" followed by high-pitched laughter. It's Fred!

"What the hell are you doing here?"

"I'm yoah Fust Mate. Didn't David tell you? And don't you know thea' whales fighting on th front deck? You betta' get 'em off or they'll scatch the paint with theyah bahnacles and the Captain will be mad."

He's right. I pick up the canned air horn and blast it at them. It blows them right off the bow and triggers an unexpected DING-DING from the telegraph beside me.

"That's not how it's supposed to work Fred! My telegraph is always silent. The engine room's the only one that makes noise!" I turn to tell him that someone screwed up the wiring, but he has disappeared. I grab both handles of my telegraph and force them forward, signaling back to the engine room that it's time to warm up the engines in preparation to leave Mahone Bay, but I have completely forgotten a Fairmile has no neutral. The thin air is filled with the sound of the propellers ripping the water apart, the ropes ripping Sondra free of the pier. Fiery smoke rings are being forced out of the smokestack's holes. I know I've made a big mistake. I try to pull the telegraph handles back to the 'Stand By' position but they come off in my hands. I pitch them overboard. I feel the fight-or-flight juices pumping through my muscles. I sense my skin hitting the cool night air as my slippers hit the deck running and I bolt towards the engine room hatch in an attempt to yell down to whoever is there.

"Hey you! Hey Engineer! Slow down the gray monsters!"

Nothing is changing. I yell at God, "Please make him slow down!" Still nothing. I slide down the fire pole that has replaced the metal ladder. No one is there. There is no engineer. A deafening noise is rising above the tapping of the engines—a sharp whistle. Someone has also replaced the compressed air's holding *tank. It looks like an oversized pressure cooker and it's about to blow! I dash for the back exit ladder to escape the danger and scramble on my hands and knees back to the wheel. The searchlight has been turned on. Must've been Fred. It's lighting up the black silhouette of land, dead ahead. I try to turn Sondra away but the wheel is caught up in my nightie made of flowing skin.*

"Oh no, we're gonna' crash! We're gonna' crash! Manthelifeboatmanthelifeboat!" The wind roars around inside my wide-open mouth, scooping up my screams, scattering them over the massive wake as we rip towards shore, full-bore.

Too late. A thousand mahogany Tama Drums are jettisoning through the air and an explosion of disconnected beats fills the bay. I'm flying beside an anchor. David's organ is on the other side of me playing "Sweet Dreams Baby," and I'm thinking, 'Everything was out of control from the start—why did David put me at the helm? I didn't practice—I wasn't ready.'

My own screaming woke me. I was standing beside the lifeboat with a survival suit in my hand. David was holding me, stroking my hair, telling me, "I'm sorry. It's okay. It's okay. Everything will be alright."

I took comfort in his arms and put mine around him to let him know I was finished being angry. I asked him to take me into the wheelhouse and explain exactly how things were going to work on the day we would set out to sea—never having started the engines before or practiced the routine.

He took my hand and led me there, lifting me up and perching me on top of the chart table. "I will be at the helm on the bridge. Fred will be standing on the pier instructing some line boys as to when to untie *Sondra* from the bollards. We will have deck hands at either end of the boat to receive the lines. Fred will also instruct me as to when to fire up the engines and which one first. I send the signal down to the guy in the engine room using the telegraph. Starting and stopping the engines is not as complicated as it seems. I know the fact that there's no neutral has you worried, Marni, but we can accomplish everything we need by various combinations of forward and reverse using the two engines. Even though my experience has only been with more modern boats with all the controls at my fingertips, it's really just simple math. I've talked to Andy Thomas a lot about this and he thinks I'm totally capable."

"But the engineer can't see anything and we don't even have one yet."

"He doesn't need to see anything. *I'm* his eyes. And I didn't want to get your hopes up for nothing, but Andy thinks he has found us an experienced ship's engineer. We'll know soon."

David made love to me that night and I told myself that he was doing his best under the circumstances. For some reason we had chosen to crawl along the edge of a straight razor together, and being the type of people we were, we *would* survive.

The Ship's Telegraph in the Engine Room

11

THE MOTLEY CREW

Mahone Bay, Nova Scotia
August, 1978

"There are three sorts of people; those who are alive,
those who are dead, and those who are at sea."
-LD CAPSTAN CHANTEY
ATTRIBUTED TO ANACHARSIS, 6TH CENTURY BC

BECAUSE *We Could*

OUR motley crew miraculously began to pop up out of nowhere. First it was a former junior-level schoolteacher from Ontario who, bored with kids, was looking for something to shake him up a bit. Stewart simply appeared at the bottom of the gangplank early one morning. Once invited aboard, he walked up the plank with purpose in his stride, accompanying his introduction with a convincingly firm handshake undoubtedly designed to offset his lack of experience. I studied him as he approached. His body was sort of non-descript—not tall, not particularly muscular or fit as indicated by his slight paunch, but his overall appearance was certainly striking. Great shocks of Irish-red, shaggy hair and complete facial 'fro the texture of a Brillo pad juxtaposed with his Ralph Lauren fashion statement. Overall, there was a softness about him that I liked—slow-moving mannerisms, quiet speech, full lips that smiled easily and green eyes that listened. I had a feeling he would be good for David. Over coffee, we discussed the fact that no pay would be involved, that it would simply be room, board and uncharted excitement in exchange for work. We took him on, and because he was a guy and this was the 70's, he was instantly made First Mate. I didn't like it, but decided that David's decision was a means of making Stewart feel welcome and important. For once in my life, I kept my mouth zipped because I knew from the racing scene that crew status changed like poll positions.

The next to arrive were the children of a local friend. Both were meek, in their early twenties, slender, dark and very handsome. Greg, in lumberjack red plaid, stiff jeans and sneakers fresh out of the box, sported black-rimmed coke-bottle-bottom glasses leaving only the lower half of his clean-shaven face visible. His total visage was one of a man who seemed to be sporting swimming goggles containing blue-striped pool balls. He constantly pushed his ocular nemesis back up the bridge of his nose with his middle finger and shuffled and slumped his posture in an attempt to shorten his 6'4" height into proportion with that of his shy demeanor.

His sister Sarah gave off the aura of a hot car with no engine. They were nice kids but, like Stew, had not a seafaring bone in their bodies. However, their arrival did *not* alter the chain of command. I envisioned Greg as my personal gofer and Sarah as, well, a ship's figurehead I could always strap to the prow if she got underfoot.

As we began our last two days of preparation, things were not looking too promising in the squad department. Basically we had a collection of Disney dreamers with absolutely no grasp of anything nautical, especially the perils. If you put us all in a blender, you still wouldn't have one bona fide jack-tar, even if you did add sea salt. By comparison to *Sondra's* former status as *HML 119*, outfitted with a Navy crew of eighteen drilled sailors, this was dire.

Then there was Ron, the real deal. He marched down that pier and straight up the gangplank, warping it gravely under his three-hundred-plus pounds, like I imagined John Wayne would have. Although it was a crisp day, his un-tucked sports shirt with overworked buttons was soaked under the pits as though he were finishing a marathon. The legs bulging from the bottom of his shorts were as big around as my waist. His baby-thin hair featured a serious receding line and meager strands were plastered to his head with sweat droplets that escaped into his narrow dark eyes.

With no ado, he began, "Andy Thomas sent me. I was an engineer in the Navy in Vietnam and I'm here to volunteer." Those words turned David into the best listener he'd ever been and the interview went faster than buying a burger at McDonalds!

So now *Sondra* had her full crew, or at least enough: someone to steer the boat, someone to run the engines, deckhands, a cook and a Ferrari. The Captain was ready to take his Lady out to sea. Although *Sondra* was registered in my name, I realized that I really only owned the turf known as The Galley. But somehow just knowing I was *officially* the owner, according to the little blue British Registration Book, felt amazing to me. I was truly grateful for that, even if only for the amusing power it gave me to shoot people that came on board without my permission, ex-wives included.

All that remained now was the dry dock work at a shipyard down the coast. We would never need the outer layer of wood protecting the hull from ice. None of that nasty frozen water where we were headed.

The night before we left Mahone Bay, we shared our first dinner together as a crew. Ron had insisted on treating us all to steaks on the BBQ and I topped it off with a baked potato bar, Caesar salad and peach shortcake. While we stood around talking and laughing and enjoying the tantalizing smell of smoldering mesquite, David disappeared for a moment and returned with a surprise bottle of Dom Perignon. The cork flew up into the star-studded sky and raucous cheers echoed out over the bay. With plastic champagne glasses filled and raised, he first proposed a toast to *Sondra*, our sexy little warship, then to me, his sexy little partner, and finally to the brave members of our gallant crew.

Downing his glass in one gulp, Ron hollered out, "Bring it on Mother Ocean!"

She would.

12

AND WE'RE OFF!

Mahone Bay, Nova Scotia
11:00 a.m.—August 19, 1978

"As we voyage we are creating new stories within
the tradition of the old stories; we are literally
creating a new culture out of the old."
-NAINOA THOMPSON FROM *THE WAYFINDERS*

CAPTAIN David Richard Keller took the helm of the *Sondra II.* She had journeyed to him from her proud beginning as a submarine chaser in an *aggressive war culture*, through to a patrol vessel in the RCMP Marine Division in the *protective coastal culture*, through to auctioned-off surplus in the *wasteful post-war culture*. David would navigate her into a final metamorphosis in her lifelong journey—into that of a Hippie Super Yacht in the *peace culture*.

The big day had finally arrived. We were ready to cast off on our maiden voyage to Shelburne (at the tip of Nova Scotia) some 200 kilometers down the rocky coastline. There, we would pull our ship out of the water into dry dock to prepare for our Caribbean destination.

The thick gray wooden gangplank, having seen a year of traffic removing and replacing *Sondra's* parts, had been dragged on board and securely strapped to the wheelhouse. The starboard side of the ship still remained lashed to the large cleats on the pier and her graceful bow was pointed to the journey ahead. I wondered if she was afraid to leave this secure place that she had called home for so many years, or was she happy to be called out of forced retirement?

For *Sondra's* last scene in this mid-morning theater-in-the-round, the main characters were all in position, awaiting her performance.

David was on the bridge looking strong and confident with his hair and beard indicating the prevailing easterly breeze. He was waiting for the final moment when, with one hand on the large mahogany wheel and the other on the brass telegraph, he would put our departure into motion. Big Ron, who could not be seen below deck in the engine room, was sweating in his own steam waiting for the sharp DING-DING that would represent David's commands to power the ship. Stewart, with his back to the wind and haloed by a hood of red hair, was on the bow waiting to catch the bowline from one of the volunteers on the pier. Greg and his sister were at the stern waiting to receive the stern line. Greg, in his caricatured glasses, exuded nervousness. His adorable sister, in matching everything, looked languid and totally expendable. Food wasn't on anyone's mind, so I was pretty much free to lean mid-ship against the wheelhouse, wallow in my perceived obscurity and take in the show. I noticed that the air was filled with an odd mélange of pungent ocean, joyful apprehension and whiffs of L'Oreal mousse drifting from the ends of my loose hair. The score from *The Good, the Bad and the Ugly* came into my head and I remember thinking it was an excellent choice for an adventure soundtrack.

I turned my attention to those actors not on the boat. Fred was decked out for the occasion in meticulously-prepared fatigues complete with angled beret. He was standing on the pier about 25 feet from the boat holding a vintage megaphone, which was actually just a cone-shaped piece of cardboard painted military green. We held a matching one. Watching him, I could see he was wired stiff and poised to holler maneuvers at David or anyone who might listen. I imagined he had play-acted this moment many times since *Sondra* had entered his life as a kid. Slater had his arms folded on his chest and was gently rocking from toe to heel. His slightly raised chin gave him a look of pride, but I knew he was saddened to see another man live his dream. The volunteers stationed at the cleats were both enjoying a casual smoke while still maintaining an air of importance as the chosen ones.

The shore's fall foliage, hundreds of cozy jackets and fishing boat escorts made for a vibrant palette. The 10:45 a.m. sun threw silver glitter on the cerulean bay's surface and warmed the crowd's faces. Most of the town had turned out to bid their landmark of 30 years farewell. The quiet of waiting was layered by the crisp snapping of our oversized Canadian Maple Leaf flag off the stern, softly idling outboard motors and storytellers' guffaws.

Being sea-faring folk for many generations, their collective expressions favored amused dubiousness. The losers who had bet against this day's arrival were paying their debts. Twelve months after David and I had landed in the village of Mahone Bay, we knew them as kind Nova Scotians who readily offered up advice, sea stories and warm hospitality, and they knew us as a couple of crazy beatniks that didn't know shit about going to sea, but we were going anyway.

There, from my observation point, I imagined a curtain being raised on Scene 1 as I, like an understudy, watched from the wings.

SCENE 1

FRED: **(Raises the megaphone to his mouth.)** Captain. Prepayah to sta't yoah engines.

DAVID: All systems a go, Sir.

FRED: **(Turns his face first to the left and then to the right.)** Bill. Scott. Cast off de lines. Quick now lads. **(There is a pause while all eyes are on the line handlers.)**

FRED: Toss 'em hawd to de deck hands.

Chorus falls silent.

(Cue ropes whistling through the air.)

Deck hands catch ropes and immediately busy themselves making neat circles resembling pioneer rag rugs. The boat begins drifting out from the pier on the incoming tide.

FRED: Poht engine low speed ahead, Captain.

Chorus looks from Fred to the bridge.

RON: **(Below deck in the engine room talking to himself.)** OK, Skippa'. Can't see bugger all down here but my hands is at the ready. Give me the ol' signal and let's let 'er rip.

CHORUS: **(Glances sideways at each other with pinched brows and questioning eyes. Words are launched into the sea breeze.)** Oh boy! Dat's de wrong dang engine!!!

David takes a quick look at Fred and then one at the crowd on the pier.

Chorus nods, to confirm David's doubt.

David's right hand quickly moves the leaver on the telegraph as commanded.

(Cue blast of air; port engine firing and water exploding.)
Sondra responds instantly to the churning and begins moving
forward towards the pier.
CHORUS IN DISTANCE: Loud cheers.
FRED: (Almost immediately after the first set of instructions,
yells over the sound of the engaged engine and the Chorus.)
Cut the poht engine! Stahbuhd engine full speed ahead!
CHORUS: (Everyone talking at once now.) Oh shite – too
late! Oh my gawd! Dey'a gonna' take a pieca' dat dock ta sea
wit' dem! I told ya dat buncha dumb hippies didn't know theyah
arse from a hole'n de ground!
David follows Fred's command signaling Ron.
Ron stops the port and starts the starboard.
David hard-cranks the wheel to port. He looks over his right
shoulder and sees *Sondra* ding the end of the pier.
(Cue wood crunching and cameras on shore clicking like
mad, attempting to record history.)
The pier remains but with a new corner design.
Fred salutes *Sondra*.
Sondra roars off in an arc to the left.
David attempts to straighten *Sondra* out by signaling Ron to
restart port engine.
Slater gives his head a long slow shake.
CHORUS: Politely chuckles and begins muttering embellishments.

With embarrassment left behind in the wake, our
Captain's attention turned to the feel of the helm, and the deck
hands turned their attention to the local boaters escorting us into
the 12-mile bay. In response to my raucous blasts from our little
canned air horn, their blares and cheers danced in the air and
filled our hearts. I was so moved and so filled with pride that my
eyes swelled up. I started to sing my favorite Jimmy Buffet song
about Mother Ocean as loud as I could into the oncoming wind,
and while still belting it out, turned to make eye contact with
David. He winked and I flashed him my warmest smile along
with a strong thumbs-up. We had done it. We were underway
and, as the French would say, "Love puts on a new face every
day."
Ten minutes into her maiden voyage with her new

owners, *Sondra II*—now cruising solo—was cutting smoothly through the frigid dark waters. Unfortunately, the time had come for Scene II, and nobody had read this part of the script, let alone rehearsed it. An unseen hand quickly lowered a plot twist between bow and horizon: the infamous Nova Scotia fog.

Protocol flew out the portholes and chance ruled. No telegraph signals went to the engine room this time. They would not have been heard anyway because Ron was on deck behind the bridge checking out the scenery and chatting me up, both of us with our backs to the oncoming weather.

SCENE II

Ron & Marni are talking in front of the smoke stack.
DAVID: **(Leaving the helm, he flies past Ron and Marni towards the bow while screaming.)** Cut the engines! Cut the engines! **(He is absorbed into the fog.)**
Ron quickly disappears behind the smoke stack.
(Cue cacophony.)
Marni follows the commotion and finds Stewart and Greg desperately trying to assist Ron in getting through the closest hole down to the engine room. Although it is the quickest access point, it is obviously too small for Ron's bulky body.
STEWART: **(With one foot on Ron's left shoulder, hysterically talking to Greg.)** Put your foot on his other shoulder and *push* him through the damn hole!
GREG: **(Breathing heavily.)** He'll never fit through there in a million years. I think he…
RON: **(Clambering back onto the deck on his chubby hands and knees.)** Get outta' my way! **(He stumbles to his feet and bolts stern-bound to his usual, larger, square entrance into the engine room, yelling as he disappears frantically below deck.)** Someone take the wheel and keep 'er on a straight course!
Stewart follows orders.
Ron cuts both engines; throws them both into reverse; quickly starts them for a moment and then abruptly cuts them again.
(Cue engine and water churning noises followed by silence.)

Sondra eerily flows through the solid cloud while everyone holds their breath.

(Cue water droplets falling from *Sondra's* hull into the water.)

Marni moves quickly to the bow and finds David stock-still in a ready posture for heaving the anchor he holds in both hands.

Greg and sister follow Marni in time to see David's mighty hurl and watch in dumbstruck unison as the line pays out rapidly and the bitter end follows the anchor's lead into the ocean. The line was not made fast to the ship.

MARNI: **(To the audience.)** I wonder if this was part of David's "No Need to Secure Things Down on a Ship" program.

David snappily ties the other anchor to the bow cleat and wings it into the wall of pea soup, almost launching his body with it. The crew stands still and waits for it to catch. It does, easily.

Sondra begins to slowly pivot around the line that now roots her to the earth until she finds the trough between the waves where, without the second anchor to stabilize her, she takes on a personality unbeknownst to the crew and begins to pitch and roll.

So began twenty hours of hell, with everyone except Ron succumbing to seasickness. None of us new sailors had developed sea legs yet and we had no experience with this kind of scenario. It was relentless, with the five of us throwing up until we couldn't imagine where another heave would possibly come from. Everything sitting on shelves or counters fell off and was rolling around down below. There was broken glass and spilled food all over the galley. Eating was out of the question anyway and keeping water down, impossible. None of us could sleep, not because of losing sight of the horizon, which normally provokes this illness, but because we were on the fly to "Call Ralph" again moments after we got tucked in. Thank goodness no one was sick down below. Finally the shroud lifted and *Sondra's* ship of fools, all with our freshly earned Green-Gill sailors' badges and a few pounds lighter, was off once again. As quickly as it overcame us, the seasickness left. We made a joke about the fact that we were wise to *Sondra* and the reason she was fired from her last position. She was a naughty girl in waves of any size!

Rather than heading for Shelburne, our Captain changed plans and decided to make a run for the much closer port of Lunenburg. I don't recall what minor adjustments we were stopping for, but I do recall they didn't include fixing the uncooperative radar. Now that I knew what being without radar was really like, the apprehension it could induce and the consequences thereof, it became foremost in my mind.

Unfortunately, the stop could not include "tweaking" the compass either (as this could only be accomplished while in dry dock). Without an accurate compass, our charts, courses, and even cardinal directions, were useless. There were two challenges to our navigation: magnetic variation and compass deviation.

Every mariner must understand magnetic variation, which is the difference between true north and magnetic north. To chart a course from point A to point B, it's not enough to simply pull out a compass, watch the needle swing northward and plot a path. Compasses naturally point to magnetic north, a physical location in the arctic regions of Canada. Essentially, Earth acts on a compass as a huge magnet, attracting the tip of the needle. However, "true north" deviates from that magnetic point by hundreds of miles. True north is a geographical point at 90 degrees latitude at the top of a world map. Seafaring folks use latitude and longitude to express where they are on Earth and where they are going, but a compass only recognizes magnetic poles, not nautical coordinates. Thus, each time a compass is read, the navigator must compensate for magnetic variation.

For landlubbers like us, this was confusing, but manageable. The real zinger of navigation was "tweaking the compass." Oh, that Earth was our *only* magnet! But like all boats, *Sondra* herself carried a magnetic field. Her copper rivets, brass props, iron engines, and all miscellaneous metallics further influenced the compass needle, and the degree of influence changed with our heading. We desperately needed a technician to draft a customized deviation table for *Sondra* to compensate for her metallic field. Each compass reading required a consultation of this table to calculate our heading accordingly, compensating for the magnetic variation as well as the compass deviation.

So far, this was all theory. We had somehow managed to get from Mahone Bay to Lunenburg with no radar and no compass deviation table. Our decorative sextant was as useful as a religious icon: no one knew how to use it. Ron was the navigator, and we had run along the coastline without incident. I started nagging David as we approached the pier at Lunenburg.

"Jesus, David! The bloody wind, the tides, all this... compass stuff... I've never done any navigation in my life! David, what *is* your list of *minor adjustments*? We don't have a working radar, and the compass issue and the radar, and the... Do we even have charts for it all? This stuff would be on anyone's list no matter whether you called it a minor, major, or panic list. We can't go back out there again without doing something. And besides, I thought that Mahoney piece-of-crap-radar was newly installed by the RCMP and that it *definitely* would function at sea. It's supposed to have, what, minutes of duty on it? Surely fixing it won't take much. What the hell is a *minute of duty* anyway?"

Annoyed, David barked across his beard, "Not now! Go help Greg with the stern line."

I knew speech without eye contact meant that the discussion was over. I took my pouty slouch back to the stern, and transferred my aggression over to Greg.

I went straight for his exposed worry button with, "Oh my god, Greg. He's going to park... he's actually going to try to dock this thing at the High Liner fish factory's jammed up pier between two other boats!" Then reality kicked my own ass into real anxiety. "Shhhhit, Greg! This is the first time David and Ron have attempted this. There's no way." I couldn't stop ranting, "I've had nightmares about the *no-fucking-neutral thing* for a year and I don't think...WHAT THE HELL IS THAT SMELL!?" The pong from the fish house was so strong it assaulted our nostrils like a punch.

The tension was broken. Greg and I turned to each other, each with our mouths and noses buried into our jacket sleeves, and laughed while Greg choked out, "That smell never showed up on the picturesque postcards of the home of *The Bluenose* schooner! Man!"

I pulled his arm down. Regardless of my drama and despite the stench, we had a job to do. "We'd better get ready back here annnnnd—guess what?" No answer on the breeze. "We get to use the ingenious monkey's fist! Yahoo!" Greg's eyebrows appeared in puzzlement above his black rims. Reaching into my parka's oversized pocket, I produced a spherical knot made of thin rope resembling a small bunched fist with a line attached. "Don't worry, Buddy, I practiced how to use it last week. I got this!" Greg flinched.

"First, you tie this thin rope attached to the monkey's fist to the heavy stern line, about five feet from the end. When we get really close to the dock and David gives us the signal, I'm going to swing the ball over my head and throw it as hard as I can past that guy on the dock waiting to catch our line. The fist acts as a weight at the end of the ship's line and makes it easier to throw. He'll grab it and haul up the stern line by way of the fist. Just hope I don't conk him on the head with it! Too bad Slater isn't the guy on the dock—I'd love to deck that sneaky bastard right about now."

With the ship parallel to the pier, David's nod signaled me to proceed. I swirled the ball over my head like a cowgirl and then let her rip as hard as I could.

Greg was all smiles and awe, "Hey! That was perfect!"

Sondra was busy starting and stopping, forwarding and reversing her 112-foot hull into the 140-foot berth. The owners of the boats fore and aft of this berth were frantically yanking on their lines trying to give us as much space as they could on such short notice. There were a lot of shouted orders and people flying around. The others on shore looked on in sheer disbelief as David and Ron parallel parked her like there was nothing to it. They could tell we had no neutral. Head-shaking admiration followed. Requests and invitations to board were exchanged and the crew basked in another moment of limelight.

After the newly acquired fans left, David and Ron quickly began fixing the *minor* things. Much to everyone's surprise, a radar technician showed up out of nowhere. On the sly, I'd taken leave of *Sondra* to flush out an expert from the many men working on the dock.

After having a good look at the equipment with Captain and Engineer looking over his shoulder the whole time, Radar Guy announced, "Yer radah is toast, man." Slater's neck was instantly in danger. Everyone knew this by the look of sheer bloodlust on David's face.

"I paid the seller $12,000 extra for that thing!"

"Sahry, man."

Without another word—not one word—David assailed a cab and rode straight back to Mahone Bay where he demanded a refund within one week from the old man or, failing that, Slater would be facing a lawsuit of $25,000 for the radar and all of the other things that had not been as he'd represented them in the Buy/Sell Contract.

While David was gone, the boat behind us left, and a huge fishing vessel attempted to defy physics and dock at the available space. *Sondra* got her first kiss, which bent the piece of metal protecting the gunnels. David returned from his unsuccessful negotiations with Slater, having decided to let him live to see another day, and at the sight of the bruised stern, he visibly deflated before his crew's eyes.

I immediately came to the rescue with strong Cuba Libres, loud rock n' roll and a great halibut fry-up. This fixed nothing that was broken, but it certainly helped soothe the trials and tribulations of the first leg of our journey. Because the rum was 110 proof, the threads of the stories quickly became the warp and the crew's wonderful sense of humor the weft, weaving the beginning of our Sea Yarn's fabric that would hold up for the rest of our lives.

The next morning, David and I, soundly sleeping in the V-berth, were awakened at 6:30 a.m. to the sound of our generator purring away in the engine room, building up compressed air for later use. The weather was perfect so Ron had decided on his own that it was time to run the rest of the way down the Nova Scotia coastline to Shelburne.

After a hearty breakfast along with diesel-strength coffee, Stew and Greg positioned themselves to handle the lines. This time, they would watch with calm smiles as the Captain and the Engineer worked in unison to maneuver the boat flawlessly back out of the tight docking space. I decided to join Ron and observe how he worked. On our maiden voyage, David had become familiar with how *Sondra* would respond with the twin props turning in any of the various combinations available. Ron was a master at subtlety—not too much precious air used for each start-up and not too much fuel so that each firing produced small amounts of smooth velocity. All of this was done with no words, just DING-DING...DING-DING...DING-DING.

The concerned crowd that had gathered on the dock expecting to see an unavoidable payback nudge to our pushy rear neighbor, looked on with stunned fascination once again.

Seeing their faces through the small engine room portholes made me murmur loud enough for Ron to hear, "We may not know everything yet boys, but we sure have coming and going down pat, with class."

Mother Ocean was magnificent that day. Her four-foot swells of varying blue shades were coming at the stern in a following sea that gently surfed us past the shoreline. The autumn sun danced joyful light off the water's surface once again, and we all found ourselves swaying and singing to large speakers David had mounted on the bridge—the only, but not unimportant, *minor adjustment* made.

While the Eagles sang "Hotel California," I nuzzled my face into David's beard and cheek and kissed him long and sweet.

13

THE DRY DOCK BOAT-FORT

Shelburne, Nova Scotia
August—September, 1978

"Several men are standing on the pier, unloading the sea."
-DAVID GASCOYNE FROM *THE END IS NEAR THE BEGINNING*

SHELBURNE, a quaint Loyalist town on the southwest shore of Nova Scotia, is a historical home of shipbuilding and maritime craft. *Sondra II* was about to become part of it. No Fairmile had ever been assembled or dry-docked in this shipyard, and the owners looked upon her arrival as a special occasion. The mission was three-fold: make a deviation card specific to her magnetic field, finish work on her hull by hauling out and bang out the dent in her gunnel.

In preparation for our arrival, the shipyard crew had constructed a huge cradle to our specs. This support was attached to an angled railway system that would ease the boat out of the water while the men adjusted the shores to her sides to keep her upright as she hovered dry on her keel.

Having arrived the afternoon before our scheduled haul out, it was necessary for us to dock at the far side of the shipyard. The winds were blowing pretty hard from shore, so timing was going to be everything in getting our boat alongside the pier and made fast before the bow was blown back out by the wind. There were no other ships docked in that area and only one short but wiry guy on the pier. In we went at a pretty good clip, slick as pros. Stewart threw his monkey's fist first. It landed with a snappy clunk about three feet to the left of Pier Guy who just stood, feet nailed to the concrete, staring down at it. The only thing moving was the ship's bow.

David hollered, "Hey!" in an attempt to shock him into action.

Knowing why he had been "Heyed," he yelled back, "There's nothin' te 'tach it to Capin."

Sitting at intervals of 50 feet along the edge of the wharf

were massive bollards that looked like solid iron, specifically for the purpose of securing a ship to the pier. We all exchanged glances of confusion.

"Wrap the line around a bollard," David responded frantically.

"The bollards ain't screwed down Capin!" he hollered back with a slow tongue.

I couldn't help but laugh to myself because even if they weren't, it would take a hurricane to blow the ship to where she could drag any one of the bollards over the edge let alone the three we would be tied up to. Of course, while all of this was going on, the bow had snuck out to an angle too acute to muscle it back in. Round two was signaled to the engine room with David cussing throughout the complete circle we made to get into docking position once again. Now he had the cardboard megaphone covering his mouth, amplifying himself to macho authority while he bluntly and loudly instructed the man to tie us up to the bollards anyway. With an amusing little salute, he got 'er done.

Down went the gangplank and we all scuttled to formally meet and thank our helper. I took a quick detour to see if the enormous four-ton bollards were indeed screwless. They were. Being from Newfoundland, where the most polite people in the world are born and the strangest version of English (known as Newfinese) had also been born, our lineman was all apologies and comical anecdotes. By the time he finished, we were enjoying a good down-east laugh. We invited him to join us for beer and dinner after work, and Screech, as we nicknamed him after his homeland's signature liquor, arrived with a dozen large, freshly caught North Atlantic lobsters.

Greg's sister politely bailed out the moment we hit land and unfortunately, due to family complications, so did Big Ron, our coveted engineer. No one was sure how the hell we were going to manage without him, not only because he knew more than all of us put together, but also because this left us with a crew of only three—Stewart, still eager, still clueless; Greg who was pretty much just ballast; and myself, a mere notch above Stewart. Knowing this, I had spent a lot of time on the hush-hush in the engine room with Ron—just in case. The engines seemed to be the size of Volkswagen vans. Their loud tapping rockers combined with the generator's humming had the overall edge of a Led Zeppelin concert. My racing team stint and natural aptitude for mechanics along with Ron's intermittent coaching had allowed me to absorb the mechanical simplicity of the twin diesels' operation.

The next morning, I was full of excited anticipation. Today, we hauled out. Fresh coffee in hand, I perched my daisy dukes on a pile of stacked beams near her designated space. As the sleekness of her whole bow began to slowly glide by me, I was mesmerized. And then, there she was—out of her element and completely exposed. She dwarfed and awed me with her magnificent hull. Her four-foot bronze propellers looked even more ominous than the spares we had wrestled onboard. Our *Sondra II* was definitely a boat designed for performance and speed, and age had taken her from function to legend.

So began the Disneyesque Swiss Family Robinson life onboard our boat-fort some 20 feet above the Shelburne Ship Yard. Resting in her cradle, *Sondra* had become a two-story house, a towering castle of mahogany, a nautical stronghold. I was surprised we were allowed to stay living onboard but I wasn't about to rock *that* boat! We now accessed the deck by a ladder leaning against *Sondra's* starboard side, which unnerved everyone except David. A block and tackle arrangement was used to get stuff onboard. From the deck, we looked out over the entire shipyard and could see all the comings and goings: hundreds of multicolored hard hats moving around like billiard balls after a break, enormous cranes resembling giant mechanical praying mantises swinging beams through the air, ships of all shapes and sizes creeping out of the water or splashing back in like giant reptiles. The air was abuzz with men chatting and laughing, loudspeakers cackling, and Scottish-influenced traditional music peppered with some modern Anne Murray and April Wine. The smells of arc welding, paint, decaying barnacles and food wagon soup wafted on the ocean breezes. We brought a spare table and two benches up on deck and created a wonderland cocktail and dining area set off by strings of tiny twinkling lights. Sunrises and sunsets over the Atlantic were spectacular from up there. Meals always consisted of fresh seafood barbequed on a little hibachi I'd rescued from the shipyard—succulent halibut, cod, tuna, and various crustaceans, all topped off with ice-cold Nova Scotia beer. The mood was one of childlike wonder and holiday gaiety.

Before I approached David about the possibility of taking over as engineer (as if he had a choice), I decided to take advantage of the further knowledge surrounding me. Being the only female within sight and an expert brain-picker (my preferred and finely tuned way of learning), I began infiltrating the shipyard below us. Initially the men thought they were simply being blessed with the company of a bored, sweet, young piece of eye candy and welcomed the flirting. But soon word spread, thanks to Stewart, that I'd been part of a Formula Atlantic team and was "A 'looka' with brains!" I loved being down in the yard among the men—a warm study in weathered faces, torn coveralls, strong bodies, and nicknames. Although it was like being in the middle of a Norman Rockwell painting, I knew I was privileged to be in their midst, accepted because I was a woman who loved boats and respected because I could talk shop. They proved to be thorough teachers.

Three weeks later, with the work completed, we threw a big party for the workers, who had become our friends. I cooked up a pot of Mom's delicious creamy, buttery, bacony clam chowder. The boys brought another feast of mouthwatering lobster and their wives sent them with homemade bread and fall apple pie. David topped the menu off with a couple of 26'ers of good ol' Canadian Club Rye Whiskey, the first shot of which was used to toast the men and their prodigy, *Sondra's* new engineer. I thought I would burst with pride and failed miserably at staying dry-eyed. We finished the evening off with a Nova Scotia jam session complete with fiddles, accordions and spoons accompanying the B3.

Early the next morning, with an explosion of water, *Sondra II*, Ship's Registry #193893, was re-launched to roaring cheers and raised fists. Over the past year, both she and I had shaped up and I must say we both looked pretty darned good as we set out on our big journey to Key West. David took the helm, and I, waving a final goodbye to those who believed in me, disappeared down into the engine room to start up the Grays for my first solo implementation as her Engineer. It was always dank as a dirt basement down there and especially dark when descending from the intense sunlight reflecting off the deck. I won't deny I was apprehensive. The generator that created compressed air would always daunt me. I never lost the fear it would overwork and its holding tank would explode like a grenade. Nevertheless, it was as if I were born to do this, for I followed each of David's many commands instantly and was able to start those massive diesels with what he later referred to as "a meager fart of air."

Once we'd maneuvered our way out of the shipyard, we motored on over to Yarmouth Harbour on the lower west coast of Nova Scotia using our adjusted compass and a pre-mapped course. There we would await fair weather for our passage to Portland, across the mouth of the infamous Bay of Fundy and into the massive open water of the Gulf of Maine.

14

THE WATERS FROM HELL
The Mighty Bay of Fundy and the Gulf of Maine
September 15, 1978

"The small force that it takes to launch a boat into the stream
should not be confused with the force of the stream that carries it
along: but this confusion appears in nearly all biographies."
-FREDRICH NIETZSCHE

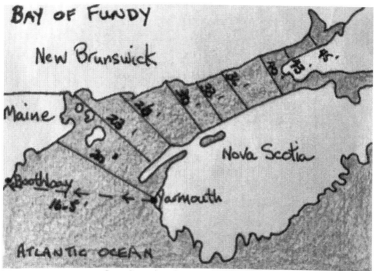

**Our Crossing from Yarmouth, NS
to Boothbay Harbor, Maine at the 16.5' line**

Bay of Fundy: A 270-kilometer-long ocean bay located on Atlantic Canada's coastline. With the highest tides worldwide, 100 billion tons of seawater surges through it in one tide cycle. www.canadiangeographic.com.

Under this immense load, the tidal surge actually tilts the countryside slightly. Known as one of the Seven Wonders of the Natural World, the flow and ebb of the tides of the Bay of Fundy are equal to the output of 250 nuclear power plants.

ACCORDING to our Captain's calculations, conditions were as perfect as they get for our first big open water journey. Although leaving in the middle of the night seemed odd to the rest of us and we did not know exactly where he'd taken these calculations from, he *was* the Captain. I found it hard to imagine that the Marine Authorities would allow a 112' vessel, manned by a small bunch of rookies with no papers, to go out there with the big boys and cross that body of water. Back on the lakes of Ontario, the red tape a small boat must go through is enough to make you stick to swimming. We were amazed no cease and desist order arrived for *Sondra*.

It was with risk and anticipation, with nervous stomachs and heartbeats up, and our imaginations fired with possibilities, that we set out into the dark of night. I sensed that we had all, for the moment, forgotten both *Sondra's* and our shortcomings. Being the innocents that we were, we actually believed we could just aim the ship in the direction of Portland, Maine and eventually that city would show up. Unbeknownst to us, a fourth crewmember had stowed away onboard last minute for the ride: Murphy of Murphy's Law.

Murphy's Law: "It is found that anything that can go wrong at sea generally *does* go wrong, sooner or later, so it is not to be wondered that owners prefer the safe to the scientific."

During the shoving off maneuvers, Murphy went straight to work and pushed Greg's outsized glasses off our crewmember's nose into the sea to become the first piece of jetsam we would unwillingly offer up to Mother Ocean. Unfortunately, this sacrifice took with it Greg's sight and every last ounce of his pint-sized courage. After pawing his way to the inside of the wheelhouse, he pretty much stayed there for the duration of the crossing, earnestly gripping the rail.

Getting underway with the new Captain/Engineer combo of Keller & Craig was as smooth as if executed by *Sondra's* original crew of eighteen. Stew managed to handle both bow and stern lines with poised efficiency. Twenty minutes out to sea, the Grays purring and no duties calling, I tuned into the allure of sea and sky. I headed straight for what had become my favorite perch, the prow, where I sat straddling the lead stanchion, legs dangling out over our parted path through the ocean. I inhaled deeply all I could of the salty air, air so intense that the back of my throat felt the briny exoticness. I imagined that its subtle condiment of fishiness came from the kelpy hair of mermaids swimming in the darkness below us. I became *Sondra's* figurehead as the ship rhythmically dipped and rose as though bowing to placate the Gods of the Sea to ensure our safe passage. Leaning back, my long hair dusted the deck as the light of the moon illuminated my serenity. *How many days of my life could possibly be like this?*

In spite of the desire to stay there until sunrise, I abandoned my post to try my hand at some long-distance navigating. We had just passed a buoy and were well outside of Yarmouth Harbour. I ran my fingers over the lifelines as I moved from stanchion to stanchion towards the wheelhouse.

I thought of the day David removed them to paint the gunnels and, in a moment of delusion, announced his plan to leave them off declaring, "The boat looks less cluttered without them."

Accidentally bumping him overboard to win that argument seemed like a good counter plan. I always grinned when I recalled the image of him treading water wearing sheer surprise on his face and me saying, "With nothin' to grab onto, I guess that's what happens, eh Captain?" Without another word about it, the posts and lines were back in place by the end of the next day.

Stewart and David, looking like two cartoon characters with their red heads sticking out of their puffy down-filled parkas, were happily chatting it up at the helm on the bridge. They brought a smile to my face and I passed them singing "I'm Popeye the Sailor Man," while ducking through the wheelhouse door and down three steps to join Greg.

The wheelhouse was my favorite room on the ship. Like Greg, I felt safe there. Four of the seven portholes, all now restored to their original brass luster, were larger than those down below and together provided a 270-degree lookout. The hardwood that covered every surface in the wheelhouse was natural and lush, undeniably red mahogany. The wheel, an iconic sculpture of oak and brass, held the fingerprints of hundreds of men and their stories of defense. The chart table, with a small tray-like edge, was made from honey-colored pine and featured worn pulls and ten thin drawers, mostly empty. The absence of charts there echoed David's words "There is no sense in buying charts for every harbor when you don't know which ones you will be going into."

The Atlantic Ocean chart that included the Bay of Fundy and the Gulf of Maine was in the top drawer. I lovingly laid the mysterious graphical representation of data out on the tabletop, smoothing it as I took in the adornment of symbols and nautical information that was supposed to ease the job of navigation. I began studying the paper with the naïve confidence that accompanies one's first day of Driver Ed. Starting with the buoy we had just motored past, I made numerous calculations as outlined in the enormous Bowditch bible on going to sea, factoring in the tides, currents and our medium cruising speed. I drew light pencil lines from that buoy to the next and the next making notes along the two lines. I then adjusted the given compass reading on the chart with *Sondra's* new deviation card to determine our actual heading. Dead on! *This navigation thing is a piece of cake.*

All was going well until about 1700 hours. The low winds gently accompanying us were instantaneously replaced by a nasty sou'wester. Riding on the back of black clouds highlighted by the moon, it brought with it a bitch of a blow and frothing water.

The crew started appealing to David to turn back or at least run in close to the shoreline so that we could keep our bearings using the lights there or, better still, find an island to hide behind. David responded with simply, "No and no."

He was right—the last thing you want to do during a big storm is go closer to land. Due to the riled surf hitting the shoreline, the oceans become more confused and the land more dangerous. Without radar, it would be next to impossible to detect indistinguishable unmarked rocks breaking the surface. My abandoned ten-foot high perch at the bow disappeared under water with alarming regularity as chaos began to rule the open bay. In the stormy darkness, liquid rose up like a backward avalanche and *Sondra* collided with a rogue wave—the sea devil feared by all seasoned sailors. An explosion of roiling white water crashed down on the deck, pelting our huddled bodies with icy shards. In unison, we looked down as we felt the deck timbers undulate in a shock wave beneath our feet. All necks turned an Exorcist 180 degrees to see if the boat would buckle under the stress and crack in half. Under the burden of a 25-foot aquatic wall, *Sondra* shuddered, recoiled and reared her proud prow resiliently. Her land-fashioned form had been challenged by a furiously angry sea and emerged unscathed. Our momentary awe jolted into fear. With no land in sight, and titanic depths, we were aliens in a hostile world. The wind clocked and crushed our own diesel exhaust into our lungs while the scream of the storm howled into our ears.

David fought to bring *Sondra* around to quarter the sea. The white-capped rollers pounded with equal fury but by putting the swells at a 45-degree angle to the bow and slowing down the engines to a crawl, we could mount and surf with some degree of control. Our pride in *Sondra's* speed was replaced with dismay when we realized her five-foot draft gave her a handling capability barely superior to our floorless life raft. Waves rocked the ship alternately inundating the gunnels with frigid Atlantic water. *Sondra* pitched and rolled, but continued to weather the storm like the high performance girl she was. The words of Jim Dowell echoed over the squall's banshee-like caterwauling, "She was a good ship, if you disregarded the comfort of her passengers, that is."

Hanging on became a workout-and-a-half and moving about the boat on the slippery deck a dangerous challenge. No one, except Greg donned a life jacket, as their antiquated bulkiness made them impossible to work in. No thought had been given to tying off with lifelines. It was amazing nobody went overboard. I thanked God that night for my insisting on the re-installation of the stanchions and their connecting safety wires.

Hunger hit us in the midst of all of this drama, and David suggested I put on my chef's hat and whip up something to eat. I crawled to the hatch and surveyed the mayhem below. One look at the disaster pretty much kyboshed that idea. The contents of the kitchen were everywhere—the fridge door flapped wildly back and forth, jars rolled around, glasses and dishes were smashed and the mattress, still in the galley area, had been thrown across the galley counter. I remembered a little quote from a book I'd seen in Slater's office by The Fairmile Association that said, ". . . when they first put to sea, even in moderate waves, hardened sailors became seasick and cooks gave up any hope of preparing proper meals." Seeming to have become more seasoned sailors after our Mahone Bay fog, no one was heaving yet, but I had definitely given up all hope of even a bowl of cereal.

Propelled by a combination of stupidity, curiosity and self-righteousness, I gripped the side of the companionway and cautiously descended, leaving its safety only when the handle of the living room bulkhead door was within reach. The horrific noise I heard through the thick wall gave a hint of what I might witness, but I could never have imagined the frenzied dance taking place on the other side. Dropping to all fours and spreading my limbs for better balance, I opened and secured the heavy door and began to cautiously crawl through. The uneasy truce of half-secured furniture and poorly-lashed instruments had been shattered. I should have known that the compromise between David and me would never be acceptable to the sea. The twin props had fallen over from where David leaned them against the hull and they, with their tremendous weight and sharp edges, were careening back and forth across the floor with each roll of the ship. There also, the disarray of drums, the organ, and the top-heavy sewing machine crushing its notions—everything akimbo except for the screwed-down items. Each moving object was leaving its trail in a fine white dust that appeared to be absolutely everywhere—graceful to and fro lines flowing across the floor as if a child had finger painted them. Once I realized my hands were resting in this substance, I put a spot of it on the end of my tongue to test my suspicion. I then looked for the large fire extinguisher and sure enough, it was out there, now lightened of its load, jockeying for position with the rest of our battered possessions. There, on my hands and knees with no view of the horizon through the portholes, bile suddenly rose to the back of my throat. I retreated quickly to the stairs and ascended to the wheelhouse, where the men had gathered in an attempt to dry out.

"Where's the food, Marge?"

"Everywhere!" I snapped with bulging eyes. "Right now, it's a bit of a mess down there, Cap'. All we got is crow dredged in fire extinguisher." I frantically waved my dusty white hands at him. "Just came up to check on how you'd like it. Medium rare?"

That is how we entered our next drama: hungry, exhausted, sea-salt wet, cold and breathing resentment-filled air. Stew left the wheelhouse in a brave attempt to take a leak over the rail. He returned like a drunken sailor, clutching the walls. "The tower's rippin' the deck up!" We knew it was serious just by looking at his ashen face.

The three of us staggered to the radar tower. One of the steel guide wires, which attached the weighty tower to the large smokestack, had snapped. The 30-foot brass tower could no longer rock in sync with the waves. Consequently, it was ripping up the deck with each roll, exposing laughably short bolts that were slowly losing their hold. No matter which way it might fall, the weight would bring about disaster and, possibly, death. Even though he was terrified, Stewart still had command of his sardonic wit. "Those Mountie boys may be able to put on one hell of a show with their horses, but carpentry is definitely not their bag."

The comic relief sparked us to action. Stewart rushed to the engine room to slow the Grays down to a dead crawl and David brought the ship about to take a following sea. He instructed me to take the helm at the bridge and to hold a steady course so he could clamber up the tower to secure the loose guide wire. Although determined to fulfill my job perfectly, my initiation at the helm was short-lived. I'd been instructed to hang on tight no matter what, so I did, but the wheel jerked violently in the confused seas and flung me through a cartwheel, dumping me on the deck with arms flailing in a desperate attempt to grab onto the ship. Luckily I caught hold of one of the heavy-duty cowl air vents near the engine room hatch. Holding on for dear life, I scrambled down the hatch and within seconds, Stewart was at the helm.

"Ouch! Ouch! Ouch! Damn! Shit! Fuck-fuck-fuck!" I yelled into the noise of the engines. There were going to be some colorful bruises. I collected myself and set about checking the gauges. All was well. I was oiling the tappets when an unexpected DING-DING, DING-DING rang out from one of the telegraphs. I looked up to see that the helmsman wanted the speed increased on the starboard engine. I responded quickly, feeling the ship begin to turn to port to re-establish the sea-quartering pattern. DING-DING, DING-DING again, this time signaling equal power to the port side. With the help of those wonderful Sea Gods, David had managed to secure the guide wire. The tower was stabilized somewhat, but we remained under the risk of disaster.

We were beat up already and still far from our destination. When would it end? Each of us privately began making deals with Fate. *I swear if I make it through this, I promise....* Our pattern of quartering the sea in erratic zigzags combined with Fundy's infamous tidal surge negated my weak navigational skills entirely. Spirits had run aground. Morning finally dawned and brought with it more angry skies, more big swells but no rogue waves. We continued to quarter the seas but the reality was, we were hopelessly lost. When at sea, the horizon is always seven miles away due to the curve of the earth. No land was in site. With no navigational equipment, we didn't know if we were still in the mouth of Fundy, in the Gulf of

Maine, or if we'd been pushed out into the Atlantic Ocean. We spent the rest of the daylight hours bobbing and motoring west without seeing a single thing. I managed to scrounge up some fruit and cheese for us and then I grabbed a little shut-eye late afternoon by assuming the shape of a spider monkey on our bed.

I awoke to darkness. It was only 1800 hours and already the sun had set. I returned to shift on watch with Greg and, within minutes, David and Stewart literally passed out on the floor at our feet. They had not rested in close to 36 hours. David had tossed the anchor and it trailed obligingly like a useless tail in water more than 1,000 feet deep. At that point, I considered myself Head Of Operations. I decided to play with the ship-to-shore radio for the first time, even though I deemed it would be a hopeless attempt at successfully ringing up the Coast Guard. The damn thing actually worked! I sprang to life and began answering questions asked by the most beautiful male voice I'd ever heard. He first requested our identification and a description of the boat. Then came the dreaded question.

"What is yoah location *Sondra II*?" he asked in his adorable accent.

Sondra didn't have a clue and neither did I. "Welllllll," I dragged out, "bobbing around somewhere in the Gulf of Maine—hopefully near Portland? I can't see any shore lights but I think I can see a buoy off to starboard in the direction of north-northwest."

"Can you identify the buoy Ma'am?"

Silence—one Mississippi, two Mississippi, three Mississippi—all the way up to five.

"Ma'am?" Louder and very clearly this time, "Can you identify the colluh of the light on the buoy and its flashin' sequence?"

I looked as hard as I could out the porthole with the binoculars but had lost the ability for such fine focus. The buoy looked like three buoys clumped together and glowing. I could see red, green and white flashes all at the same time. I told him this in the thin voice of a very tired, lost and scared young woman.

"OK Ma'am. Just stay calm. Could you launch your dingy and have one of yoah crew membahs motah on over

119

thayah to get the numbah off the buoy?" I cackled, rather like a crazy-person. I couldn't help myself.

I figured the officer was probably one Mississippi'ing it now as he waited for my answer. Looking down at David snoring at my feet, I would've knocked him out if he hadn't already been comatose.

"No, Sir," I said imitating him a bit. "That would not be possible. We don't have a secure anchorage and I'm the only one left standing of our four-man crew." I felt obliged to mention Greg but not the embarrassing details about the yellow life-donut.

A plan was conceived: I would keep talking while the Coast Guard boys tried to use my voice as radar to get a fix on where we were. This seemed pretty cool. I didn't know about that technology, but I hoped it would work better than *Sondra's* version of radar. It didn't. Then, they decided to light flares from their Portland base in five minutes' time and I was to look for them out of the West. I saw nothing.

"Negative on the flares, fellas."

We resorted to a new plan. I was to keep my eyes open for the car ferry, *Caribe*, which would be leaving Portland Harbor soon en route to Yarmouth.

"They've been asked to keep an eye out for you as well," he somewhat weakly assured me, both of us knowing it was a needle in a haystack scenario.

As commanding officer of the ship, I drafted Greg into service. He had silently observed this entire escapade. It appeared as though he'd not moved an inch since the loss of his glasses.

"Greg, move over two feet and keep a watch out this porthole for the Yarmouth ferry, okay Buddy?" I said as I gently tugged on his coat sleeve to position him. His now small eyes and gentle dark, beard-shadowed face smiled wan hope at me.

I stepped back over the wheelhouse's new carpet of limbs and wind-whipped hair to take my watch at the starboard porthole. What a sight this was for Mother Ocean: anchor dangling uselessly about 800-feet above her floor, one of her Captains and his First Mate sprawled out and snoring in defeated harmony, and Greg—sans glasses—and I glued to opposite portholes looking out over her vastness for a comparatively minuscule white object. In the void of action, I began to sing, ad-libbing my own silly lyrics to my favorite Zappa song:

Dreamed I was a Sea Goddess-o
Salty winds began to blow
Under my glasses and around my glow
The rip that tore at the deck below
It was of the tolerance named 'Zero'...

And my old man, King Poseidon, cried
And my old man, King Poseidon, cried
Aphrodites, a-no-no
Aphrodites, a-no-no
Don't be a naughty Goddess-o
Save your coins, don't go in Fundy's show

Well I turned around and I said oh, oh oh
Well I turned around and I said oh, oh oh
Well I turned around and I said no, no
And the great winds began to blow
And the great tides began to roll
And he said with a fear in his eyes,
Keep watch where the phosphorescence goes,
and never go below
Keep watch where the phosphorescence goes,
and never go below

It seemed like an eternity passed before Greg finally mumbled something into the thick glass of his porthole. The words became "historic" *Sondra* folklore.

He simply said, "I think I see something." (No exclamation mark.)

Quickly crossing the wheelhouse, leaping over body parts like a football player in tire-jump practice, I put my head next to Greg's and stared out. Absolute disbelief shaped my whole face. *You've got to be kidding me!* Crossing our port side was a ship so big that *Sondra* must have looked like a rowboat to those aboard it! And Greg just thought he saw something! All three decks of the Caribe were lit up like the Times Square Christmas tree. I turned and looked with empathy into Greg's eyes and realized what a blind nightmare the crossing had been for him. I was moved by compassion and respect. Looking at his sadness, I wanted to surround him in bubble wrap.

Back over the bodies, I grabbed the ship-to-shore to ring the Coast Guard. With no prelude, but absolute joy, I shouted, "I see it! I see it!"

Before they could answer back, the Caribe gave a blast of her horn, the shock of which just about caused my knees to buckle. Judging by the grunt I heard over my shoulder, it had resonated with Greg. Surprisingly, it did not stir the Captain and First Mate.

"Yes, *Sondra II*, they've spotted you too. Yoah not too fah off Boothbay Hahbah, due East of Portland."

"So how long before you guys can get here?"

"Well, Ma'am, (I was starting to hate that word), we will be theyah in about an owah, or two—dependin'."

In spite of myself, in a rather loud voice, I threw back "Dependin' on what?!"

There was another silence before he had the gall to clear his throat and deliver his response, "Ma'am. The Ali/Spinks fight is on the TV, and well, Ma'am, you'll be okay till we get theyah. You ah' in very deep watah. Just keep your runnin' lights on—and relax."

I was confused. Wasn't this illegal? Should I, with authority, simply tell them that this was not acceptable? Or, maybe I should whine, beg, flirt? Or, should I simply yell, "You are the US Coast Guard! Get your asses out here. Now! You can watch the re-run tomorrow, for god's sake!"

Instead, I decided on assertive flirtation laced with guilt and within half an hour, their little Guard vessel was beside us. By then, David and Stew had risen from the dead and were on deck to receive them with utter relief and gratitude. I stayed with Greg and opened the porthole so he could enjoy the action too.

Their Captain spoke to us using his steel megaphone— loud and clear, "*Sondra II*, staht yoah engines and pull up along ouah poht side."

My facial expression barked a silent "HA!" into Greg's face.

Captain Coastguard went on, "One of my men will boad yoah vessel, take the helm and pilot you into Boothbay Hahbah."

This time, I gave Greg a big shoulder nudge saying, "Oh, I am really interested in seeing this scenario play out." Punchy tired, I started to giggle. My laughter was infectious.

"Sorry, Captain, but this ship has no neutral," David bellowed back through our cardboard megaphone.

The seconds passed—waves lapping, *Sondra* bobbing, Coast Guard motor purring...

"Okay then. We will come along side, thrah you a line and ouah man will..." More time out.

Greg and I pondered about how the heck they would get that poor sucker from their much lower deck to our deck, without a ladder, while we were still rocking and bobbing like a mammoth cork.

Greg finally spoke, "Short of launching him out of a cannon, I don't think this is gonna' happen." The laughter rose to hysterics.

While backhand waving us to be quiet, "That won't work, Captain," David replied with authority, camouflaging his few days of experience on the high seas. "I suggest we just follow you to the anchorage."

This became the strategy. Following the USCG into that harbor in the dark was like playing a video game with real life consequences. Objects kept passing by but somehow, always at the last minute, we managed to dodge them—rocks, little islands, moored boats and lobster traps—plenty of each. And then finally, we were in the placid water of Boothbay.

As David threw our anchor overboard, I called out, "Thanks, Boys, and sorry about the fight. Who won anyway?"

"According to the boys back at the office, Ali—in the 15th. First guy to claim the Heavyweight Championship three times!"

"Oh, that's nice." And more to myself, "Stupid sport anyway."

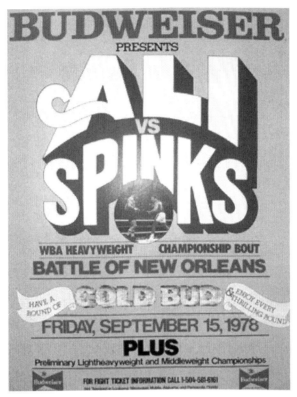

Advertisement for $350 tickets to the Ali/Spinks fight.
Sixty-four thousand fans packed the Super Dome
to watch the highly anticipated rematch.

Telling this story years later, I tried to make sense of my foolish choice to go to sea so unprepared. Another sailor observed, "Young people don't know when to say *NO*—don't think of the consequences and don't seem to mind them. They know no boundaries and approach high seas with great focus and determination. For you, going out to sea in hurricane season had no experience to which to relate. You had a total lack of fear. I say we toast to the brilliance of human adaptability."

"The sea's only gifts are harsh blows... and occasionally the chance to feel strong. Now, I don't know much about the sea but I do know that that's the way it is here... and I also know that it is important, as it is in life, not necessarily to be strong but to feel strong—to measure yourself at least once, to find yourself at least once in the most ancient of human conditions facing the blind deaf stone alone with nothing to help you but your hands and your own head."

-from film *Into the Wild*, quote by Primo Levi

15

BOOTHBAY HARBOR: A LOVE STORY WITHIN

BOOTHBAY HARBOR, MAINE
SEPTEMBER, 1978

"It is in the solitude of love that we learn to drown."
-ANNE MICHAELS

SAFE at anchor our first night in Boothbay Harbor, too tired to eat, undress or even talk, we used our last ounce of energy to lift our mattresses back into their wooden berths. Within seconds of flopping down, a jazz concert of harmonious zzzzzz's echoed throughout the ship, complete with broken time, bridges and changes.

We awoke to the soft voices of the American Customs agents calling up to us from their little motorboat while they lightly tapped on the wooden area around various portholes. "Helloooooo. Tap. Tap. Tap. *Sondra* Twoooooo. Tap. Tap. Tap. You sailas' awake yet?"

Then I heard them giggling. I knew from living in Mahone Bay for a year that the story about the local Coast Guard's rescue of the hippies on the Canadian Gun Boat would have immediately followed, over morning coffee, the blow-by-blow review of the same night's Ali/Spinks fight. What I didn't realize was that it was yesterday's coffee and yesterday's news. We had slept 36 hours. How considerate the officials were to let us rest past the legal registry deadline for entry, and how inexperienced we were to have thought that we could enter this American port without some form of scrutiny and interaction with the Rubber Stamp Man.

The four of us emerged from our quarters, lined up at the stern and stood at sloppy attention looking down at the customs officers in their official dory. I suspected only two were required for the job and that the extras, likely the balance of their department, were along for the entertainment. Our appearance alone would have satisfied them—miles of hair and beard matted by salt and wind, faces and clothes imprinted with sleep, grimy hands, and eyes blinded into slits by the early morning sunshine. They were gawking at us. We were smiling, just happy to be alive.

David started talking to them using a lot of "Yes, Sirs" and "No, Sirs," an old Southern habit that surfaced on occasion and, of course, annoyed me. As previously drilled to be, the rest of us were quiet. Passports were checked, papers were inked and the necessary questions were asked about any illegal cargo. Of course they would've asked about drugs, but they also asked about smuggled immigrants and fish. This struck me as funny as I imagined a huge aquarium of people and halibut sloshing about below.

Thinking that it was okay to talk by then, I started to jokingly say, "No, there's just the cat," but it turned into an exclamation of panic directed at David. "The cat!" And I went on, "The cat! Where's Rhett?" Normally our mascot would be in the middle of all of this, being nosy. "Oh my god, David, we must have lost him. I'm sure he slipped off the deck and drowned."

Greg touched my shoulder and pointed at the tarp mid-ship mumbling, "I think he's still hiding in the lifeboat."

I ran forward and ripped up a corner of the tarp covering the pathetic excuse for a boat. There he was. Rhett wasn't "Gone with the Wind." All of us watched in silence as Clark Gable's namesake—fat, furry and orange—slinked to the edge of his refuge, yawned, stretched, and then head-butted the closest authority's leg to encourage a much needed scratch. That brought on a round of warm New England laughter and pet stories. I served up the best coffee I ever made to go along with the many inquiries that finally worked their way into some embarrassing ones.

"Is that really yoah lifeboat?

"So, why didn't you guys screw anything down below deck? You was lucky those spayah' props didn't go right through yoah hull."

I was smugly smiling into my coveted cup and enjoying the cowed silence.

"And good luck cleanin' up all that fiah extinguishah dust. It's a buggah."

I wasn't smiling anymore. I shot David a raise of my eyebrows that said "Welllll?" as a new angle of my increasingly stronger personality edged its way to the foreground. Before David could comment, I decided I was going to shore—alone. I was pissed, really pissed, that our Captain had injured *Sondra* and damn near killed all of us with his willful ignorance. I figured every aspect of the mess was due to his negligence or stubbornness, so he should be the one to clean it up. And, like any hardass sailor still standing, I was in dire need of tequila, music, companionship spiced with laughter, and unmitigated raw sex but *not* sex with David. With the American authorities witnessing the disaster that had taken place below, along with the obvious fact that there was negligence in the lifeboat department, I felt my opinions had gained authority (at least in my own mind).

The first order of my day was to get a ride to town. I hadn't been on the ball when the authorities left with Greg, who had given up his dream of a life at sea and quit while he was ahead. Quickly throwing some clean clothes and toiletries together, I resurfaced on deck and said, "I'm going ashore."

Although knowing something was going to happen that he didn't want, but deserved, David smart-assed me with, "Just how are you planning to get to shore, Marge?"

Without a word, I walked past him to the bow with knapsack slung over one shoulder. I threw my chest, hip and thumb out in a don't-you-even-think-about-not-picking-me-up-fashion. Funny, I didn't realize at the time that such an attitude was redundant. What sailor wouldn't pick up a big-boobed blonde babe hitchhiking from the bow of the most talked about arrival in the harbor? I was gone with the first passing boat of fishermen.

I planned to stay on shore until I found a little runabout and until he had cleaned up the mess and secured *Sondra's* contents for real.

The shower at the local marina was sheer bliss. The steaming fresh water penetrated my matted hair and warmed my chilled breasts. The heave-ho of the boat still in my bones, I found myself amused at the struggle necessary to maintain balance when I closed my eyes. I scrubbed until the salt-water-filled flashbacks, one by one, disappeared down the drain: that first rogue wave, the horrifying chaos below deck, the intimidating dark and lonely helm, the loss of our bearings and the constant damp cold and hunger. I realized with a degree of astonishment that I had never once been afraid. How could that have been? Too busy just hanging on? Too naïve or just plain dumb? Or, had I developed an unconscious confidence in *Sondra* and myself during that passing? I took a minute to give thanks to everyone and everything that had made my safe delivery to Maine possible.

Loosely coiffed and clad in tight Levis, a baby pink cashmere sweater and cowboy boots, I strutted out of there singing the lyrics to Rare Earth's "Get Ready." I had conquered an ocean, lived to tell about it, and was ready for whatever dared to come my way next.

The manager at the marina told me that McSeagull's Bar was the most popular haunt in town. Overlooking Boothbay Harbor, it featured quaint marine décor, and the old knotty pine walls made it warm and welcoming. I headed straight for the bar. The late morning Miller felt crisp, cold and rich as it chased after a generous shot of Jose Cuervo. Gulping down the beer far too fast resulted in the need for an immediate second. Before I could order, it appeared, and following the waitress's gesture towards its origin, I slowly turned on my bar stool to glance at its sponsor. Enjoying an early liquid lunch in the back corner were six locals with slouched, leg-spread postures, grinning at me as if I were a big strawberry sundae. Deciding to play their game, I Marilyn Monroe-mouthed, "Thank you boys." They all squirmed in their chairs, and I turned back to my fresh beer.

Once full of liquid confidence, I left my place at the bar to join them. I sensed they all knew I had come off the big gunboat and was the registered owner. "So boys, where could I find a little boat, to buy?" There was a long pause as they bounced their gazes off my breasts and each other.

Finally the young cocky-looking one spoke, "Well, Bradley Simmons, he's th Top Dog Tunah Man in th Habah, he has one foah sale. He should be heah soon."

Over another round, I began to get acquainted with these New Englanders.

Soon the Top Dog did arrive and Cocky Boy escorted me to his booth. Had I not been led along, I would've turned back to buy some time to catch my breath. Wow! Bradley Simmons looked like a Marlboro poster boy: six feet, buffed, tan, untrained honey hair and a smile like an invitation. I could have stared for a thousand years. Later, even David and Stew admitted he was the Top Dog Hunk.

Bradley took me to the waterfront, where boats lay on their sides in the mud as if taking a siesta before flood tide. Not only was he gorgeous, he had a caring charm about him and a quick-witted sense of humor. He was the sort of person that constantly refocused the conversation back to the person he was talking with. I felt important, funny, pretty. Unfortunately, his boat was too big and heavy for our needs, but he was going to Portland. I was going with him because there was also the issue of David's old red panel truck. He'd previously ferried this antique from Yarmouth to Portland on the *Caribe,* for future transfer to Key West, and now he wanted it in Boothbay.

When I left *Sondra,* David had expressed doubt in my ability to take care of this. "She probably has four flats." He had forgotten I was part of a formula racing car team.

After a long, slow walking tour of the small town of 2,500, followed by a delicious halibut feast, Bradley and I returned to McSeagull's to join up with our ride to Portland. The ride was a no-show. The evening being young, we decided to head to another bar to throw some darts and throw back some tequila. A loud mix of guys talking, women laughing and The Police belting out "Roxanne" greeted us. Smoke, popcorn and the smell of fishermen filled the air.

While taking a few practice shots, Bradley casually asked, "What ah' th stakes, Canadian Lady?"

Still chewing the cud of revenge, my sassy answer flew unguarded at him from somewhere below my waist. "Winner chooses the position—bottom or top." His eyes said yes. I wanted him to undress me. I wanted our skins to know each other. Without a word, he threw the first dart.

I lost the game and won the best romp a battered sea witch could've dreamed of. After a year of no-frills sex with my Captain, I just couldn't get enough of the real thing. The 'Coca

Cola' of sex. Naked poetry. That fast, I fell in love.

Our ride to Portland finally showed up on Bradley's doorstep the next day at noon, and we spent the afternoon rescuing the old clunker. Of course, the tires were flat but I never would admit that it wasn't me that changed the damn things. We drove the truck back to Boothbay and parked it where David could easily see her from the deck of *Sondra* and then headed to McSeagull's for a cold one. Over pizza, Bradley invited me to join him and his mate Jeff early the next morning for a day of tuna fishing.

Boothbay Harbor was delicious in the autumn sun, the sad, sweet smell of late September; fall colors splashed vivaciously among the maples and elms by the ghost of Jackson Pollock and a gay medley of boats gently bobbing on their moorings. The shoreline, spotted with pastel New England-style clapboards, was battered rugged by the Gulf of Maine's temperament. I wanted to live there. It felt extremely strange to motor past *Sondra's* stern. I was very relieved that no one was in sight. That morning, there was no wind and not a single whitecap. Once out in the open, we headed for the Gulf Stream, a virtual river of dazzling blue water within the ocean that reached temperatures of over 80-degrees, an oasis of life suspended in the surrounding cold Northern Atlantic. This warm water had all the essential life sustaining characteristics for our target, bluefin tuna. These elusive, powerful, and formidable giants of the sea could weigh up to 1,400 pounds and we were going to harpoon one.

I was invited to join Bradley and Jeff on the tuna tower. It was a second helm on a small lookout platform built for two. To me, it appeared to be a hundred feet above deck and was accessible only by a ladder that stood right beside the burning-hot smokestack. The most fearful part was the one-and-a-half-foot gap between the top of the ladder and the floor of the lookout. *Really, Marni? This is what you're afraid of?* Trying not to show my anxiety, I slowly white-knuckled my way up, as the tower repeatedly swayed through each wave's peak and trough. Finally safe between them, I exhaled and flashed a goofy grin. Joining their silence, I immediately began to help scan the calm ocean skin for the typical movement of a cluster of bluefins.

It was divine up there, early morning warm breezes tossing our hair around and a sunrise palette reflecting in our sunglasses. The lingering waning moon behind us was weaving its way through long thin clouds. Without a word, Jeff changed our course by 45 degrees and slightly increased the speed. He had spotted them below the surface and it wasn't long before I saw the smooth rise and fall of dorsal fins. Bradley had already slipped down the ladder and was taking his place at the end of what they called the swordfish plank, a sturdy narrow beam extending some 12 feet out over the water. At the end was the coveted harpooning pulpit, surrounded by a safety guardrail which allowed the harpooner to brace himself when throwing the spear. Then the monsters disappeared into the darkness. We kept our course. Bradley was ready, harpoon in hand.

Jeff was the eyes. "Twenty-five feet." That was all. Then, "Twenty feet. Fifteen feet."

Now Bradley could see them. "Got 'em."

Our speed had been adjusted so that we were gliding directly behind the graceful swimmers. Bradley, now poised like an Olympic javelin thrower, put the strength of his whole being behind a perfectly choreographed movement. The harpoon whistled through the air and implanted itself deeply into its target. A large barb affixed to the end of the long pole embedded in the flesh and locked in. Bradley's primeval grunt was matched by an eerie void of sound from the water below us. Instantly a long piece of quarter-inch line tied to the barb uncoiled from the deck and launched an attached basketball-sized buoy overboard. This marker allowed us to follow the wounded tuna until it became fatigued and drowned. Although I was taken aback by the magnitude of what had just occurred, I was a seasoned lake fisherwoman who savored these moments. It was the timeless, almost holy, simplistic act of fishing in the presence of the sea's heartbeat, an ancient native conception with seemingly equal odds between a sea beast's instincts and man's titan ingenuity.

When the red ball was still, barely bobbing in the small swell, we pulled up alongside it. Bradley grabbed the buoy's line and began to pull in the 800-pound tuna as Jeff slowly motored in the direction of the fish. Once alongside, Jeff joined Bradley to bring the catch on board. All they had was the gaff, a rope and their gloved hands to muscle that lifeless weight up and over the gunnel onto the deck. Looking down at the magnificent creature we had just killed, blood spilling out from the harpoon wound and between its lips, I was filled with emotions I'd never experienced before. Visions of the gaping mouths oceans away, deriving hedonistic pleasure while devouring greedy amounts of this sashimi flesh at my feet, made me feel ashamed. More surprising, the woman in me wanted that harpoon man in a way I'd never desired a man before. The brute strength of his conquest had actually aroused me.

With Jeff motoring the boat back to harbor, Bradley and I slipped down below and we tore at each other like sharks in the most instinctive and urgent sex I'd ever had or would ever experience. His rough hands shocked my soft skin as he grabbed my thighs and pushed hard into me—wild sex in the forceful Atlantic current.

Towards the end of that week, I returned to the boat to get some more clothes and check on David's progress with the cleanup. The boat was starting to look good and everything had been returned to its now permanent place. I was delighted to see that he had added a good-sized suspended boarding platform at the stern—one that could be pulled up on deck when we were underway.

Over a civilized afternoon beer, he stunned me with his plans to throw a big party for all of the locals. Yup, including local Bradley. I'm not sure why I trusted that he wouldn't kill the latest flavor in the Variety Club, but I did. David also insisted on organizing everything. All I had to do was invite the guests and hostess the party.

Two days later, the hordes of partiers arrived. Their skiffs and dinghies, tied to each other off our stern, looked like party streamers waving under the brilliant night sky. Their contagious mood fell upon *Sondra* like fairy dust as they clambered on board. In true Crazy David style, they were greeted by healthy shots of his signature Captain Morgan's 110 proof, along with thumping rock n' roll that vibrated from our oversized woofers and tweeters. I was in the galley, uncovering plate after plate of cold lobster, pickled herring, smoked halibut, fresh bread, cheese and decadent desserts. This station made me privy to the looks and comments of awe as one by one our guests politely descended the companionway. Our home looked so warmhearted and alluring, intriguing and amusing. I felt very proud of the work we had done over the past year.

One boatload of guys thought to bring huge green garbage bags filled with ice from the dockside icehouse to chill the never-ending stream of beer cases that were also arriving. This transaction was duly reported to the Coastguard by some nosey do-gooder as a suspicious transfer of what was undoubtedly marijuana. The local law enforcement, natural rivals of the gang on board, arrived in the familiar rescue cutter.

While bobbing up and down below us off our port side, the officer spoke, "Captain, it has been repoahted to us that some rathah lahge bags of suspicious goods was seen transpoted onto yoah vessel."

This brought the whole party to *Sondra's* rail. An anonymous male voice rang out, "Hey boys, that canastah on the fah side of the lads deck looks like it could use a hosin' down. Looks kinda dirty t' me." With that, half a dozen guys unzipped and began pissing towards the deck of the authorities. "Whoa, careful you don't piss on Bobby there, Bibbah."

The young officers were now in on it, "Is that all you got, Bibbah? No wonder yoah wife left ya."

After much guffawing, name-calling and exchange of lewd jokes, Bradley managed to convince them we were not smugglers. I was pretty sure they knew that, but they were ignoring their certain knowledge of the many joints brought to the party in shirt pockets. Satisfied no real crime was being committed, they roared off to a chorus line of crotch grabbing, victory-raised fists and a melody of mocking laughter. I felt bad that their jobs had rendered them ineligible for invites, but I knew I would be able to make this up to the Coast Guard boys the next morning with the round of coffee and sticky buns I would take to my now daily secret training in navigation at their office. It was nice of them not to mention this at the alleged crime scene.

Eventually the musicians in the crowd took stage and a top-notch jam session graced the harbor, with The Beatles, The

Stones, Cat Stevens, Rod Stewart, all covered. It was the first "official" party held on board *Sondra*, and after her Bay of Fundy experience, I imagined she enjoyed having her planks massaged by the vibes of music and dancing feet.

Sometime during the evening, David talked to a guy with a small runabout to sell. When the party ended David, Stewart and I returned to shore with the salesman. After one quick look at the tiny wooden boat tied to the wharf, our Captain bought the damn thing right then and there. It must've been his altered state. I decided to return with them to *Sondra* to assist with the post-party cleanup and was the first one to carefully step into the middle of this little oar-powered six-footer. She rocked like a canoe and before I could finish with my "Whoaaaaa!" both boys clambered in. We were in the sobering icy water in a flash and Stewart and I surfaced choking on salt water and laughter. Once back up on the dock, which was no easy feat, I suggested to Stew through chattering teeth that maybe we could stick the new addition in the middle of our floorless donut to make one whole boat. More drunken hysterics from Stew and me. Knowing he had just bought a useless piece of deck décor, David's embarrassment turned to anger. He quickly grabbed me and sent me flying through the air, splashing back into the water. He then commanded the First Mate to get back in the wooden thimble and agitatedly oared them off into the moonlight, leaving me behind on the dock.

Looking like a wharf rat, I grabbed a cab to Brad's house where I would stay for another two weeks. On the evening before David was to set back out to sea, he came ashore looking for me and found me at McSeagull's enjoying a beer with Bradley.

Politely standing before us at our table, looking sad but wearing the spirit of a proud man, he spoke quietly. "*Sondra's* ready. Are you coming with us or not?" I nodded yes, and told him I would be there early the next morning.

Bradley and I left the bar and walked down to the rough-sculpted shoreline to sit together under Maine's midnight sky one last time. With arms and legs entwined, we shared dreams for our future while acknowledging the many obstacles. The next morning he would be leaving for New Orleans to fulfill a work contract running supplies to an oil rig and I was leaving to fulfill my commitment to David and *Sondra*. It was the first time that we dared to fast forward into uncharted territory revealing what we really wanted. We were so smitten that we talked of marriage and children. We worked out a feeble plan for the future that featured penniless me attempting to get off the ship and travel from Key West to New Orleans to visit him often. We wanted it to work, and if we were to part with our hearts even remotely intact, we had to believe that it would.

All through that night, we made the kind of love that can only be shared by two people that want to give—an aching desire to penetrate through the physical into the realm of possibilities so far beyond sounds, smells, sights and touches.

I returned to the ship before daybreak, emotionally spent. That night when I lay next to David, all he said to me before he succumbed to sleep was, "Did you get the kind of sex you wanted?"

I answered only "Yes." I felt so sad and confused that he could not, would not give me what he was referring to. What road in life brought him to this? And why couldn't he express it? I wondered if he had allowed himself to absorb the fact that I might have needed something more than just foreplay.

The next morning, David knew enough to leave me alone with my misery while he prepared to depart. I vanished to the private place at the stern's boarding platform, as close to the water as I could be, where I sat down and wrapped my arms around my bent knees. While gazing at my red toenails painted with a color ironically named "Does Anyone Want to Party?" I languished in my coffee and told it my sad love story, version after version. When my gaze was drawn by the sound and then the sight of a boat passing from our bow to stern and my eyes connected with the driver, my lover, I never imagined that I was seeing him for the last time.

It was sunset before we finally pulled up anchor and the boarding platform and left Boothbay en route to Key West with yet another entourage merrily escorting us out of their harbor— folks that would likely never forget The *Sondra II*, or her sparse crew of three.

Although Bradley and I tried to see each other again,

distance, cost and obligations prohibited us. Our affair slowly slipped into the category of unfinished love. As the years went on, I came to realize that my true love was adventure—something only *Sondra* could give me in those years.

16

KEY WEST HERE WE COME!

The New England Coast
October, 1978

"Don't cry because it's over, smile because it happened."
-DOCTOR SEUSS

BECAUSE *We Could*

DARKNESS having engulfed Boothbay, I needed the distraction of work and the adventure that lay ahead of us to sooth my pining heart. We were planning for a long run this time, from Boothbay Harbor, Maine to Key West, Florida, all 1,646 miles of open sea alongside the big boys. This would take us roughly five days if we motored around the clock. We had no plans to stop along the way but I already understood that this was not something we had much control over.

I busied myself at the chart table in the wheelhouse, mapping our course as far south as the Cape Cod Canal, some 150 miles. Using my newly-acquired navigational skills, I calculated that if we left by noon and cruised at a speed of 18 knots, we would arrive at the entrance to the canal around 1900 hours, approximately a seven-hour voyage. This would have us going through the waterway after sunset. Although a scary thought, being obscured by the veil of darkness was probably the best way for us novices to attempt the passage. Studying navigation on the sly with the Coast Guard of Boothbay was one of the more intelligent things I'd done over the past year. David was both impressed and delighted that I'd accomplished more with my time in Boothbay than just falling in love.

Stewart and I joined David on the bridge where all was silent except for the engines. The loyal diesels below us were doing their work with steady grace and rhythm—the tap-tap of the tappets, a crisp beat miraculously converting fuel into power for the propellers that pushed us forward. I came to realize that the movement of *Sondra* was a fine art. Charting, I took into account changing tides, currents, wind, waves and ship traffic along with the setting of the engines at a precise pace. Unlike most vessels her size, which could be expected to reach between 10 and 12 knots, *Sondra* could comfortably cruise at double that. So many demands were made of the helmsman, alone in the vastness of ocean and sky, and *Sondra* had made it quite clear she would *not* suffer fools lightly.

David standing on a step oiling the starboard engine

Stewart, sweet man that he was, had secretly planned a celebration breakfast for our new start to our old journey. The menu consisted of Boothbay's ridiculously decadent sticky buns, fresh squeezed OJ, crispy fried fish, scrambled eggs, and coffee from some exotic place. No easy feat from a little galley equipped only with a two-burner propane camping stove and a toaster oven. We took turns eating at the captain's table with Stew. He smiled at me and, as he ate, he hummed the way one does when the pleasure of the food is beyond words. Capturing the moment perfectly for me, *The Band's* "I Shall Be Released" floated in from the living room speakers, assuring me that I *would* be released from the grasp of my aching heart.

The Captain's Table

17

THE ANIMATE PROPELLERS

Vignette 2: Growth

"A single day is enough to make us a little larger
or, another time, a little smaller."
-PAUL KLEE

INANIMATE—*adj*: not endowed with life—i.e. no capacity for self-replication, growth, metabolism, or reaction to stimuli

WE were off the southern coast of Maine en route to our passage through the Cape Cod Canal. On one of my hourly visits to the engine room to check gauges and give a squirt of oil to each of the 40 tappets, my trained ear detected something amiss—one of the cylinders was not firing.

After only a few hours at sea, we sought refuge in the already dark Kennebunkport harbor. We needed a repairman and an obscure part for a circa 1956 engine, two serious challenges. As we entered the harbor, we unwittingly ploughed through several lobster trap buoys. We felt bad that we had separated traps from their markers but thought it was a dumb place to set them anyway.

Stew and I were sent ashore for the treasure hunt and literally within minutes, flushed out an engineer who claimed "No problem!" To our delight, he worked on Coast Guard vessels—a job I knew paid as much as a Captain's position. I figured negotiating his fee while onboard *Sondra*, who oozed man appeal, might fetch us a better price. I was right, he did it for a beer and satisfying his curiosity.

Early the next morning, having accomplished the impossible, we headed back out to sea, zigzagging through the now visible minefield of remaining buoys. The engines were purring on all cylinders but our props were vibrating like go-go dancers. It seemed that the night before, a few of the snared nylon trap lines had fouled the props.

Once again, David and I found ourselves squaring off over the props. This time, David wanted to volunteer me for the job of removing the unwanted rope while bobbing in the waves off Massachusetts. All I had to do was put on my brand new full-body wet suit (a virginal experience for me), jump into the October North Atlantic Ocean with knife in hand, swim to the stern, free-dive the props, and cut away the melted nylon. Having recently watched Jaws for the second time, the sea's midnight blue color seemed ominous. Coincidentally, I had also just read this written by Peter Benchley: "Since writing JAWS, I've been lucky enough to do many television shows about wildlife in the oceans and, yes, I have been attacked by sea creatures once in a while."

One might wonder why this assignment fell into my lap. I got the job because my hair was shorter than David's and I also didn't have a two-foot long beard. Therefore, it would require less fresh water to rinse the salt water out of my hair. This was some of our skipper's most warped logic ever. I proposed we get the scissors, but the Captain had spoken.

I became claustrophobic just trying to get the damn wetsuit on. Stewart, whose abundance of hair automatically took him out of the running for the job as well, diligently heated up some water and dumped it, along with words of encouragement, down the front and back of my suit's neck. Over the side I went, just like Jacques Cousteau, but that's where the similarities ended. A poorly executed jump from the 10-foot high deck dislodged my mask and due to the shock of the icy water that immediately chased out Stew's, I gulped salt water the way I'd been known to go at a margarita.

After the coughing ceased and my goggles were back in place, I put my face in the water and did a tenuous 360-degree scan looking for Jaws while hyperventilating. I heard David coaching me from above. "Marge. Get down to business." Easier said than done without weight belts—something else I knew nothing about. At least I had fins.

I filled my lungs, kicked like hell and suddenly two monster propellers appeared out of the deep blue. I met them in their intended environment for the first time. I knew that things looked bigger through a mask underwater, but the scale of our props seemed to have doubled! Seeing them attached to the shaft, giving them the ability to annihilate me in a split second, was as frightening as I imagined a shark sighting would be.

My first job was to catch hold of the boat as it moved in the North Atlantic waves and hang on without being sliced in two. I calculated my timing, took a big breath, dived and tenuously grabbed the port prop with both hands. Much to my surprise, as soon as I let go of the prop with my knife hand to begin the hacking, my butt headed straight for the surface with amazing determination.

"Wrap your legs around the prop!" David yelled.

I angrily yelled back through my snorkel what came out as "Fuff off!"

Knowing that flapping around in the water attracted the finned fish I was trying not to think about, I dived back down and dutifully wrapped my legs around the prop. Flailing and hacking with a kitchen knife, I freed one prop and came up for air. In my newly acquired serial-killer fashion, I took care of the sister prop in half the time.

The last ensnared lines floated free and I popped back up to the surface and gasped for breath, clinging to the rope David had lowered to the waterline. Once on deck, I collapsed, blue-lipped and shaking with cold. Stewart doused me in fresh water and wrapped me in blankets while David fetched me a stiff shot of Captain Morgan, normally forbidden while at sea.

I'd met my working props up close and personal and had a solid understanding of just how much inanimate objects could actually grow underwater.

18

THE CAPE COD CANAL

Cape Cod, Massachusetts
October, 1978

"East of America, there stands in the open Atlantic the last
fragment of an ancient and vanished land.
Worn by the breakers and the rains, and disintegrated
by the wind, it still stands bold."
-HENRY BESTON

OUR next challenge was getting through the Cape Cod Canal, a 17-mile shortcut through the ancient cape, in existence since the early 1900's. Sky and sea were clear and calm. Everyone agreed that the anticipation of motoring through a large and famous canal by the seat of our pants was right up there with the angst that comes with final exams in university, but we simply approached it as if cruising through any narrow body of water.

I passed most of the seven hours en route in solitude reading Bowditch's chapter on the significance of a ship's lighting, studying charts and polishing the engines. Of course, I was also reliving my recent love affair. In the middle of this reverie, the sharp dinging from the telegraph jolted me back to reality. We had arrived and David wanted *Sondra* slowed down for the approach. I responded and David lined us up for the entry behind a Russian-flagged ship.

Suddenly, riding on a rogue sound wave, we heard the voice of authority: "*SONDRA II*, TURN AROUND NOW AND GO BACK OUT TO SEA."

Poseidon had spoken from some thundercloud or, more accurately, those designated to protect the canal had us on their radar. A bright spotlight had also burst through the night. Our ignorance had once again led us to believe there was no order to the high seas, no protocol, that we could actually take our 112-foot subchaser under a foreign flag through the Cape Cod Canal in the dark of night unnoticed. We were busted.

Luck was with us in that it was slack tide, we were now alone, and the canal was some 500 feet wide. Turning around was possible. Various combinations of start, stop, forward and reverse on the twin engines later, we finally completed the 180 and, with her Canadian flag hanging limp at the stern like a naughty child, *Sondra* headed slowly back out to sea. The canal authorities joined us. Lots of bobbing in the waves, questions and explanations later, permission was granted to re-enter the canal.

We decided, since we no longer had to sneak through, to toss anchor off the canal entrance, get some sleep and make our pass through in the morning.

Once underway shortly after breakfast, David came down to the engine room and much to my stunned delight asked, "Would you like to take the helm, Marge? I have some work to do. Stew can man the engines."

I knew this was his way of trying to pull me back in, to get something close to what we had before Boothbay. His awkward sweetness moved me and put a wide grin on my face. We hugged before I danced my way through the engine room and up the ladder.

Although the water in a canal is calm, a helmswoman must still be astute. After being in the ocean two miles offshore, motoring through a canal only 170-yards wide with the possibility of oncoming traffic is a challenge. The things I saw seemed as close as if passing by car. I maneuvered *Sondra* alongside sparkling harbors filled with resting sailboats, fall pastures dotted with grazing Jersey cows, and quaint shops opening for the day. I heard the metal against metal ting-tinging of the sailboat mast lines and smelled the chimney smoke rising from the rainbow of clapboard homes.

I can still envision myself up there on that bridge, all alone, with the wheel of my sleek, white, luxury subchaser in my hands, feeling like the coolest chick in the world. Much to my disappointment though, we had the whole canal to ourselves from one end to the other. I wanted so much for someone to bear witness to my initiation. I wanted to be able to turn my blond head, fashionably clad in Jackie Onassis sunglasses, to the captains of bigger ships passing by us and nod.

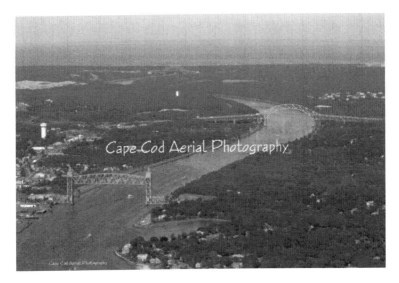

19

NEW YORK, NEW YORK

Atlantic Ocean, New York State
October, 1978

"Each man reads his own meaning into New York."
-MAYER BERGER

I was at the helm again when we began our pass along the south shore of Long Island. As we floated past the huge beach mansions I started thinking about the celebrity and rock star owners and wondered how they found each other in such big houses? I envisioned Fairmile-like brass telegraphs in every room for DING-DINGING each other with commands. For example, a DING on the right bell might mean "Come downstairs via the center hallway. Fast!" DING on the right and left bells: "Stop all forward movement! Back up and get your sister." And after whistling attention through long brass talking tubes that snaked through thousands of feet of walls, they would chit-chat: "What are you wearing to the party?" "My new black dress." "Oh great! So hot!" I tried to imagine their daily lives and conjure up who they might entertain on this privileged island just minutes from the compact, bustling hub of the US. Could our Prime Minister Pierre Elliot Trudeau be sitting down to a poolside luncheon making pleasantries with his friend President Jimmy Carter? Likely sharing his gift of a Niagara Pinot Grigio, Pierre would spot the flapping Canadian flag on our sexy submarine chaser and proudly expound upon her history as we motored by.

Ahead of me in the direction of New York Harbor, the sea's horizon was beginning to meld into the clouds. Brininess suddenly found its way into my mouth and a pungent smell into my nose. I'd read that this musky odor came from a gas produced by ocean-dwelling bacteria and was now even thought to play a role in the formation of clouds. A chilly wind had also come up. I leaned into it and felt surprisingly alive. My heart was toughening up. I would be okay.

The sea-air suddenly smelled like nothing at all. I was strangely unnerved, sensing that something was silently screaming a quickly-approaching change. It seemed only minutes before it became visible—a vast gray beast of burden carrying the city's grime and odors was rolling towards us. Fog.

I muttered, "Oh no. Not again." We couldn't continue. We still had no radar and we were headed for the mouth of one of the world's busiest harbors. And, of course, we had no charts for any of the safe havens of Long Island. David's words came back to me, *Marni, there is no sense in buying charts for every harbor when you don't know which ones you will be going into.* Damn!

The boys joined me at the helm. David had studied the main chart and announced his decision to duck in behind Jones Inlet, minutes from where we were. He took the helm, Stew went down below to man the engines, and I took up lookout on the bow. It didn't take long before I saw the outgoing current surging against us. Things didn't look good. I ran back to the wheelhouse to call the Coast Guard to make sure we could enter the bay safely.

I lunged for the ship-to-shore. "This is the *Sondra II*, a Canadian ship of 112 feet, drawing 5 feet. Due to the fog, we're forced to make an emergency entrance through Jones Inlet. We have no chart. Will we clear?"

"I'm sorry, Ma'am. We're not allowed to advise you on this matter."

Incredulously I blurted, "WHAT? Don't be ridiculous! We've passed the entrance and are now approaching the buoy. Is there enough water for a 5-foot draft?"

"Ma'am, I cannot help you."

Finding calm in my panic I quickly said, "Okay then, answer this. Will you likely be coming out later to rescue some Canadians swimming like hell near the buoy if we continue?"

There was the "one Mississippi, two Mississippi" Coast Guard silence. David had reduced the speed so we were almost in neutral in the current in front of the channel marker. "Come on, man. Things are happening fast here and I have a crew and a ship to think about."

"Off the record, you won't likely be swimming today,

Ma'am."

The choice to turn around and go back out to sea was not an option, regardless. *Sondra* was incapable of such a maneuver in that narrow channel with its ripping current. I ran back to the bow, hollering at David as I passed him, "It's a go!"

The engines were given a little more juice and, turning sharply to port at the marker, in we went. I was in a sweat. Looking at the shoreline on the backside of the island, I imagined that its sandy beach just kept on going through the ocean's skin, becoming wet desert. Anchoring in sand with one hook would be tricky business. *Sondra* carried a kedge, the ancient, massive, traditional anchor espoused in tattoos, not designed for sand but for rocks. For this bottom, we needed a plow anchor designed to dig itself into the ground by use of its deep burrowing flukes.

Once out of the narrows, the water's rage gradually turned to something more playful. David shouted at me to take the helm, as I would not be able to lift the anchor (let alone heave it).

Passing me on the front deck, he threw me a "Good work mate." In that moment, that tiny moment filled with only three words, I felt some return of the old intimacy.

He stood on the bow directing me with pointed fingers at arm's length. I knew to keep my steering minimal. Reaching what looked like a good out-of-the-way place to anchor, he sliced his hand across his neck followed by two thumbs back on either side of the neck, signaling to cut the engines, throw them into reverse and restart. I immediately moved the position of both handles on the telegraph to STOP and then to SLOW REVERSE. Stewart executed both commands in quick succession. David signaled the second neck slice, which I telegraphed to the engine room.

He gave the anchor a good heave and the heavy plunge filled the air. We began drifting backward in the slight current that remained, just enough to help set the hook. The tautness we breathlessly awaited soon followed and by some miraculous stroke of luck, old faithful dug in and held. We must have found a rocky oasis down there. David and I stood in silence, waiting to be sure we had a good hold. Finally David approached mid ship and beckoned Stewart to come up on deck. I felt obliged to call the Coast Guard again, probably more to share my relief than anything.

"This is the *Sondra II*. We are safely at anchor."

"Thank you for informing us, *Sondra II*."

"No problem, and 'mum's the word,' Sir."

Unbeknownst to us, shifting sand bars and shallow waters had given Jones Inlet a reputation of being one of the most treacherous for boaters to navigate.

Going to shore on Long Island was appealing, but without making sure the anchor would hold through both tides it was too risky. We couldn't really afford a drink anyway as we were collectively down to our last scratch. Part of this was in the form of a gold coin personally given to David by the President of Switzerland years ago for opening a Swiss bank account. The three of us stayed with the boat and took turns standing watch.

Early the next morning, the Port Authorities visited us. This was a much different version than we had encountered in Boothbay. They rudely zoomed up alongside us and unnecessarily using their megaphone, demanded to come aboard. According to them we were supposed to check in each time we entered a US harbor whether we set foot on land or not. Showing our stamped papers should have been sufficient but they insisted on boarding.

The two guys that clambered up the back were greeted by the bluesy sound of B.B. King and the smells of bacon, toast and coffee wafting up from below. We were dressed in our PJ's and housecoats but as they stood before us, I imagined myself in a uniform similar to theirs, but hanging in the middle of my braless chest would be a huge gold medal awarded to me for surviving The Bays from Hell.

After lots of unfriendly questions and paper checking, the two jerks began a full search of our home and all of our personal belongings. An hour into this exercise, one of the officers began rooting lingeringly through my underwear drawer. I was hovering, supervising. David and Stewart were behind me, which only added to my embarrassment.

Breaking the awkward silence, the head officer hollered from the main quarters, "I found your stash!"

"What stash?" David exaggeratedly mouthed to Stew and me. His face had transformed from Mr. Congeniality to Mr. Thunderstruck. Stew and I answered with wide eyes and dumbfounded shrugs. We all turned and headed forward as casually as we could, trying to disguise our nervousness, knowing this could be big trouble with terribly unbalanced odds. The pervert followed us.

Mr. Authority's fat self, covered in a mix of white anti-cockroach dust and fire extinguisher, was awkwardly crawling out of the bilge using one hand while the other frantically waved a tiny little plastic bag above his head. He was so excited that his mouth-spray could be seen flying through the air as he repeatedly yelled his words of conquest, "I found your stash! I found your stash!"

Not having to pretend in the least, I interrupted with, "What on earth is that?"

"It's a bag of marijuana seeds! Seeds! And I found it hidden in your sewing kit!"

Finally on his feet, he was pointing to a rusted antique cookie tin on the floor. I glanced over at my old treadle sewing machine with its cute little drawers full of my needles, buttons and spools of thread and wondered *Who put that there? And what idiot would hide their stash in a collector's tin in a damp bilge anyway?* I had no idea about any of it.

By this time David had found his voice. He denied that we had any knowledge of the man's prize and Fatso denied that he believed David. Billowing toxic dust into the cabin, he plunked his sweaty body down on the leather sofa with triumph. He then yanked what looked like a traffic cop's ticket-book from his back pocket, grunted as he bent over the coffee table and began writing. The "no-dope rule" while underway was thoroughly understood by the crew, so we were totally mystified as to who could have done this. I read the name on his jacket. Ricardo Guerrera. I knew enough Spanish to know that this translated into Richard the Warrior.

Finishing up with an exaggerated period-hit on his page, he grunted louder as he leaned forward and handed me a $100 ticket for possession of a minor amount of illegal substance. He, of course, confiscated the seeds and I smiled to myself thinking

Those dried up old things couldn't get bilge-dwelling insects stoned even if they swallowed the works, bag and all.

Racing off with puffed up chests, they gave us one last sign of authority by rocking *Sondra* with a big broadside wake from their oversized speedboat.

The whole scene was re-played over beers and dinner with all of us piping in. "Whoa, the big New York shakedown and all they'll get out of us is $100 bucks!" "Yeah, maybe they were really pervs or muggers in costume." "By the way, Marni, what size o' batteries does that pink thing hiding in your undies drawer take?"

The next day, knowing that the anchor was holding well, David carefully oared the two of us to shore in the "thimble" and we headed for public transit into the heart of the Big Apple. Not exactly how I would've planned to visit the most exciting city in the world—chastised and pretty much penniless—but I was going nonetheless. David and I dressed as well as sea-hippies can and took the train to Manhattan to pay the fine and cash in the coveted gold coin. I felt bad leaving poor Stew behind to babysit *Sondra*.

Arriving at the Port Authority building, we took the elevator up. As the registered owner, I alone was escorted to a private office with a chair that I suspected was intentionally too high. The Man, gray from head to scuffed shoes, rolled his stool too close, put his face in mine and delivered his canned lecture with New York spittle on the loose once again.

"Bla-bla-bla...dead-end street if you smoke pot...bla-bla-bla...turning into coke addiction...bla-bla-bla."

I wanted so much to lecture back at him about the dead-end street aspect of his Vietnam War and becoming addicted to actual drugs in a hostile country. However, faking remorse, I hopped down off my chair and nodded my way out of there to the teller's wicket.

We escaped into the pawnshop district and began our wheeling and dealing. It turned out that $100 was the going rate for the Swiss coin. We couldn't return to *Sondra* without at least splurging on one cheap beer-for-two in New York! Outwardly, I was making light of our day while inside, I was troubled that the last symbol of "Crazy David" was gone and *David* was actually broke. We had enough food and fuel to get us to Florida, but then what?

The fog had lifted and we had timed our return with the second slack tide of the day. I cooked up a pot of Autumn Soup with New York bagels and some of my aged Canadian cheddar. The three of us started talking about the functionless radar unit still dangerously perched on top of the tower. Soon a scheme was conjured involving a quick side trip into New York Harbor, where we would disconnect the component and heave it overboard. We assumed this would be easier in the harbor than in the inlet (where we were rather conspicuous) or worse, in unpredictable open seas.

Once again, we had no chart, so we ducked in behind a commercial boat that seemed to know what it was doing and hoped for the best.

New York Harbor

I was in the engine room in another cold sweat, a state that was becoming too familiar, as I watched lights of enormous boats pass closely by my portholes. The signal to stop the engines came down and after hearing the splash of the anchor, I poked my head up into the night air. There was Lady Liberty. Her 450,000-pound righteous facade, veiled in a thin copper patina, dwarfed the harbor as she had for nearly 100 years.

With no delay, David climbed the radar tower and, using a system of ropes and pulleys, slowly lowered the heavy component to the deck. With much grunting and strength sparked by the fear of being caught, we executed our challenging plan. The radar splashed awkwardly into murky shadowy water, joining a 350 foot steamship, 1,600 bars of silver, a whole freight train, mob slot machines, a virtual fleet of auto carcasses and who knows what else. Had I known at the time the magnitude of how much junk was down there, I may not have felt so guilty about our crime.

Leaving the harbor was even more intimidating as we imagined that somebody *must* have seen us. Surely someone had binoculars focused on *Sondra*. Much to our relief, we cruised back out of there in the same obscurity with which we had entered. As we slunk our way out of the harbor past the last buoy, my anxiety faded and it was replaced by pleasant thoughts of a long overdue stint of smooth sailing that was sure to be ahead.

20

SMOOTH SAILING

**Atlantic Ocean—New York Harbor to Fort Lauderdale
Late October, 1978**

"My experience of ships is that on them one makes
an interesting discovery about the world.
One finds that you can do without it completely."
-MALCOLM BRADBURY

WE left the lighted night of New York Harbor, cranked the Grays to 22 knots (leaving a trail of black smoke), and headed straight for the shipping lanes. This imaginary corridor, although marked on the charts, has neither signs nor aids to navigation on the actual ocean surface. These seaways are approximately five nautical miles wide in total and consist of two lanes, and a separation zone. We traveled on the inner side of the southbound "lane," removed from the northbound by a 3-mile-wide separation zone. By staying on the edge closest to land, we were out of the dangers of going aground or of being run over.

We were all in the wheelhouse, relaxing, enjoying an evening coffee and reveling in the fact that all was calm. David was at the helm, Stew was sitting on the floor, and I was slouched over the chart table reading tanker tips in Bowditch's American Practical Navigator. Because I was punchy tired, the pointers struck me as funny.

"Hey guys, listen to this advice on sharing the shipping lanes with tankers. 'Number one: big ships do not turn very well and certainly not on a dime.'"

"Two: big ships will not stop.' Imagine being stupid enough to think those monsters even could. They'd just run over you like you were one of those remote controlled pond boats. Oh and here's a surprise: 'Big ships often have foreign speaking crews.'"

David got into the act. "I knew we shouldn't have let Anna and Greg leave. Between her Spanish, your French and Greg's Mumble, *Sondra* would have been a polyglot!"

This made me laugh out loud. "Ohhhh, big word

Captain. Wait, there's more. 'Four: Assume the big ship cannot see you.'"

"Probably more accurately they can't see you because they are on autopilot and down below gambling," David said.

I couldn't resist, "Ah, and we can't get close enough for you to board and show them your stuff. Bummer. How's that gambling book working out for you Captain? Rich yet?" Before he could answer—"'Nummm-ber five: Watch out for the big ships' wakes.' We'd better tell *Sondra* that one. And the last one's my fav: 'Never play "chicken" with another ship.'" We all burst out laughing.

"Imagine having to tell somebody that," Stew cackled. "What do those suckers weigh, like thousands of metric tons?"

"Yeah, about 200,000 to be precise and they motor along at 25 to 30 knots. Says here some of them are now over 1,000 feet in length. Really? Never play "chicken"? But you know, I bet more than one of those hormones in their cigarette racers have given it a go."

We were disappointed to find the channels empty that evening. We wanted to see at least one and have the opportunity to play-plan our chicken strategy.

David took the night watch. I tenderly kissed him goodnight on the little bit of cheek peeking out between tufts of facial hair, and Stewart and I shared a hug. I reveled in the paradise of our large V-berth, its soft flannel sheets against my bare skin. Releasing a sleepy sigh, I surrendered to the soothing carousel swell, all but forgetting that I was a mere two planks away from the ocean and its constant changes. Slowly, all my day-to-day challenges became suspended and my thoughts drifted beyond the bizarre reality of my life to the irrational fantasy of dreams.

Too soon, rising sunbeams bounced off the water into my porthole and playfully jumped around my face. The Beatles suddenly began blasting out of the four giant speakers in the adjoining living area, singing "Here Comes the Sun." David's sense of humor was right on. I couldn't get out of bed fast enough, anxious to make coffee and enjoy it with the guys on deck.

I poked my head up through the galley hatch. All I could

see beyond our boat was the cloudless sky and the calm sea in multiple hues of blue. The water was dotted with sparkles as if tiny droplets of mercury had been scattered over the ocean's surface. I couldn't have felt better.

After a hearty breakfast of scrambled eggs and maple-syrup-soaked cornmeal muffins, David turned over the helm to Stew and disappeared below. Looking over at his red hair and flushed freckled face, I realized that, although I'd been to hell and back with Stew, I didn't know much about him. For a teacher, he was not much of a talker.

"So, I can't believe we never talked much about this before, but what on earth really possessed you to join this ship of fools?"

"Well, Mate Marni," he said with a grin, "I needed something that would snap me out of my mundane life in Ottawa. I was tired of being surrounded by kids all day and going home to a predictable long evening in my stale apartment." He looked down at his feet and continued, "Girlfriend left. Another guy. Anyway, I'd taken to blurring everything with booze, knowing all along where that was going, or *not* going." He paused to reflect. "In August, I just got on the train with a one-way ticket to its farthest eastern point. Boy, that was a depressing bunch of scenery. The empty bar car was even more bleak. By chance, someone had left a travel magazine aboard with an article on Mahone Bay. It looked so picture-perfect. Just like that, my mind was made up. I hopped on the first bus rolling south outta' Halifax and, of course, the second my feet hit the village, I headed straight for the local pub. It was there that I heard about you guys and how you were looking for volunteers to crew your boat to Key West." His face lit up as he turned it towards me. "I couldn't stop thinking about it that night or over breakfast at the B&B the next morning. I asked my hosts if they knew anything about this. The husband told me in his thick down-east accent that the boat used to belong to an older gentleman named Slater, a respected resident of Mahone Bay." Stew and I both chuckled at that description of Slater—certainly not the adjective we would have used.

Stew continued, "His wife told me that Slater had sold the boat to a couple of hippies from Toronto and that although the two of you looked as wild as the sea, you were good hard-working kids." Stew smiled here as he added, "As the man left the dining room, he'd muttered that, in his opinion, you were naïve idiots."

"Wow! Is that what people thought of us? Imagine!" I stuck out my tongue.

"Yup. Half an hour later, I was standing at the foot of your gangplank. The minute I met you and David, I knew I'd found something that would pick me up and throw me against the wall. I didn't realize at the time that this would turn out to be so literal." We laughed and shook our heads in unison at the memory of our Bay of Fundy crossing. "It has been quite the ride so far! But, I do love my new life on board this crazy boat. It's been more than I ever hoped for, and I'm pretty much over the girlfriend. How 'bout you? Are you holding up okay with Brad in the wake?"

I smiled at his kind eyes and looked out over the water, took a deep breath, and thought about the right thing to say. "I don't suppose I'll ever be over Bradley, but I don't feel like anything is missing in my life. Just about everything I ever fantasized about over the past ten years, along with a lot I never knew to fantasize about, is happening. Hell, I live in nature with abundance, challenges and creativity everywhere. It's tough with David sometimes, you know that, but it's worth it. And I have a wonderful new...what exactly are you, Stewart?"

"Whatever's needed in the moment, Ma'am."

"You truly are a Jack-of-all-trades."

Finally we passed the starboard side of a tanker at a distance, about seven times the size of us, flying a flag I didn't recognize. We couldn't help but wonder what they must be thinking as they inspected us via binoculars. I told Stew I'd read that at the turn of the century, passing ships would use flags to share info back and forth: where they were coming from, where they were going, or if there was sickness on board. "How does one say with a flag, 'We have no idea where we're going most of the time, look out'?"

"Very funny," he said with a grin.

After scarfing lunch, he asked if I would man the helm alone; he'd not slept well the night before. I gestured towards the calm beauty around us and nodded yes.

Settling in for my solo cruise down the coast, I put on my favorite Leonard Cohen tunes and started singing along to the words from "Suzanne." I loved that poet. He always captured my experiences in such a unique and moving way. Today was the day I'd anticipated for two years: warm brilliant sunshine, a picturesque sea and clear sailing ahead, with me at the helm.

Rhett soon joined me, flopping his overweight orange bulk down onto the warm floor, ready to soak up a few hours of afternoon sun while enjoying a giant catnap. It amazed me how well he'd adapted to life at sea. I guess he figured that as long as he still had us and his little space under the life donut, all was well. Factor in the attention that came with being the ship's mascot, it was no wonder he was Cheshire content.

A mottled brown sparrow-like bird landed next to the wheel in search of a place to rest on his journey to who-knows-where. The cat and I squinted at him—Rhett, in his habitual state of satiation, simply too lazy to care, and me simply thrilled to be that close to our visitor. He just stood there, feathers ruffled by the breeze, cocking his head occasionally as if enjoying the music. When I looked up at the distant shoreline of North Carolina, I knew, based on the detail I could see, that we were about three miles offshore. Quite a distance for this little fellow.

My mental focus shifted to what I *wasn't* seeing: miles of pavement jammed with cars, strip malls full of aimless wanderers and frenzied shoppers, obnoxious billboards and webs of overhead wires. Such a life now seemed so contrived. I brought my gaze in closer and turned to watch the shadow of *Sondra* cancelling out the sparkles on the water's surface as it raced with us along our port side. We moved, but time didn't seem to. It had become a meditative traveling companion.

I detected the introduction of a new sound, not a part of the music. I stopped the tape and knew instantly I was hearing a sound that all sailors dreaded—water breaking. In an instant my bliss turned to high-alert panic.

"What are you breaking on?!" I cried. I thought of changing course but had no idea which direction to turn. I was left no choice but to abandon the wheel to investigate, and because no one was in the engine room, this had to be done without slowing the ship down. Who the hell would design a ship that you couldn't slow down from the helm? Only Brits!

With adrenaline exploding into my veins, I flew towards the bow, imagining a gut-wrenching crunch. I kept repeating, "OhshitOhshitOhshit! Please god, please!" Dodging the anchor and its coiled rope, I reached the lifelines and began to look for a reef. Immediately I realized that the noise was coming from directly below me. My face was instantly pulled down, like iron to a magnet, down to where the bow met the churning water. And there they were—a small school of bottlenose dolphins— bow riding! They were enjoying the day just as I'd been, in their dolphin way—because they could. With childlike glee and wonder, I slowly lay down on my belly and watched them turn to look up at me looking down at them. Was it the music that drew them to us—the vibration of the props—or was it their idea of a sport? I smiled at the thought of a father dolphin teaching his son, *If you don't swim fast enough at the right moment, son, the boat will knock you senseless and you'll lose points!*

Like *Sondra*, their strong, sleek bodies were beautifully designed for the hunt. I couldn't help but wonder what they were thinking behind those dolphin smiles. It was enchanting to be in close contact with wild creatures that for thousands of years have been intimately involved with the fundamentals of human existence. I stayed there for as long as I could, singing to them about Susanne and her place by the water. Reluctantly, I blew them kisses and returned to my post. Minutes ago, I'd been thinking my day was absolutely perfect—and then, half a dozen dolphins swam into it!

> "...man had always assumed that he was more intelligent than dolphins because he had achieved so much—the wheel, New York, wars and so on—whilst all the dolphins had ever done was muck about in the water having a good time. But conversely, the dolphins had always believed that they were far more intelligent than man—for precisely the same reasons." -DOUGLAS ADAM

21

THE ANIMATE PROPELLERS

Vignette 3: Metabolism

"Genius depends on dry air, on clear skies—that is, on rapid *metabolism*, on the possibility of drawing again and again on great, even tremendous quantities of strength."

-FREIDRICH NIETZSCHE

INANIMATE—*adj*: not endowed with life—i.e. no capacity for self-replication, growth, metabolism, or reaction to stimuli

AH, the propellers' wake—truly something for a sailor to contemplate and enjoy. Ours, at the hands of all three crewmembers, started out with the usual rookie-style, snake-like pattern. Keeping the ship on a straight path without constantly over-steering the wheel to starboard and then immediately to port was a skill. As navigator, I was more conscious of our zigzag trail, which made it more difficult to keep on course. I thought I'd raise the stakes on our learning curve and make our steady course a competition. I presented David and Stewart with an envelope announcing the challenge.

NOTIFICATION BY THE RIGHTFUL OWNER OF SONDRA II OF AN IMPORTANT COMPETITION

THE COMPETITION:	FIRST CREWMAN TO STEER IN A STRAIGHT LINE
LOCATION:	THE HELM ON THE BRIDGE
ELIGIBILITY:	COMPETITION IS OPEN TO ALL HELMSMEN OF SONDRA II
WHEN:	1100 HRS. WITH COMPETITORS ROTATING EVERY TWO MINUTES
GRAND PRIZE:	A FIRST-CLASS DINNER PREPARED BY THE LOSERS

The contest raised eyebrows and prompted teasing digs. We all decided that it was only right if each contestant began 45-degrees off course. David suddenly turned on his heels, and without a word, headed towards the stern with his index finger in the air. He disappeared for a couple of minutes down the back hatch. I turned back to Stew and caught him sneaking in a little practice so I gave the wheel a good yank to port.

"You little bugger, Marni!"

"You big cheater, Stewart!"

David, grinning ear to ear, returned with a plank over his shoulder. He rested the board on the bridge's crossbeams about five feet up in the air. Stew and I sensed that our gambling-spirited Captain had just upped the ante.

This simple addition (which I think had already been in the planning stage) made for an amazing new vantage point, allowing us to actually stand above the wheel, with the radar tower for support, and see over the wheelhouse and beyond the bow. Now the competition had become: FIRST CREWMAN TO STEER IN A STRAIGHT LINE USING ONLY YOUR FOOT. David further set the scene, singing Donovan's tune about getting your bearings and knowing your time.

We flipped a coin to see who would go first. Winning the toss, Stew awkwardly clambered up onto the board and tentatively pulled himself to his feet. He looked like a Canadian flag up there with his long red hair and white jacket gently billowing out behind him.

"Good thing it's a calm day!"

With his left foot, he attempted to maneuver the wheel. It was hilarious watching him try to balance while using an appendage that had no fine motor skills. His two minutes passed quickly leaving the worst-ever wake trailing behind the boat. David, although more agile as he mounted the board, turned in poor results as well.

There we were, just the three of us on our old battleship with nothing in sight but sparkling navy blue water, laughing our heads off as we attempted to finally learn one of the basics of seamanship. The straight line remained elusive and the competition continued until my fourth turn. I then had an epiphany. I thought about the disabled artists who paint with their toes. Removing my shoes and socks, I took my position and placing only my big toe on the uppermost spindle began to feel a connection between *Sondra's* movements and my foot. Suddenly, because I was feeling rather than thinking, my adjustments became subtle—almost undetectable. I had brought *Sondra* to heel! I didn't need to look over my shoulder to see her perfectly straight wake and, without looking down at my competitors, I casually said, "I'd like a steak, medium rare please, a baked potato and a Caesar salad."

"You got it Marge," David said reverently, "an' with the rest of the morning off. Stew, make the Champ a fresh coffee and serve it to her on the back deck, where she loves to sit."

Hanging out in the warm Indian summer sun, feet dangling off the stern, I sipped on my yummy coffee that Stew had spiked with a clandestine shot of rum. The boys had eliminated their snake-like pattern too. I imagined that I saw the shedded skins of our Hippie yacht's past floating on her track of turbulence.

I fixed my gaze on the mass of bubbles churned into the wake by our formidable, yet comforting propellers. Leaping out to the sea with a cheerful crackling sound, the twin screws' wash was as mesmerizing as fire flames. I began to ponder the physics of *Sondra's* propellers and my steering. Together we had metabolized a wake. Once again, the propellers appeared to be animate.

22

SWIM GODDAMNIT SWIM

Fort Lauderdale, Florida
Saturday—October, 1978

"When you go in search of honey
you must expect to be stung by bees."
-JOSEPH JOUBERT

MANNING the ship for three four-hour watches per day became our jobs on the journey of 1,400 miles from New York to Key West. Life during this weeklong voyage consisted of routine blue-ocean days and black-ocean nights, punctuated by two incidents of acute risks. Mother Ocean's skin could never be a place of complacency.

We were off the coast of a large industrial harbor. I was alone at the helm in the middle of the night, navigating, steering and checking the engine room. I never felt relaxed on these watches. No matter how many stars there were in the sky or how big, beautiful and bright the moon was, I was still the only one awake with all that responsibility. The added task of having to leave the helm every hour to descend into the pit of power and noise to inspect and lubricate kept me on edge. Often there were no stars and no moon, no land, no horizon, nothing but *Sondra* and me in a colossal aquarium of black ink.

I'd just come up from the engine room and readjusted my eyes to the darkness. Dylan was singing "One More Cup of Coffee." The violins were as soulful as the haunting whistle of the wind passing through the sights on our searchlights. I never liked the sound of the wind in any of its forms. It carried unrest. The air smelled like a combination of diesel and that oily sardine-like smell of fish feeding. A few miles off my bow, I spotted a configuration of lights suspended in the obscureness. The longer I stared, the more confused I became, because their configuration was slowly changing. I couldn't make any sense out of what these lights were conveying to me, the helmsman. I froze, gripping the wheel hard as *Sondra* moved up and down on the waves. I struggled to discern the meaning of the lights. *Could it be a ship crossing my bow at a 90-angle?* For some unimaginable reason, our crew had never discussed ships going in any direction but north and south. If so, I would have been looking at one bow light, two stern lights and either a red or a green side light, depending on the ship's direction. But my first sighting indicated *two* sets of stern lights. *What the hell was it? Was it a ship and buoys? Why would a monster ship be crossing my bow? I was in the shipping lanes!*

I didn't know how I'd screwed up, and if I turned around, then what? How could I establish protocol in this confusion? *Sondra* was approaching this mystery at 24 knots and I couldn't go below to slow her down.

In a complete state of panic, I grabbed the air horn and gave it one long blast to signal David that I was in trouble. He came flying out of the hatch behind me in his undies, took one look at what was ahead of us and cranked the wheel a full 180-degrees while ordering me to go below and slow down both engines.

I had been approaching two freighters that were passing each other in front of us, one leaving a U.S. port, the other motoring towards it. Why that scenario had never entered my head is beyond me. We had avoided a catastrophe by seconds. It had been *too close*.

Two nights later, while navigating around Cape Canaveral, I faced another serious peril. The cape is actually a headland, a point of land that extends out into a body of water. Notorious for coral shoals and currents, Cape Canaveral extended lightless into the obscurity of night. At the eastern tip, once in sight, the lighthouse looked like no more than a candle.

I was heading for a buoy in this black void, my course carefully calculated to avoid these dangers. I felt as though I had been blindfolded, spun until disoriented, and told to head due east through a minefield in search of something the size of a small pickup truck. I was over my calculated sighting time by about fifteen minutes when Stewart appeared beside me with two steaming cups of sweet tea.

"What's up Mate?" I was thrilled to have another pair of eyes on deck.

"Well Stew, it's more like what's *not* up!" I took him to

the chart table in the wheelhouse to show him where I thought we were and the location of the marker I was looking for. This was the first time we had experienced not spotting our charted buoy. I didn't need to hide my anxiety and fear from Stewart. He was well aware of the responsibility; the welfare of the ship and the lives of the crew were in my hands.

"What about slowing the engines down?"

"I thought about that, but with the strong current, it would likely just take us off course. I'm pretty sure I've held steady. Oh, Stew, what I wouldn't give for a functioning radar on top of this old tower. Turn on the searchlights, will ya'? Keep an eye out for breaking shoal water or a sign of land."

Stew look worried. "Do you think these buoys ever run out of power? Maybe it's out there bucking the seas lightless."

"I thought of that too. I've been scanning the horizon. Damn it, Stew, sometimes I wish I were anywhere but on this boat. I hate being up here alone at night."

"Well, you're not alone now, Marni. We'll get through this."

For an eternity, we both strained to spot the marker or some sign, sharing the binoculars. Ten minutes later, there it was: a 10-meter high Lanby buoy, bobbing and blinking against a canvas void of color. The relief was almost a physical sensation.

"Oh, I'm buoyed up now, Matie!" We laughed at Stewart's timely pun and hugged.

The rest of the journey down the coast was pleasantly boring. We hadn't let loose since Boothbay, and we hadn't been off the boat in almost a week. When David injected an exaggerated air of excitement into his proposition of afternoon margaritas in one of Fort Lauderdale's famous beach bars, Stew and I jumped all over the opportunity. We knew that David's little rowboat could never have made a safe landing in the surf, so we decided to swim. Unfortunately we overlooked the fact that it would be a *long* swim through pretty good-sized swells before we could belly up. We stood in a row surveying the shore and contemplating the situation. Stew left the scene and returned with his bathing suit on.

"I don't know about you guys, but I am heading to the

bar."

I was anything but intrepid as I plunged maskless into the unknown water. Sharks and barracudas are predators and, I, like most other Canadians dropping into their environment, was still convinced these creatures were waiting for me to deliver lunch. The waves were bigger than I thought—big enough to block my view of the shore when I was down in the trough. My stronger right stroke and lighter weight caused me to drift a few hundred feet away from the guys. I was doing the crawl and focusing on swimming with smooth strokes and bubbleless kicks. In the midst of one of those strokes, my reality shifted to pure, intense pain. Thousands of bee-like stings were firing at machine gun speed into my neck, over my shoulder and down the soft part of my inner arm. I had no idea what was attacking me, injecting some kind of venom, but it was too entangled in my long hair to escape.

I screamed, flailing wildly in agony.

David headed towards me yelling, "Swim goddamnit swim! Marni! Just keep swimming!"

"I can't! Something's biting! It's around my neck!" I was crying and swallowing salt water. "I can't swim anymore."

David kept his distance and shouted encouragement. "Yes you can! Just focus! I'm right here! You'll be okay. Stop thrashing and swim hard!" I could tell by his voice that he was scared too.

I thought of a quote I'd heard by some saint about physical pain being the greatest evil. This quirky little bit of wisdom might have been what saved me. I desperately tried to regain my efficient crawl and swim to shore. I had to escape the water.

We must have been quite the sight coming exhausted out of the ocean—two hairy red headed guys supporting a woman that looked like she had been severely whipped. We stumbled into the closest bar—barefoot, wet, sandy and half naked. My hair was tangled with purple-blue slime. The bar's smells of rancid cooking grease, cigarettes and burnt unsold coffee only added to my feeling of nausea. Jimmy Buffet was singing about blowing out his flip-flop to tables of teens swigging icy Millers and generally having a great time. Our arrival brought a quiet to the room, causing a group of surfer-looking dudes hanging out at the bar to look up. They instantly approached us with familiarity in their urgency. After examining me, they said I would be okay, explaining that I had collided with a poisonous man o'war jellyfish. I was lucky to have encountered only one, because lately these wretched creatures had been seen floating in groups of a thousand or more and their long tendrils could extend 165 feet in length below the surface. It could have killed me.

Portuguese Man O' War

They unanimously agreed that the best remedy was either a shower of pee or ammonia. My pride wouldn't allow the former option and the latter only left me asphyxiated. My skin felt raw like a severe burn and my anxiety level had risen to that of a broke junkie. Thank god the gratuitous shots of Tequila numbed my brain and, shortly after, the pain. As the sun set and the cocktail hour band began playing great cover tunes of beach themed music, I was drawn to the dance floor. There I was, bikini clad, wild looking, smashed, giving my best rendition of Saturday Night Fever dance moves, blocking out my horrifying afternoon.

David had found a Captain (in the usual Captain-meeting bar stool space) who said he could give us three pathetic drunks a lift back to *Sondra*. The lift would be on his night-fishing boat, complete with an array of chubby tourists hoping to land a keeper. His low-to-the-water boat and the swells made a deck-to-deck transfer impossible. With David hollering, "Come on Marge!" my shipmates leaped off the gunnel of the fishing boat and started swimming the couple of hundred feet towards our rocking home. I remember thinking how strange it was that we had left *Sondra* unattended, in the dark, with only one anchor.

David began screaming at me for the second time that day only this time it was, "*Jump* goddamnit *jump!*" I couldn't imagine how he and Stewart were going to board our boat because the loading platform was on the stern's deck and there was no ladder—something we hadn't thought about when we left to go ashore. I watched in absolute amazement as David rode up with the swell of a wave, stretched hard to grab the rim of the porthole with his left hand (another four feet) and pulled his whole body up. On the momentum of this, he quickly gripped a stanchion with his right hand and, then, using all his strength, swung his long lanky right leg up onto the deck. It was absolutely amazing, like witnessing King Kong scaling the Empire State Building. Then we watched Stew attempt this feat. It took him a few tries, splashing back into the water with each failure, but in the end, he did it too!

The boat full of camera slinging, ball cap wearing, extra pound sporting tourists chanted from behind me, "Jump! Jump! Jump! You can do it! Jump! Jump! Jump!" I couldn't. I was glued to that fishing boat like a child's tongue on an icy pole— man o'wars, sharks, barracudas. Who knew what lay below the black surface of this piece of ocean? I did!

I slunk back down onto the bench, humiliated. I tried to become invisible and was determined not to look over my shoulder as we pulled away.

Fishing was lovely, especially when one of the clients

hooked a ling. This fish, a large member of the cod family, is every charter captain's nightmare. Once a ling has taken the bait, it circles the boat in a frenzy, entangling all of the lines and tricking the fishermen into thinking they've all hooked their own big one. I actually started chuckling.

Sleeping on board the Captain's personal boat, tied up somewhere in the backwaters of Fort Lauderdale's inland waterway, was awkward. He was cute, but I felt it might not be a good time to use my Variety Club card. Morning coffee and aspirins helped everything a bit. We waited for slack tide and mid-morning headed out to open water past an array of sparkling white luxury boats that exuded smells of luxury-hour breakfasts. As we neared *Sondra,* bobbing in the early morning sun, Captain Helpful and I realized that she was actually moving. As in leaving. As in leaving without me!

The slow words, "You mother fucker!" escaped my lips.

The details of how I ended up on our deck were scorched from my memory by flaming anger. "What the hell, David? Were you actually going to leave me behind? Just like that?"

"It's late and I thought you weren't coming."

There was a ring of sadness to what he had said. We both apologized, hugged awkwardly, and shook our heads at the absurdity of life on our outrageous boat.

23

THE ANIMATE PROPELLERS

Vignette 4: Reaction to Stimuli

"The difference between the impossible
and the possible lies in a man's determination."
-TOMMY LASORDA

INANIMATE—*adj*: not endowed with life—i.e. no capacity for self-replication, growth, metabolism, or reaction to stimuli

THE voyage from Fort Lauderdale to Key West was smooth and uneventful. I think all of us had had enough 'events' to satisfy any lust for trials and tribulations for months to come. As we surfed the following sea past the Keys, although not officially in the Caribbean part of the Atlantic Ocean, the water's colors began to change. Due to the shallower depths where the glorious sunlight was being reflected off sand and reefs near the surface, we were gliding through what looked like mystical, flickering marble—the deepest of aquas, the lightest of turquoises, and the truest of blues. Exhilaration filled the air onboard as we neared the island we'd all been dreaming to call 'home.' It seemed like the memories of the efforts necessary to get there were being churned up by the props and left behind in *Sondra's* wake.

For our first night, we decided to anchor across from Mallory Square between Christmas Tree Island and the main Key West channel buoy, the only area around the island populated by other pleasure boats. Due to the current, the constant traffic, *Sondra's* having only one anchor and our dinghy having no engine, David felt that it wasn't safe for us to stay there another night. Thus, we decided it best to motor around to the Atlantic side and throw our hook in front of a bar known as The Sands (which, I now suspect, was named after the consistency of the bottom). The first evening that we went to sleep in our new neighborhood, we were unaware that our old friend Murphy had joined us once again. That bad boy had quite the busy night because we woke up a mile or so north of where we'd gone to sleep. This involuntary changing of locale became an experience I instantly added to my repertoire of "seamares." Surprisingly, *Sondra's* sleep drifting did not move our Captain to return to the rocky-bottomed harbor on the other side of the island—a decision that led to even worse consequences.

During a spell of calm weather, we left *Sondra* unattended to go seek out a café. While leisurely enjoying a delicious Cuban coffee, compliments of a fiver David found in his shorts pocket, a nasty southern blow unexpectedly and quickly engulfed Key West. Without even paying, the three of us bolted from our chairs and ran the two blocks to The Sands where our little rowboat was waiting on the small stretch of beach. *Sondra* was bucking her anchor line like a bronco, but the hook was still holding. Unfortunately our lone neighbor's anchor was not. The owner had arrived seconds after we did but we all knew that if you are not on your boat once she is in serious danger, there is nothing you can do. His unmanned boat, now a mere 200 ft. away, was headed straight for the rock-strewn shoreline just to the right of the beach. Within minutes, right before our eyes, his lovely wooden forty-footer was smashed to smithereens. It was horrible; the noise of the exploding hull absolutely unnerving and the sobs of her owner heartbreaking.

While our attention was diverted, *Sondra* had started to drag *her* anchor. Luckily, Stewart noticed. We scrambled to get the wee rowboat launched and Stewart sculled like a madman through the waves to the platform at *Sondra's* stern, about 500 feet out. Fortunately we didn't capsize. The plan was for David and me to jump on board. This was one hell of a challenge in rough seas as everything was moving up and down out of sync. Timing was everything. We both made it safely and hit the deck running with David yelling "Start both engines immediately." I flew down the engine room ladder without hitting a rung and, faster than I imagined possible, had the Grays fired up. We began moving forward, slowly dragging the anchor over the sandy bottom out to deeper waters where we would be safe. Feeling relieved and beginning to relax, I became aware that we were vibrating just like that morning off Kennebunkport. I instantly knew something was wrong with the props. I'd done a lot of snorkeling off the sands and had spotted the only underwater boulder. It was huge and only a couple of feet below low tide water level. Murphy must have introduced *Sondra* to it and while flirting with her new toy, she likely bent a blade or two.

The storm subsided almost as quickly as it had arrived and we shuddered dejectedly around to the other side to stake out a rocky anchorage back in the boat colony. Now we had a serious problem requiring a major repair. When we dived the propellers to inspect, we found that both had suffered severe impact. Without a dry dock (we lacked funds regardless), we would have to remove the submerged props that likely hadn't been taken off since *Sondra* was launched more than 30 years ago.

In a Key West minute, every sailor, chandler, beach bum, and barfly had heard about the dilemma and they offered as many solutions as there were ears. Dynamite was popular, but those pushing for that obviously had no vested interest in *Sondra's* well-being; and those dreaming of underwater hammering as the solution were obviously people who'd never worked underwater.

It was David who finally concocted a viable plan.

"Let's use a small hydraulic lift made for changing tires and *push* them off."

After all of David's bungles and lapses, I was impressed. It was brilliant. The plan was perfected when I proposed using empty gallon jugs as floatation for each 100-pound prop.

Everything went off without a hitch and that night at the pier-side bar, we were treated to rounds of tequila and toasted for our success. "Nice job fellas. The props slipped off like a new bride's pajamas and those blades popped up like a happy groom."

The propellers *did* react to stimuli.

24

HARVESTING THE MANGOS IN KEY WEST

Key West, Florida
November, 1978

"I'd love to try to sell a blank white canvas to an art dealer. And when he asks what it is, I'd tell him, 'It's a landscape painting of Key West, from the perspective of an optimistic blind man.'"

-JAROD KINTZ

IN Key West during the 70's, there were about 50 bars but, in my opinion, only five fell under the category of '*the* scene': Sloppy Joe's, Captain Tony's, The Pier House, The Bull and Whistle, and The Monster (the lavish gay hangout). All featured exceptional live music, a packed house and more memories than you thought possible to gather from the end of America.

"Last Mango in Paris." Remember that song? Jimmy Buffett? It was written in the 80's about Captain Tony Tarracino, a famous Key West saloon keeper. It told the true story about Jimmy going down to Captain Tony's bar to get out of the heat and Tony inviting him to have a seat beside him at the bar. At Tony's it was easy enough to rub elbows with the rich and famous of the creative world (authors, artists, musicians) all melding into this scene as brother and sister hippies, but each with the talent to transcribe the essence of all of those memories into stories, paintings and songs that would last forever.

Jimmy perched his butt on an all-star stool line-up, each sporting the name of a celebrity who had perched there before, like Truman Capote, John F. Kennedy or Earnest Hemmingway. He had been invited to take up afternoon court with the most notorious man ever to tread around barefoot on Key West's crushed bones and coral. I too had the pleasure of sharing a stool many a night beside this old seadog. Let me take you back through this flamboyant man's life. We'll begin with a scene on a cool Saturday evening, "somewhere past dark-thirty," as Jimmy would say, in November of 1978.

Captain Tony's Saloon, a quirky bright yellow bar purchased by Tony in 1961, located at 428 Greene Street, Key

West, Florida. The interior is decked out in ultimate camp with a hodgepodge of eclectic tidbits donated by the bar's equally flamboyant clientele. A century old tree, adorned in the lacy essence of Victoria's Secrets and the souls of hung pirates and murderers, is growing in the middle of the dimly lit tavern, its limbs disappearing through the ceiling into a tropical sky. A live band, playing Chicago blues, is kicking ass. Lots of booze is heard plunking down. It's clear that most of the patrons had visited some other altered state department prior to walking through the oversized front door ornamented by a monster hogfish trophy. Turning back the pages of Tony's life, we see years of running: running fishing boats, arms, CIA agents, mercenaries, refugees and three different households punctuated by 13 kids. Forever passionate about taking chances, Tony's life is also peppered with gambling. We see him running from a successful cooked up scam, driven to a dump, and left for dead by his 'partners'. Two days later, Tony is back in his pink Cadillac with his cute girlfriend running south to a new life. We stop for a moment in 1948 to watch them show up at The Tropical Park Racetrack in Florida. In flight mode and pumped up on whiskey, he gambles away all but $18 of his fortune.

Anthony 'Tony' Tarracino 1916 – 2008

Fast-forwarding, we see 73 year old Tony running for Mayor of Key West. In response to those who objected to his use of the word 'shit' in his campaign slogan, *"All you need in life is a tremendous sex drive and a great ego. Brains don't mean shit"*, he unapologetically said, "I just hope everybody in Key

West who uses that word votes for me. If they do, I'll win in a landslide."

Having arrived in Key West with that measly last dollar in *Sondra's* coffers, the immediate decision that one of us had to find a job was obvious. David was the only American among us, but he did not feel comfortable leaving the ship with the one anchor, the current and tides. Keeping a girl like *Sondra* safe under these conditions was a big responsibility. Stewart was a teacher. What else can I say? Guess who was elected? I actually didn't mind as I was anxious to get off the boat and mingle with the locals. I wanted to have some fun. I knew that Sloppy Joe's was *the* bar in town and would therefore produce the biggest tips per night but I also knew there were four owners, four bosses and four decision makers, all up against one Canadian with no green card. Captain Tony's on the other hand, had only one entity to coax into hiring me. I strutted in there mid-afternoon and with snappy confidence, asked to see The Captain.

The two girls behind the bar looked at each other with an expression I did not understand and finally one of them screened me with, "Why do you want to see Tony?"

I wasn't about to be interviewed by them so I shot back a cocky, "Because…"

"Well, if it's about a job, Tony doesn't hire girls like you." There was a weird emphasis on girls.

"What the fuck does that mean?"

They both smiled and one replied through her smirk, "You're petite and straight, sweetheart."

"Just get the guy, will ya? I'll wait right here on top of, let's see, Truman. And, I won't get off of him until I'm walking out the door with Tony. Ok 'boys'?"

Two minutes later, I was face to face with 'The Man'. I asked Tony if he could spare ten minutes to go for a walk with a pretty girl. He studied my eyes, ran his bony tan fingers through his gorgeous Italiana salt and pepper hair and answered my question by sweetly escorting my elbow through the front door. On our way out I apologized over my shoulder to the bartenders, thinking I might need them later. I led Tony over to the pier and pointed at *Sondra*.

"See that big war ship over there, Tony?"

"Yeah. Boy, she's a beauty. She's new in the harbor. Know who owns her?"

"You're standing beside her. *Three* of us just brought her down the outside from Nova Scotia. With only a compass. And no neutral. (I threw that in for effect knowing that, being vintage himself he would know about these kinds of setups and understand the added challenge). Now we're broke and I'd like to work for you."

"Tomorrow night. 8:00. I'll see you then kiddo." He turned on his bare heels and left me standing.

As soon as he was out of sight, I jumped up and down screaming, "I DID IT! I DID IT! I FUCKING DID IT!"

And, not a word was ever mentioned about being an illegal alien.

The deal was that I would get $10 a night for an eight-hour shift and the rest was up to me. That first night, I pocketed a hundred bucks and had the time of my life—flirting and making people happy. I'd found my calling and I was in love with Key West.

My having a job changed life on board immediately. It meant champagne and hamburger dinners at Burgers Plus, a stash of weed and the much needed second anchor! Or, was it the second anchor and the much needed weed?

Unfortunately for me, the blues band finished out their contract three weeks later and Tony decided to take a break from booking talent for a while. Business was slow, my tips took a big dive and boredom was setting in. I was grateful to Tony who, always the perfect gentleman, understood I needed to go where the action was. About 12 years later when he became the Mayor, Tony also became the 'Conscience of Key West'. His goal while in office was to retain Key West's mystique and to keep its reputation as a refuge at the Mile One address for the culturally extreme. I was lucky to have known such a man.

With experience under my belt and a grasp of the unreliable drugged-up nature of my beer-slinging competitors, I headed straight for the top bar. I figured I had nothing to lose. By then I knew the players at Sloppy's and targeted the cute divorced owner. As he hugged me the aroma of his previous nights highlights greeted me via his lip kiss. I knew right then that this was going to be a shoe-in. I gave him an all-knowing look and changed my strategy from, "I need a job," to "I'm coming to work for you." I boldly continued with, "I'll show up sober, on time for all my shifts and I'll make you money—lots of money. Just ask Captain Tony." And with what seemed to be a bar owner code, he responded with, "Tomorrow at 8:00!" But in a code I was not familiar with, this new boss opened his brief case to reveal four powdery lines. I simply winked at him, turned away, and once outside, burst into my 'I fucking got it' dance again. I felt good. I had just landed the most coveted waitressing job on the island and was back in the juicy money.

Much to my surprise, working half of a square block size bar was not as easy as I'd expected. The clientele was different from Tony's slightly sophisticated patrons. Sloppy's didn't attract the locals. It was a mix of university students on spring break, seamen and fishermen, and they were all looking to get drunk and laid on a budget. They moved around the bar constantly, cruising of course, and usually did this before I could get back with my big tray full of their orders. And, they weren't tippers.

I made about fifty bucks that first night and it seemed I'd worked twice as hard as I had at Tony's. The next night I showed up braless in a backless red Tee-dress with a matching red hibiscus in my long blond hair. I was also armed with some new rules for the mostly male partiers. While reciting these rules, I was nonchalantly flipping empty beer cans underhanded into a large garbage pail some fifteen feet away, hitting my mark every time. Who knows where that talent came from, but combined with my new look, I got their attention.

Between tosses, "Hi everyone. My name is Marni and I'm your bossy waitress for the night." Pause for a toss and a flash of my smile. "If you want me to be your beer slave, here's how it works. First you tell me what your pleasure is. Then you pay me including a nice tip for the great job I am going to do. Next I scurry on over to the bar, get your drinks as fast as I can, return to this very table, put your drinks right here [every eye followed my finger to the table top and then back up to my mouth] and leave, whether you're here or not. In Key West, we work for tips. No tips, no work. Any questions?" I ended with another perfect toss.

Sometimes there was groaning and occasionally a few of them swore under their breath while passing me on their way to the bar to get their own tip-free drinks. I didn't think it was my job to inform them that only those actually sitting at the bar got served by the bartenders. Eventually these wandering sheep would slump back to the fold, thirsty, and place their prepaid orders with me. I never let them down. I worked hard, knew everyone's name, danced with them when I could and brought cute stray girls to their tables. Everyone was happy. Plus, I made cash on the side from bets placed on how many cans I could wing into the trash before I missed!

That night, I went home with a wad of a hundred and fifty bucks. High on a couple of after-work pina colada slushes, I skipped and sang my old favorite conquer-song all the way to the pier where David was waiting with our little ship-to-shore to take me home. Whoah! I felt good and I was na na na na na na na'ing it.

25

THE BUM'S CRUISE TO THE BAHAMAS

North Bimini
April, 1979

"The lovely thing about cruising is that
planning usually turns out to be of little use."
-DOM DEGNON

FOR some reason, we thought we could simply anchor between Christmas Tree Island and Key West and stay there through eternity. When we were informed by the ever-badgering Marine Patrol that *Sondra* had to get her British hull out of American waters for a minimum of three days every six months, we were definitely caught off-guard. This called for some major brainstorming. Cuba was not an option unless we wanted to smuggle David, a U.S. citizen, into and out of Castro's domain. The next-best possibility was the Bahamas, but they were so far. The main issue of course was lack of money, and no money meant no fuel. I had been working steadily since we arrived in Key West. David and Stew had started up a Bed & Breakfast on board, but *Sondra* was an expensive mistress. What we did manage to save went towards a new anchor and a used 16-foot Zodiac featuring a brand new 20-horsepower Mercury—a safe and fun ship-to-shore and bona fide lifeboat. Finally!

Need A Place To Stay?
You Are Invited To Spend The Night ...
on board Crazy David's 112 ft. private yacht anchored off South Beach. Lots of bunks and good company. Cost: $10.00 per person per night. Breakfast available.

Wait here on South Beach Pier at 8:00 P.M. or 12:00 Midnight for launch to the boat

Crazy David's Pirate Hotel

That evening, over copious beers, tokes and a mouth-watering dinner of Cajun shrimp, we conjured up "The Bum's Cruise to the Bahamas." Ideas rose on the exhaled smoke and melded into a plan. We would run an ad in the *Toronto Star* offering an adventure-filled week on board Crazy David's yacht at an all-inclusive price of $100, drinks not included. We'd meet them in Miami, load our cargo of hipsters, rockers and artists onto the ship, and make for international waters. If we found twelve intrepid travelers to fill the bunks on our 110-mile round-trip cruise, we'd make some dough, have an adventure, and placate the marine patrol.

Thanks to us, *Sondra* was well appointed for a rock 'n roll cruise with the jammin' room's dance floor, fishing gear, an abundance of masks and snorkels, lots of sun tanning deck space and, of course, a good cook.

David and I, 1979

In no time, we had the numbers we needed and their 50 percent deposits in our welcoming hands. We armed our newest crew member, Allen, with a handful of cash, and sent him ahead to Miami for party supplies. Allen had come into our lives as a paying B&B guest who never left. After a few months, he became a prime candidate for head gofer position on the ship of fools. He had all of the established crew qualifications, i.e., virtually no nautical experience, no money, and longish style hair and beard. He was dark in the way Arab men are, and tall, wiry and strong with chiseled edges that were in constant caffeine-fired motion. I never really got a handle on where he was from, but he came to us full of amusing tales told with animated flair. Before telling each story, he would herd us to a table. Taking up the head position, he would lean on his forearms tattooed with black snakes that suggested listening would be a good idea. Once he had our undivided attention, his signature prelude would begin. Rescuing the remains of a big Cuban cigar from his back pocket, he would slowly and deliberately place it in the corner of his chapped lips. Then, leaning back and straightening out his left leg, he would produce his coveted Jack Daniels Zippo with its familiar smell of butane. Using a different sequence of events each time, he would make a show of lighting up that would rival any flamenco dancer's hand movements. That lighter would remain in his left hand for the duration of the telling, acting as a kind of theatrical prop. For example, he would tap it on the table matching the beat's intensity to his desired suspense level or, for emphasis, he would snap open the top with the flick of his wrist and light it in one quick motion. Sometimes, if the story were being told in dim light, he would use it for certain lighting effects, along with smoke rising in various shapes from his raw looking mouth.

Russ, our other guest turned crew, on the other hand, was the exact opposite of Allen; like milk vs. tequila. Although he was tall and sported our signature "hairy man look," he was one of those guys who you imagined worked in a zoo lovingly tending animals. Unlike Allen, he kept his cards close to his chest, was measured and observant. The few times he did pipe up, Buddha-type wisdom flowed from his sensuous lips. His deep crow's feet foretold that he saw life through an amusing viewfinder. I loved Russ. Everybody loved Russ. He had worked for David as the in-house artist in the T-shirt business and it was through this medium that his clever sense of humor shone best. Before we left Toronto, we'd given him an open invitation to join us on the boat and when he spotted the Bum's Cruise ad, he took us up on the offer. Unfortunately for Russ, he was enlisted as our official Zodiac driver and the new Mercury turned out to be a real lemon, conking out more than once while crossing Key West's fast-moving channel. On a number of occasions, poor Russ—appropriately nicknamed Dinghy O'Rielly—was rescued by the Coast Guard while drifting off to Cuba. We put a sticker on the side of the damn motor that said "Go Johnson and Evinrude."

With dusk approaching and Allen on a provisioning mission, we began orchestrating our departure for the rendezvous in Miami. After six months on the chains, we repeated the familiar ritual only this time with Russ hauling hand over hand and David hollering commands. Stewart was in the engine room awaiting signals via the telegraph. Russ hauled up the stern anchor without effort, but the larger bow hook was firmly wedged between large rocks. It spooked me, because I feared I'd be suited up again to do some more hacking on *Sondra's* behalf. By this time, I knew the waters of Key West *were* shark-infested. Thankfully after some fancy maneuvering with lots of engine starts and gear changes, the anchor slipped free and I saw it emerge, that faithful piece of iron that literally marked the beginning of a passage and symbolically indicated the end of another.

I'd taken up my observation position at the prow. I gave thanks skyward for everything and added a wish to never be asked to participate in anything that had to do with anchors. No one was listening.

While Russ busied himself coiling the lines and David and Stewart slowly moved the ship forward, I turned my face into the warm evening breeze and basked in the splendor of the mango-skin sky and the anticipation of the journey ahead. David sounded a short and then long blast on the air horn, a noise that triggered my adrenalin and made me look lively. I turned to see what was up and saw him waving big-armed at the shore. The ritual sunset party on Mallory Square was waving us out. There was that feeling again welling up inside my chest, my throat, my eyes. Turning back to David, I wiped tears from my cheeks as I laughed, relishing the bittersweet moment of departure and the birth of a new adventure.

Beneath thousands of layers of stars, our passage up The Keys was so smooth it reminded me of midnight boat-putts around Go Home Lake back in Ontario. The scent of a familiar sea was tinged with soft conversation, giggles and mellow tunes. We cruised at 10 knots, taking turns napping, and were offshore of Miami by daybreak.

As we turned towards the harbor entrance, the outgoing tide raged through the narrow harbor mouth. I was on the bridge beside David ready to enjoy the scenery of this notoriously opulent harbor when alarm invaded the ship. It was frighteningly reminiscent of our difficulties in Long Island. Without a word, I flew down to the engine room, the sting of apprehension enveloping me. Below in my dim station, I saw nothing out of the portholes for orientation. The flood tide bullied our boat into speeds I was uncomfortable with as we pitched wildly into the surging sea. The aggressive sound of the current against our hull and the rigorous working of the engines made me edgy. Instinctively, I responded to David's numerous signals; with *Sondra*, we were one finely-tuned machine. We turned to starboard into the harbor itself; the water around us became instantly placid, and I began seeing the decks of other yachts tied to the pier. Although I knew we were out of danger, we still had the challenge of nosing up between the money against the pier. We had once again entered an inland waterway successfully without charts.

David's voice came down through the brass tube alerting me that the docking maneuvers were about to begin. Once the telegraph started Ding-Dinging, I was barely able to get one engine up and running before he would send me another signal to stop the one I'd just started and then throw it into reverse and start it again. I was panting and sweating and nervous as hell because I knew he was putting us in between two yachts worth millions. Later, we learned our neighbors were the Chicago Blackhawks and Peter Fonda's party boat. If I used too much air with each start, we could run out of that essential ingredient necessary to slow or stop our boat's momentum. Hitting the ultimate in floating luxury with no insurance would be bad, really bad. Luckily we docked our Lady with finesse that belied our inexperience.

I emerged from the engine room to an audience on the dock. The applause paused mid-clap when they realized the ship's engineer was a blonde in a paisley bikini. I headed aft to hose off my engineer's sweat and scramble into my hostess costume while the trio of male longhairs collected on the foredeck to prepare for the guests we would receive in only a few hours.

No one expected Allen to be on time for the 8 a.m. rendezvous for supplies, but by 9:30 we were pretty sure his absence meant that we'd been scammed. In retrospect, we should have known better than to send an admitted ex-con to Miami with $300 cash. We never saw Allen again. I considered the whole scenario a stroke of luck for the guy because if David *had* ever laid eyes on him again, Allen's tale of woe would have been his last. A classic quote by Ted Turner, avid sailor, summed it up nicely. "The chance for mistakes is about equal to the number of crew squared."

Cutting our losses, Stew and I headed to Winn-Dixie. The Bum's Cruise clients were to board at noon. I started to chop veggies for the build-your-own taco bar in the back of the taxi. I'd just finished mixing up pitchers of jalapeno-spiced margaritas when *Sondra's* paying cruise guests sauntered on board. I realized the female contingent thought they'd booked a ticket on The Love Boat. They were all in high platform heels. This just would not do; it was too dangerous. I politely asked them to go barefoot or put on some deck shoes. You'd think I'd asked Twiggy to grow her hair. The crew and I couldn't help but wonder *what* in the title of our ad "Bum's Cruise to the Bahamas" inferred lavishness—perhaps the word *yacht*. Once these chicks grasped that they had to bunk in the same quarters as the guys, full-fledged pouts accompanied their inappropriate outfits. They hadn't realized yet that there was no head back there. At least some of the guys looked like fun.

The tequila-laced lunch went so well that I thought our façade of professionalism would hold. Our clients, however, were not as optimistic. After dessert and flirting, the guests disappeared down below to prepare for some serious sunbathing. I'd forgotten how bad Canadians look half-naked in April—blue-tinted white. I was accustomed to the American girls coming on board and whipping off their tops as soon as their feet hit the deck but, for some reason, I was glad this bunch had Canadian modesty running through their blood—the bikinis emerged. They each found their perfect spot for max exposure to sun, stares and music, then settled in for their first cruise on the open ocean. With the women squared away, the men were free to go below and change. An assortment of Hawaiian trunks subsequently appeared on deck, punctuated by one lime green speedo. Maybe David's faded orange version had emboldened our tubby guest. Our wooden deck had become an obstacle course of beach towels, Harlequin Romance novels, Coppertone and American beer. Ironically, while they were dicking around, a cool breeze had come up and the sun disappeared behind threatening clouds. I thought about how long a week it was going to be with this bunch. If I'd known what was ahead of us, *Sondra* might have experienced her first mutiny.

Due to the morning confusion, a much more serious problem had arisen: we'd neglected to coincide our departure time with slack tide. We were heading back into the turbulent waters of the harbor's mouth, now roaring out to sea. Adding to the angst, we'd learned from another yachter that these conditions could cause a boat to pitch-pole (throw end-over-end). We didn't realize that pitch-polling was usually reserved for catamarans. I was absolutely petrified as we approached the confused seas of the narrow route.

Stew had replaced me in the engine room and I stood by David at the helm, thankful that he had the wheel in *his* hands. The guests were ordered to quickly empty the deck of their belongings, put on the chesty, mold-spotted life jackets Russ was handing out, and find a place where they could hang on. Uncertainty reigned.

As *Sondra* pounded her way through the waves, the vibration jiggled the bow anchor across the deck and, eventually, over it went. Because the anchor was tied off to a cleat leaving it a leeway of only six feet of chain, it began smashing against the starboard hull with such force that we all thought it would penetrate right through the double planks. Before I knew it, I had the ship's wheel in my sweaty hands. Russ and David were on their bellies with only their lower bodies visible as they tried to grab the frenzied anchor. They couldn't get a hold on it. I was terrified one of them would be injured, or thrown overboard, run over and possibly even sucked into the props. I couldn't stand by and watch such risk. Leaving the helm wouldn't have been recommended by most sailors but, under the circumstances, I saw no other solution than to get the fishing gaff to David. The passage was free of other yachts. I sprinted to the bow, ripping the long tool from its mount on the side of the wheelhouse en route while yelling, "David! Use the gaff!"

I dropped it between them and hurried back to my station. The round trip took only seconds and, thanks to Neptune, the ship was still on course. It was just what they needed to hook the anchor, steady it against the bow and get their hands on it. Up and over the gunnel it came, landing on the deck with a loud thud. They tied it down like cowboys finishing off a lassoed rodeo steer. By the time David joined me back at the helm, we'd passed through the mouth into open sea. He grabbed me and held me hard in his arms. I could feel him shaking. I hugged him back with all my might.

Sensing the passing of danger, the Canucks popped up like prairie dogs from their places of refuge and gathered at the rails on either side of the bridge. I stayed at the helm as we set our course to cross to Bimini. The Gulf Stream, running roughly south to north between Miami and Bimini, consists of a massive flow of water so powerful that it has its own set of wave dynamics. Flowing at two to five knots, it moves 32 billion gallons of water per second. In certain situations, the Gulf Stream produces wave patterns as dangerous as any in the world, conditions unsafe for anything other than the largest naval ships. Things did not look good for the crossing. The sky had darkened and the wind had accelerated. By mid-afternoon, we were being tossed around by eight-foot swells on the beam and *Sondra*, as was her annoying style, was rocking like a slow metronome. Many of our passengers were seasick. After attempting to find comfort in their bunks, the poor things would appear at the top of one of the hatches—eyes wild, one hand covering their mouth and the other waving about in search of something to hold onto—erratically dashing about in search of a place to heave. For some reason, they usually headed straight for the cowls: large, round, metal hoodie-like air vents whose sole purpose was to ventilate the areas below deck. I would holler, "No! Not there! Not there!" while frantically pointing down-wind.

We finally arrived at the entrance between the North and South Islands of Bimini, late but with ample light. Although North Bimini is seven miles long, only the southernmost three miles are actually inhabited. We had escaped the perils of the Gulf Stream and entered the tepid waters of the Bahamas. The sea was tranquil and a sensuous warm breeze was in the air. Floating just above the horizon, the sun had donned its pale orange filter to softly light the island that Sunday, April 22, 1979. One of the guests told me that in three hours, Mick Jagger and Keith Richards would be giving a benefit concert in Oshawa, just outside of Toronto. It was Keith's restitution for trying to smuggle heroin across our border. (Did he really think Ontario was heroinless?!) Had David still been in the business, I could just see his featured concert T-shirt—a white set of Jagger's lips on the red maple leaf of our flag with "Canadian Government Smacks Back" written under it.

The ocean was pure celestite, a heavenly blue like the milky-blue stone. It lapped at the creamy beach that rose up steeply to a grove of towering coconut palms. Their fronds stuck out from the top like green dreadlocks adorned with unripe coconuts. Everything about this island crooned, "Welcome. Welcome. Welcome."

The Biminis

Everything, that is, except the approach. The passage was filled with coral heads rising up from the shallows, only inches below the surface. It was like a Kandinsky painting of a country garden, profuse in shapes of colors exploding emotion: violet pillars, lemony brains, fuchsia fans, golden staghorns, green elkhorns, pumpkin sponges, and magenta branches. The water was crystal clear with no visible difference between a depth of five feet or fifty feet. At first glance, it is variegated shades of blue, but a seaman learns to read the colors of the ocean like a map. Turquoise water indicates a sandy sea floor. Sky blue fading to white is shallow water or a sandy shoal at low tide. Glossy navy confirms the presence of turtle grass and a soft bottom. Although a coral reef holds a myriad of colors, it appears blue-brown from the perspective of an approaching vessel. A reef is a delicate eco system, but it's surprising how quickly it can rip a hull wide open. You must never pass over the coral.

I was sent to the bow to help David guide *Sondra* through a natural channel "the cut." This was a new level of navigating for me—much more intense than the loose and forgiving guiding I'd done before. Communication on board is ancient and precise. It *must* be this way. Once again, the language was a combination of hand and arm movements. Not a single word was exchanged; my back was to David. My Captain and I again worked as one, in the moment, each trusting totally. Everyone but Stewart was on deck, but no one moved or made a sound. All we could hear was the purring of our diesels, the waters willingly parting beneath us, and a reggae-beat bouncing off a bongo in the distance. It was ethereal.

We were in nerve-wracking proximity to the machete-sharp edges of antler coral. They rose enormous from the sea floor like the bony hands of the ocean herself. The cut was unmarked, narrow, and subject to fluctuation in depth. As usual, we had to pick through the notoriously treacherous Bahama Banks with no charts or navigational aids. I imagined Columbus's galleon the Santa Maria, although half the length of *Sondra*, passing through the same reefs so many years ago, bulky and motorless.

Much to my incredulity, I was actually able to take us through what would be our most challenging harbor entrance in terms of likely—no, highly probable—chances of going aground or being sliced open. Once out of danger in deeper waters behind North Island with our anchors set, everyone cheered and hugged. Some were celebrating our safe arrival, some sharing the joy of not being ill, and all were anticipating what they had come for— a great Canuck party in the Bahamas.

Immigration was closed, but we weren't sweating it. Harry Nilsson crooned out of the speakers from below telling us to put the lime in the coconut, and as I passed around shots of rum, we were all happily yelling, "Doc'ter!" in unison. Suddenly, "The Authorities" showed up on our deck, uninvited so to speak. We guessed that because it was a Sunday *and* after hours, the boys were looking for a little something on the side. A healthy bribe later, we were cleared, an evening of jammin' was arranged and a bag of grass was lying on the captain's table.

That night, guests clambered out of our Zodiac with the girls waving their summer-colored heels over their heads, and tiny Alice Town greeted us with all it had. A harvest of odors— from smoking fish, sweet from its molasses-spiked brine, to Bimini's famous bread baking in outdoor ovens—drifted down to the docks. Inside the Compleat Angler Hotel bar, Bimini's hot spot, the fruity smell of tropical blender drinks, expensive cigars and old leather wingbacks took over. Even the music had its smell, a smell that smacked of dirty dancing.

We arrived lit up and a little randy, and descended upon Hemingway's modest 1930's haunt. "The Authorities" had morphed into the local musicians and were already setting up their instruments. An electric piano awaited David and some of our guys had brought along their guitars and harps. Drums of all sorts, shakers, tambourines, speakers, and wires were everywhere. The air was full of laughter as the makeshift band tuned up. David, being the pro that he was, sensed the moment they were ready and with simply, "Okay boys," brought silence. Suddenly his piano rang out with those distinct introductory chords to Marley's "Jammin'!" bringing on an explosion of talent and moving feet. We white girls soon found ourselves with a pair of black hands resting on our hips, encouraging our frozen northern pelvises to sway apart from the rest of our bodies. Although it resembles reggae, the music of the Bahamas holds a separate identity unique to its people—"Rake 'n' Scrape." Imagine the beat of honkytonk, the energy of ska, and the relaxed island flavor of bent knees bouncing to the backbeat. The spine is held with perfect posture and pelvises are pressed against each other.

What an evening! The weak-of-liver and faint-of-heart were in their berths by 2 a.m. while the hearty and the foolhardy (including some of our new island friends) gathered in *Sondra's* salon. The music picked up where it had left off, but now The Grateful Dead, The Allman Brothers and Sam Cooke joined the mix. All the tinny synthesizer burps had been left on shore and the glass bells of the Hammond sonorously passing through the

Leslie added to the heat of our spicy jam session. At some point, one of the invited, a guy from Chicago, walked up to the organ and cut out a bunch of lines. This also *bumped* things up, including the dance lessons and Bahamian naughtiness. The boys, with their freshly topped-off cologne du jour "Bacchus," bought the marketing jive and attempted to "Conquer the Empire" which, that night, consisted of Canadian Babes doused in Fabergé's "Partage."

David and I danced our way into the V-berth where the live jam provided a curtain of volume for our privacy. After what seemed like mere minutes of slumber, those who had prioritized sleep were now prioritizing breakfast. Over the pounding beat of my headache, I heard the knocking on the salon hatch. I told them to help themselves to coffee and cereal. I fell back into sleep as their grumbles and giggles and footsteps vanished to explore my galley. The rest of us managed to crawl up out of our dark holes in time to celebrate brunch. An abundant feast materialized when the Bahamians returned with smoked marlin, coconut rice and fresh grouper adding to our herb-scrambled eggs, bacon, warm bread and lots of coffee. After siestas and tanning, we all partook in the best cure for a lingering hangover I've ever found, a plunge into salt water from the 10-foot-high bow. The current carried our bodies from our launching spot past all of the portholes and the helm speakers (playing an afternoon Stones tribute) to the platform at the stern. We floated in the bathtub-temperature water and joked about how our depleted electrolytes were being replenished by sheer osmosis. Hanging onto a thick rope tied to the swim platform, we could look underwater using snorkels and masks. The anchor was clearly visible off the bow, tethered to the boat with its sturdy chain. Sighting along *Sondra's* 112-foot hull and following the anchor line with my eyes, I realized with a shock that the visibility of these crystal waters exceeded 200 feet. I marveled at a yellow-spotted eagle ray speeding towards me from the anchor; her graceful six-foot wingspan moving like her namesake. Within feet of me, she playfully soared through the ocean skin into the sky because it felt good, because she could. Under me, numerous turquoise and pink parrotfish crunched at lunch off a coral head abuzz with tiny, dazzling tropical fish. A school of florescent squid spurted backwards past me as they rhythmically squeezed seawater out of their bodies. Vibrant color and design surrounded me. I had never imagined all this was under the surface of Bimini's waters.

The week passed with lots of drift snorkeling, fishing, music, delicious Caribbean-flavored meals and gallons of rum. Before we knew it, it was time to head back to Miami. Again, the weather forecast for the journey was not good. This prompted the complainers, who coincidentally were most of the seasick victims, to choose to fly back. *Thank god.* While *Sondra* was rocking and rolling her way over to the US, the dissatisfied contingency was busy in a meeting with the Miami Port Authority. Unlike their Bimini version, these officials meant business. As soon as we tied off, David and Russ hopped in a taxi, not realizing what was about to happen.

I was on deck cleaning when a police cruiser pulled up to the dock. Two officers emerged and they were looking for me, the legal owner of *Sondra*. In short order, I was in the back seat en route to their headquarters. The disgruntled guests had registered a formal complaint about their vacation experience. Although the group admitted that the activities and food were wonderful, all were gravely disappointed about three things. They complained about the living conditions—how they had to sleep in mixed quarters with no bathroom. They bemoaned the terrifying experience of leaving Miami harbor and entering Bimini harbor and that *Sondra's* crew seemed to have no experience, let alone certification. They had wailed about *Sondra's* performance at sea and how each of them suffered seasickness on the journey across the Gulf. Consequently, they were forced to spend money over and above their $100 cruise ticket to fly back to Miami. Much of their tale of woe was irrelevant to the men taking the report, as a rolly ship is perfectly legal and a mixed dorm every cop's dream. These paled in comparison to the officers' allegations. We had chartered a cruise in a foreign-hulled vessel, originating from a US port, and carried over six passengers without a licensed captain. Ultimately, the objection was money. We'd made some, ostensibly, and all of this was illegal.

I was informed that I was facing fines, jail time and the

loss of *Sondra* forever. I sat in my institutional chair and listened with contained horror. After observing David's various legal escapes back in Toronto, I knew there was a slim chance at getting off and that keeping my mouth shut was imperative. In the meantime, David had returned from his supply run and Stewart had pointed him in the direction of the local brig. The authorities had just finished their laundry list of charges when the tawny mane and tail of my knight in shining denim walked through the door. I faked calm as they led him into the adjoining room, but silently I was refusing to go to jail, not even for the booking. Minutes crawl when you're facing hard time. I had always been intimidated by the US government and never imagined that we would be staying in the States, even if it was in Key West. I felt that in some way David had let me down but, at the same time, these were my choices. The piper would be mine to pay. I thought of the months and funds I had devoted to *Sondra* and how devastated I would be if they confiscated her. I also thought of the possibility that David wouldn't be able to bullshit his way out of this one, or maybe he'd only be able to save his own ass and I'd be left hanging. The image of Bradley hearing the news of my stupidity crossed my mind. That thought made me feel even more miserable.

David and the officers, along with the Chief, emerged five minutes later. The four of them came into my room. After some throat clearing, the Chief apologized to me for the misunderstanding. Handshakes were exchanged and we nonchalantly left their air-conditioned office. My feet barely touched the ground. I decided to wait until we were back on board with Russ and Stew before asking David what on earth he'd told the officers.

"I asked them if they really thought that the T-shirt mogul of Canada needed a half-dozen friends of friends to pay him $600 so he could afford to put gas in his 112-foot yacht? Then I showed them the *Miami Herald* article I've been carrying around in my wallet."

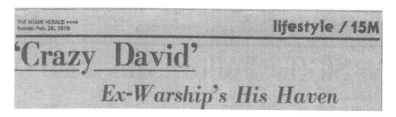

THE MIAMI HERALD ★★★★
Sunday, Feb. 25, 1979

lifestyle / 15M

'Crazy David'

Ex-Warship's His Haven

David Keller's Kingdom Is a Former Sub Chaser

By SUSAN SACHS
Herald Staff Writer

When David Keller, his waist-length red beard tousled from the wind, steered his ship into Cape Cod Canal last year, he was greeted by the pointed machine guns of a 95-foot U.S. Coast Guard cutter, whose crew warily ordered him out to sea.

It's not the kind of experience civilian boat captains are used to, but Keller owns a warship. His 121-foot Canadian Navy submarine chaser — vintage World War II — serves as home and business, hotel and fishing vessel for Keller and a crew of five.

"We took them all over the boat," he says of the New England Coast Guardsmen. "They loved it, once they realized we weren't attacking."

KELLER, known as "Crazy David" in Key West, where his ship the "Sondra II" is moored beyond city jurisdiction, is about ready to offer himself for hire as a freight shipper between Miami and Caribbean and South American ports.

The hold of the ship can carry 100 tons of refrigerated cargo, 80 tons of it in what is now the comfortable, oak-beamed living room and another 20 in a forward hold.

A load of 50,000 pounds of lobster bought in the Honduras for $3 a pound could sell in Miami for $6 a pound, he says. With investors taking most of the profits, Keller figures he still could walk away with $25,000 — at 50 cents a pound for the boat — from a single trip.

"It's the tonnage that's important," he says. "It doesn't matter if it's Campbell's soup, vaseline or cedar wood."

But for now, Keller is busy refurbishing his warship — replacing much of the rotted wood inside and polishing the brass trim and the 20,-000 brass rivets that hold the crisscrossed slabs of mahogany together.

HE BOUGHT the ship about a year ago from two old Navy buffs in Nova Scotia, who had bought it 20 years earlier, but did little more than look at it.

"They were Army surplus guys," Keller says. "They wore their uniforms all the time, and drove around in Army Jeeps. This was one of their toys."

He bought it cheap, but found the boat was so rotted that the floor was practically gone. Keller says he spent some $10,000 in lumber alone to repair the ship.

At the forward end of the ship, bunk beds for 18 crew members were tucked into small, subdivided rooms.

"If I hadn't gotten it, it wouldn't have lasted much longer," he says. "They had never opened the hatch."

At first, he says, his neighbors in the small oceanside town in Nova Scotia thought he was crazy to invest in the hulking vessel.

While he was doing the woodwork on the boat, for about a year, many of the sailors who served on the Sondra II during the war would wander by and reminisce. They'd also share their seagoing knowledge.

"Everybody in the neighborhood came by, and I picked their brains," Keller said. "After a year, I knew how to run it. They don't think I'm crazy anymore."

EVEN SO, Keller, 32, advertises himself in Key West as Crazy David, the man who offers accommodations and a meal at $10 a night onboard the long, gray ship.

Guests are referred also by the local chamber of commerce, and are picked up at one of the island's public piers by Keller in a small, motorized rubber raft.

The ship is Keller's escape from the world where he first made his fortune. But even his successful business is a bit eccentric. Keller once was the T-shirt prince of Canada, running a multimillion dollar business that eventually "drove me nuts."

"I needed a change in life," he says. "Now, with the ship, I'll never let this get any bigger than it is. I'd rather sit in Mexico for a month and soak up the sun."

THE SONDRA II still has a military air about it, especially down in the engine room, where Keller can sound the telegraph bells to signal full and half speed for his engineer. Everything in the dark room, laced with pipes and wires, is from the original wartime submarine chasing.

But there are eclectic twists to the stern military bearing of the ship. Four stereo speakers are tucked into the wheel room on deck, with a radio and tape deck. An antique sewing machine serves as a small table.

A string of small white lights hangs over the deck, making it a small ballroom where Keller and friends relax on calm evenings.

Menus for the crew are hand-printed a week in advance by Keller's girlfriend, and the live-aboards take turns cooking according to her instructions.

"You have to be a little military to run this thing," he says. "We get a little more organized every day."

IN THE oak-beamed and comfortable living room, a set of drums and an organ sit for the crew to play. Keller, a former studio musician, says he has almost a full recording studio set up in the bowels of the ship.

"This is like land — it's an island."

Standing on the deck, which one of his hands was swabbing — just like in the real Navy — Keller looked toward a large yacht.

"It's worthless," he boasted. "It costs $250,000 and you can't make a penny off it."

Knowing David, somewhere in his brief speech, using a tone full of significance, he likely emphasized that he was an American and even more likely, he wrote down their names—a small gesture big enough to shift the power. Although we won this one, I learned that Maritime Law was not so easy and it was not gray-area law. Twenty minutes in an American Law Enforcement space is enough to make anyone think hard about his or her choices. That being said, this was not to be the last time David would butt heads with the authorities in the state of Florida.

26

LIFE AT MILE ONE

Key West
1979—1980

"Life is just a bowl of oat flakes.
You wake up in the morning and it's there."
-CAPTAIN DAVID KELLER

FOLLOWING the Bum's Cruise fiasco, we were happy to return to Key West. She lay waiting for us, her glistening bleached bones in her turquoise bath, tropically restless, her 50 bars endlessly cranking out the sounds of song and carousing. Not having succumbed to cruise ship tourism, she was coquettish and guileless.

While the rest of the world was listening to Super Tramp's "Breakfast in America" and flocking to the theaters to witness Coppola's "Apocalypse Now," we settled back into an Island lifestyle where spontaneity generally ruled in our bag-of-rags populace. Key West's motto "One Human Family" summed up how this bizarrely random clan somehow worked.

Sunday, our day off, was the only time when the stability of a ritual reigned—something we all seemed to need to keep the four of us connected. We would begin the day around noon and putt-putt our way in the Zodiac around the island to The Sands, our old anchorage site on the east side. A hip beach club, it was a weathered Key West original that had been added onto over the years using whatever blew or floated by—a description that would also apply to the patrons. Laughter, bottle clinking, and the mouth-watering smell of Jack Daniel's BBQ sauce caramelizing over hot coals played in the shore breeze. Toby McGregor, David's best friend, treated the crowd to a wide variety of original music. When he banged out boogie-woogies laced with bawdy lyrics on the old stand up, the place rocked. The crowd ranged in age from the smooth-skinned babies sucking on a breast to the prune-skinned sun worshipers sucking on a Miller. There was something for everyone: dancing, drumming, Frisbee tossing, volleyball, windsurfing or just getting high and hanging out in the shallow water. I loved those afternoons.

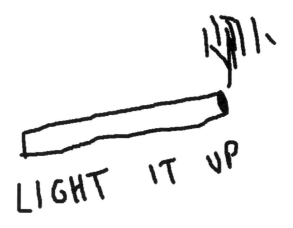

From The Sands, we would head back to the harbor-side of the island to join the hundreds of people at Key West's famous Mallory Square, where sunset was actually *celebrated*. Every night, a funky arts festival of the inimitable was staged next to the water facing the bravura setting sun. The avant-gardes were our entertainers, expanding the boundaries of aesthetics, making art for art's sake. The music—everything from ancient, droning didgeridoos to Stomp-style rhythms using everyday objects—harmoniously blended to set the mood. Moving throughout the buskers were characters like the Banana Man, who talked-sang his sales pitch in that Caribbean way, "Banana bread. Banana bread. Get ya some while it's hot. And if not, don't blame me when it's all bought." That treat was always warm and topped with crunchy brown sugar tossed with cinnamon. I liked following the psychic who floated from person to person in layers of velvet, tulle and tie-dye, gently caressing unaware palms, connecting with the owner's lines. "Marni. You are a daring woman. I see years of adventure in your life . . ." She blew me away with what she could see in my wrinkles. Of course, I overlooked the fact that she had *Sondra* in her sight and likely, in a town that size, knew exactly who and what I was. Too bad she couldn't really see into the future. All of these artistes were there to help the locals and the tourists (loaded with two-for-one piña coladas and margaritas) pay homage to the Big Star, the center of our Solar System. As it sank into the Gulf of Mexico, blazing persimmon, our eyes and expectations were united as that "One Human Family."

Sunset at Malory Square

Stewart and Russ continued to run our floating B&B, which had become a temporary home to an array of thought-provoking, international guests. Our mates were also responsible for the water taxi service and for the ever-demanding task of keeping *Sondra* spiffy and safe.

For me, working at Sloppy's was like going to a party every night and, at 29, I thought it was the perfect profession. In the fashion of a "hostess with the mostess" entertaining friends in her home, I would circulate, serving drinks, dancing, and prompting amusing conversation, all to the sound of the island's best live music. The only difference was that I was getting generously tipped for this performance. When I wasn't working, I was either riding around with my girlfriends on our funky bikes, diving, fishing, jammin' or making out with a stranger.

The music sessions onboard attracted both local and traveling musicians. If someone was walking around with a guitar case slung over their shoulder, one of our regulars usually commandeered them. *Sondra's* double-planked mahogany salon reverberated sound like an amplifier. There was weed and beer and the dress code was simply "skimpy." It always amazed me the way a group of strangers could improvise harmoniously. We seldom had a singer, so guests would take a turn at being in the spotlight with their instrument at some point within the tune. I usually picked up the drumsticks, and I could get all four limbs going at once (although every now and then, my snare attack was off). David would get his head and hair into the act, nodding on the note my backbeat should've been on. Those without instruments would help themselves to my basket of toys— tambourines, shakers, sticks, bells, kazoos—some following me, some consistently stressing the correct beat. Every now and then, a big wake would rock *Sondra,* sending my Ludwigs and me ass over teakettle for some comic relief. After hours of filling our open portholes with classic rock n' roll, we would all go for a drift swim, lay some fresh fish on the BBQ and watch the stars come out.

Key West in the 70's was also sex. After the free love of university and being a member of David's "Variety Club," I considered myself to be among the avant-garde in this department, that was, until I moved to the little three square mile island where day-to-day life was like living inside a Masters and Johnson lab. If there was a sexual desire to research, appropriate guinea pigs could be found in the mélange of aircraft carrier crews, vacationing college students, fishermen, local hippies and hot-blooded Cuban immigrants. Everyone was either sippin', tokin', dropin', shroomin' or snortin' to the groove of the 70's peace, love, and rock n' roll. Beautiful buffed bodies in all shades of human, glistening in states of undress, floated around just looking for something to get into or be ridden by. At any given moment, someone was experimenting with straight, bi, cross or gay, topping it off with the Kama Sutra and spicing it up with group sex, bondage and whipped cream. Although most heard about the sexual revolution, most never really experienced that kind of social liberty—the pinnacle of which was sex in the 70's in Key West. In the altered state of one's choice, one could have any kind of sex with just about anyone, any time one pretty much wanted, with no moral downtime.

Because my world was mostly filled with male friends, guests and clients, I was privy to their man talk. Inevitably, it turned to sex, the gist of which was sport fucking. I wanted to know if I could do this: have sex with more than one partner within hours without any emotional attachment whatsoever. The opportunity arose on an evening that started at the Bull and Whistle, a great corner bar lavished with copious shells, sponges and other treasures from the sea. A singer who did justice to Janice Joplin's songs with the perfect degree of raunchiness kept the place in a constant state of arousal. I had lost track of David so decided to perch my bottom on a stool at the bar and enjoy the show. There was a man beside me, mysterious and striking in a Latino way, examining the opening of a large conch shell he'd picked up off the bar. I was mesmerized as I watched him rotate it in his right hand, allowing his rough left fingers to unhurriedly glide over the smooth pink Georgia O'Keefe opening.

He turned to look at me, taking that extra moment that allowed for connection before he spoke, "Have you ever seen anything so sensual?"

I gave him a smile that let him know I was on to him. The waitress interrupted, "Can I get you two anything?"

He looked back at the shell's opening, turned it outwards and provocatively placed it close to her face. Then he stopped and looked closely at me as he asked her, "Do you have a drink that tastes like this?"

The waitress and I exchanged a blushing look reflecting our recognition of the likeness of the conch's outer lip. "Not now but maybe later," she flirted back.

He ordered two shots of tequila. We enjoyed the silent ritual of wetting and salting our thumb crotches, shooting back the burning liquid and sucking on the juicy lime. He then invited me out to his car for a toke. We clambered into the backseat of his red mustang and before I knew it, my panties were twisted around my ankles, binding them. My back was arched and I was enjoying superb oral sex, the kind I knew wasn't foreplay. It was the toe-curling main event.

We each exited opposite sides of the car and I returned to the bar, alone, and danced and danced and danced. Still no David. I decided to see if he'd gone to our favorite locals' bar located just past the cemetery. As I walked in that direction, a buffed surfer joined my stride and offered a hit on the joint he was puffing on. Without so much as exchanging names, I let him lead me to the grass beside a headstone. Naked strangers, we lay in the coolness. His lovemaking began slow and sweet, full of delicious kisses. He told me he'd studied tantric sex and asked if I would allow him to take me to a level of pleasure and kinds of orgasms I had likely never experienced. I answered by raising my curvy pelvis to his gentle touch and let him begin to work his magic. Taking me to a point of mad desire to have him come into me, I writhed as he pushed me hard against the earth.

We parted without promises.

Full of energy, I headed back downtown to Captain Tony's to catch the late-night set and do some more boogying. I felt I'd successfully completed my experiment. I concluded that a woman could enjoy two men back-to-back and walk away without any emotive lint *and* catch a buzz similar to a great afternoon of downhill spring skiing.

I found David playing pool at Tony's. We nodded at each other and I continued on to the dance floor. And then ...

I remember her hair
it was black
tangled crooked
flying in as many directions
as her feet
bare
tough tanned skin wringing
point of frenzy
white sleeveless blouse
white peasant skirt
chasing her naked body
wildly
she danced
at me.

Between
woofers and tweeters
in Captain Tony's bar
it began
Jenny
teasing me.

My man was not in sight
I knew this would turn him on
he loved women overcoming
dogma together.

Somehow three
became crowd
in our home on the water
legs jammed under captain's table
each of us with our own reason
for drinking more Bloody Caesars
ending up on the oversized bed
on top of nude Marilyn Monroe sheets.

God her breasts were soft
round brownness
everywhere
her tongue so so so on my . . .

Her salty smell
our untamed hair
black   blond   red
we took turns at being
the-cream-the-sandwich-the-squished
and laughed.

As the shared male told it
"The wind blew
the sand flew
I couldn't see for a minute or two
and when I opened my eyes
she was gone."

Key West aroused such eroticism. In my eyes, life at Mile One was absolute bliss. Regardless of the reader's credulity, it was (and probably still is) impossible to leave Key West without a psychic Joan Baez designed souvenir bag full of diamonds and rust—diamonds being delightful commemorations of your inner badness and rust the bit of shame you carry back to "the rest of the world." And, the little label inside this bag would read:

Diamonds - made from Pura Vida
Rust - made from the small price to pay

27

LEAVING. RETURNING.

Key West
1980

"Farewells can be shattering, but returns are surely worse. Solid
flesh can never live up to the bright shadow cast by its absence.
Time and distance blur the edges; then suddenly the beloved
has arrived, and it's noon with its merciless light, and every
spot and pore and wrinkle and bristle stands clear."
-MARGARET ATWOOD, "THE BLIND ASSASSIN"

DAVID'S main job was refinishing old Conch houses, a solitary, repetitive task of painting shutters and ornate Victorian railings. He loathed it. Once in a while, he would execute some wild moneymaking notion that had popped into his mind—schemes like dangerous bang-stick fishing enormous 200 to 400 lb. goliath groupers or netting itsy bitsy aquarium fish—both of which fell short of big cash flow and pizazz. Then there was his band, featuring him on the B3. For each gig, the crew had to lower the heavy organ into the Zodiac. Sitting on the organ bench, David looked like Captain Nemo being kidnapped. Back in Toronto, Crazy David playing the organ was something but, unfortunately, in Key West he was just a member of one of the many hired bands, no longer infamous and no longer a crowd pleaser.

All of these efforts were short-lived and a far, far cry from getting up every day knowing that you're the top dog of T-shirt manufacturing and sales in Canada. Watching David bounce from one unfulfilling and unsuccessful effort to another was like watching a child actor who'd fallen out of the limelight into its shadow.

Although we enjoyed Mile One and its safe anchorage, living there full time was *not* what we were dreaming of when David bought *Sondra*. We saw ourselves cruising her in and out of exotic ports the world over for years to come. In reality, we were living the tail-chasing dilemma "It takes money to make money." As far as using *Sondra* as a business was concerned, we'd been naïve about international marine law restrictions with regards to a Canadian-owned British hull run by an American with no captain's papers. After our Bay of Fundy experience and even our problems in the Gulf Stream, we realized that *Sondra* was not designed for open water—a true impediment to our dreams.

I was beginning to sense a big change in the air. Along with the disappointment we all felt about not traveling, living hand-to-mouth on a 112-foot yacht was whittling away our morale. I also suspected, with only room and board and very little privacy, Stewart and Russ were likely having thoughts about moving on. As for me, I was getting tired of being the main breadwinner with nothing left over for myself at the end of a long workweek. Unlike the attitude toward my initial *voluntary* investment into *Sondra*, David now felt *entitled* to my money. His control and downbeat was becoming a wedge between us.

Towards the end of 1980, *Sondra* began bravely reflecting the foreboding signs of change I'd been sensing. It was a rare occasion when her anchors were lifted to take her out for a spin. Music had ceased to drift from her portholes and her appearance was not being attended to. It was like we'd become squatters slowly taking over her rights.

The Florida Marine Patrol had even started to treat us like trespassers. Much attention was given to the fact that, like most of us, *Sondra* was *not* American and to the MPs her sleek alien hull looked like it was up to no good. They constantly surveyed her from shore (using binoculars we could see with our naked eye). We all found this infringement on our privacy creepy and unanimously agreed they must be violating *some* right. Sporadically, they would just hang out at the pier as if they had nothing to do with the unmarked car parked nearby. On these occasions, they usually performed searches of my laundry as I wagoned it past them in green garbage bags.

"I would have to be an *imbecile* to smuggle marijuana right under your binocular-shaped noses in broad daylight." Not even my outright scoffing deterred them.

They were also interested in how many fish traps we had, even though we never exceeded one. Out of nowhere, they would zoom up in their confiscated cigarette racer, swamping our little Zodiac with their big wake. Without any niceties the driver would bark, "Y'all show me yo' catch." She was a nasty-assed woman with stressed buttons, wet shirt-pits and bleached-out straightened hair that looked wind-struck. Knowing we weren't breaking any laws, I'd taken to razzing her about her bad-hair day or the fact that her uniform had shrunk.

It all came to a head the afternoon she and her accomplice roared up to our dinghy while David was tinkering with his nemesis, the Mercury motor. This time she demanded to see his Florida registry papers for the Zodiac. When he failed to produce what had no reason to exist, they arrested him *on the spot* and took him off, speedo-clad and barefoot, for finger printing and mug photographing and locked him up. Luckily the judge hearing our case was a former sea captain. He actually admitted he was *embarrassed* by this case and admonished the arresting officers by saying loudly, "Don't you Marine Patrol know a damned thing? That a foreign-registered vessel does not *ever* have to register its support boats in *any* port other than its *own*?" Without waiting for their lame response, "Apologize to this man and release him at once."

In the past, David would have seen the humor in this episode, but this time he didn't. He was outraged and incensed that his draft-dodging file had been reopened and now included a fresh set of prints. I recall looking at him in his 'Key West uniform'—faded T, skinny brown socks, black runners and that faded old orange Speedo that I loathed, and having this dreadful feeling of pity wash over me. I found myself looking at a penniless dreamer who had just been arrested in front of the people who had once idolized him. We had witnessed his succession of Key West ventures fail miserably. Each left his ego a little more badly bruised. I don't think he actually grasped that his luck with the T-shirt business had been a matter of timing and that he wasn't Midas. Not everything he touched would turn to gold.

T-Shirt Co. Head Into Disks, Pub

6, 1974, BILLBOARD

TORONTO—David Keller, whose Crazy David T-shirt company grossed over $4 million in sales in 1973, has entered the record business with a label and a publishing company, Crazy David Records and Crazy David Music (CAPAC).

The first release is "U.I.C. Blues" by the Crazy David Band of which Keller is lead singer and organist.

The record will be marketed and distributed coast to coast through the Crazy David outlets, and prior to the Canadian release, the single was issued in Germany, Austria and Switzerland through Crazy David's International of Gleisdorf, Austria.

The band is making a number of promotional appearances here and there are plans to have the band emerge in the coming months as a club and concert act.

Jim Watson, the company's promotion manager, indicates that a heavy promotional push is planned by the company for the record both in Canada and Europe. The promotion will include the production of a special T-shirt, which will be marketed nationally.

Previously, Crazy David had entered into an agreement with RCA (Canada) whereby the company manufactures and distributes T-shirts depicting selected RCA album jackets. In return, RCA provides sampler 45's taken from the albums for inclusion in the T-shirt packages. They are free to the public with the purchase of a T-shirt. The first artist to benefit from this promotion was Brian Auger and the Oblivion Express.

To my knowledge, this music endeavor never amounted to anything.

I had long known he never really was a millionaire. That façade was simply a part of his clever marketing. If he'd liquidated his assets when we left Canada, it would have been a different story. But he didn't. Sure, he'd had abundant cash flow, but that dried up the moment he drove out of Toronto. He'd also sunk what little savings he had stashed away into *Sondra*. In the beginning, everyone, including me, thought he was the quintessential version of a hippie—like a hippie super hero—something cool, romantic and alluring and rich from fan club mail or something. But we were all wrong. Although he wore his iconic T-shirts with longer hair than everyone, and he was certainly anti-establishment, he sat on the outside of the movement and made money off it. In reality, he was the capitalist he had mocked so successfully. When David lost interest in the T-shirt business after a relatively short time, he retired at the top of his game with a feeling there was no need to prove himself. David had peaked early, and his experience touched him in such a way that he actually believed his own marketing. The road to the bottom was steep and rough for David, and although it was *his* journey, he wasn't taking it alone. He was dragging Stewart, Russell, *Sondra* and me along with him.

Due to the new circumstances in his life, David was no longer simply a hard-ass. He'd become mean, with his callousness usually showing up in the form of snide remarks directed mostly at me. I doubt that he ever stopped to think about how this made any of us feel. He finally pushed me past my limit while dropping me off at the pier for work one day. At the time, he was unemployed and between schemes. The water was rough and as the dinghy went up and down in four-foot waves, I struggled to get from the slippery rubber bow to the safety of the pier. Although usually as agile as a primate, I slipped and ended up with my right side in the drink. And David, full of malice, uttered that favorite put-down of his, "I am *so* sick of being surrounded by a sea of idiots!"

I could barely look at him, my hair streaming down my face and dripping saltwater, my clothes plastered to my skin. There were a few people standing on the dock looking shocked by what they had witnessed. Right then, in that small moment, I was jarred into knowing I had to leave him. I didn't hate him—I was utterly ashamed of him. I couldn't let this man take me down another inch, and I couldn't save him from himself. In a voice loud enough for only him to hear, "From now on, you'll be surrounded by one less idiot. I'm done, David. I'm leaving."

The truth was, the entire crew was tired of walking on eggshells. We felt we had no leadership, and life on board

Sondra just wasn't fun anymore. Not only did his words give him away, but his appearance, body language and increased drinking also indicated how profoundly dissatisfied he'd become with himself. He no longer took pride in his dress or grooming. His classy posture had been replaced with a bent head and slumped shoulders. Ever since I met him, when greeted with a, "Hey David! How're you doin' man?" he would always answer with a broad smile, "Excellent! Excellent!" Now he simply muttered complaints. And too often, he drank himself into a stupor in public.

I was working full time and supporting part of everyone's life. Not partying was impacting my life too. I knew I was better than this and knew I could leave.

David in his 'Uniform' With My Dad

My attempt at a new life off the ship was short-lived. It started with a visit to the apartment of a cute guy that I'd met in Captain Tony's bar. I knew Norman had a crush on me. Weeks earlier, he'd even gone so far as to swim across the channel to *Sondra* in the middle of the night in an attempt to have a moment together. As one could imagine, this broke a couple of rules of the Variety Club. After a few punches were exchanged, David launched him back into the shark-infested waters telling him that the next time, he would shoot him. I moved in with Norman that first night I visited him.

The third night, a concerned friend told us, "David is looking for you guys. He's drunk and he's got a gun!" I was on the back of Norman's motorcycle heading for Miami by daybreak.

My new boyfriend was a caricature artist and began making money as soon as he hit the street in MiMo land. I, on the other hand, was totally lost for some reason. I couldn't get a job. I was listless and broke, living in an apartment which would fit in *Sondra's* main salon. More and more, Norman wasn't where he said he would be and I was questioning my hasty decision. A couple of weeks after my escape from Key West, I admitted to myself I wasn't really ready to forsake *Sondra*. I clambered onto the bus and headed back, leaving behind only a note on the table. Still without a plan, I wandered over to the pier like a homing pigeon. I just sat and stared at my Lady, hoping for a sign. It came in the form of a stranger who plunked down beside me and began a conversation.

"Just get into town?" Not in the mood for talking, I simply nodded. He lit up a cigarette and went on, "I've been here for two weeks. Been livin' on that big white ship over there— cool B&B. But the owner, a guy named Dave, well, he's pretty messed up 'cause his girl left him. Feel like it's time for me to move on."

I bummed the first ride I could out to the boat. I was aware of one feeling, severe homesickness, a sentiment to which I was not accustomed. I wasn't finished with David, and I wasn't finished with *Sondra*.

Luckily, he was sober and alone when I arrived. I remember him holding me in his arms for a long time, silently stroking my hair. Finally, he went below and returned with a six-pack on ice, took my hand and led me into the wheelhouse, a place where no one would find us if they returned. We sat on the floor for hours talking about the past, and where we could go from there.

"Marni, I admit I've been mean and I'm sorry. It's just that it's a never-ending struggle with money now! You know I've been trying. Please move back in. Things will be different, I promise. It's going to get better. I've decided to put *Sondra* to work with a man who swears he knows *exactly* where the *Atocha's* treasure is."

This actually sounded promising. I knew a treasure hunter named Mel Fisher had been searching for this sunken Spanish galleon for at least a decade but had found only a scattering of coins and trinkets. I asked David, "Does he work with Mel?"

"No. You see, according to my new partner, Bernie, Fisher's been looking in the wrong area all these years. Something about his using the incorrect measurement for a fathom when reading the reports from the 1600's as to where the ship sank—Spanish fathom as opposed to the British fathom. Bernie's discovery of this will take us straight to the mother lode!"

"Why doesn't he just take this information to Mel? He's already geared up for the hunt."

"Well, apparently Fisher thinks Bernie tried to run over his wife one night."

And then David proposed to me. He might as well have asked me to swim with him to Cuba. Although I was sort of flattered to be asked to marry my Captain and a tiny bit of hope had fluttered into my heart, I had to see where things were going. His latest scheme, although it afforded sensational daydreams featuring me basking in a cache of stacked gold bars surrounded by buckets of emeralds, was just a bit too over the top for me.

A few days later when I met Mr. New Partner, he struck me as an opportunist, talking incessantly about how he was going to make us rich, but in order to make us equal partners in being rich, we would have to invest in a new radar unit and some specialized equipment for the search. I was no accountant, but it seemed to me that use of a boat worth a quarter million dollars was a significant enough investment in this venture. David nodded in agreement with my observation. Before I could decide what I thought about this, the whole case was dismissed because we told him we had *no* money for these *urgent* new pieces of equipment. In a heartbeat Bernie was covertly sizing up the next sucker who had just anchored his yacht in our neighborhood.

In 1985, Mel Fisher, whose mantra was "Today is the Day" had that 'Day.' He and his crew found $450 million worth of treasure in pretty much the same area where he'd been looking all along.

While I was in Miami, Stew had departed *Sondra* leaving no forwarding address. The space that remained in his absence seemed to fill up with my memories of his sunny nature and tropical humor. He came on board knowing jack shit, but his fearless willingness and versatility had turned him into a first-class mate. He was my steadfast ally.

With the failure of the treasure hunt plan, it was no time before David slipped back into his despondent state, and his condescending attitude towards what was left of his faithful crew was worse than ever.

I'd fallen in love with "Crazy David," not depressed David. He was not on top of his game, had no cash to get there, and it was killing both him and our dream. I knew *Sondra*, that rare and stately mistress, was all that remained to attest to his former fame and fortune and that letting go of her would have completely broken him. However, I saw no other way to move forward together. We had to let *Sondra* go.

"She's not for sale! Not now or ever!"

28

WANTING MORE

**Key West to Nassau and Back
Late Fall, 1980**

"Did perpetual happiness in the Garden of Eden maybe
get so boring that eating the apple was justified?"
-CHUCK PALAHNIUK, *Survivor*

SHORTLY after Stewart left, Russ took a sabbatical. This left David and me alone with *Sondra* for the first time in years. Although I had enjoyed the company of most people who had lived onboard with us, this break came at a much needed time and it was delicious having our Lady all to ourselves. Strangely, it gave David the space to be who he used to be: the original platform shoe, the jagged edge of liberalism, my Captain Nemo. I happily resumed the roles of Duchess in the parlor, Gourmet in the kitchen and Courtesan in bed. We reconnected.

David returned to painting Conch houses, but this time he partnered up with his friend Toby whose carpentry skills made them an attractive turnkey restoration package. They were good company for each other, working hard at menial jobs while hashing out the pros and cons of more appealing pipe dreams. Often, Toby would join us for dinner and a good-for-the-soul jamming session. My work at Sloppy's continued, but because of problems with their food service division, I was switched from slinging drinks at night to enhancing the bar food during the day. My tips actually improved because I became "Mom" to the blue-collar patrons looking for a great homemade meal served by a cutie patootie. The off-season was our favorite time of the year in Key West. The town belonged to us locals as temperatures slid down to the bearable low 80's. It was great having evenings free and David mostly to myself with nothing to do but play and dream. David was still convinced that we could put *Sondra* to work at either commercial fishing or hauling cargo. He just didn't know how to get started.

One afternoon, he was unusually late picking me up from work. When I questioned where he was, he alarmed me with, "I had a business meeting."

Dreading the answer, "A business meeting? What kind of business?"

"Oh just something Toby and I are working on."

I pressed forward with my questions but he'd said all he was going to say.

Toby was David's best buddy; I liked Toby too. Everything about David's cohort was an exaggeration. He was well over six feet, massively boned, swarthy and grossly hairy. His suave baritone voice, sexy with a pot-smoking, husky New England accent, came through his wide smile to entice you like a red sunset sky would a green sailor. Toby was a thirty-something former Coast Guarder and, like David, he was just getting by in Key West with odd jobs and gigs. He was a marvelous musician who could hold a crowd with his amusing lyrics, original compositions and his ability to flip between classical guitar and honkytonk piano. I found it unusual that David had befriended Toby. Trust always got in the way for David because, like many famous people, he could never discern the genuine from the false. He thought of himself as superior to most. Perhaps the inflated self-images that they shared along with their delusions of grandeur were what triggered the camaraderie. Whatever it was, I was happy that they were friends.

Although Toby's success never exceeded patrolling the high seas, he and David shared the mutual opinion that their current work was below them and that unless things changed, they would never have the financial leverage necessary to be top dogs in the Caribbean. Consequently, Toby had become part of the discussions involving new get-rich-quick schemes using *Sondra*. These included lobster fishing on a grand scale, hauling cargo such as exotic woods, and using our ship to hunt treasure.

We were a platonic threesome, often seen walking down the street, my small frame flanked by muscle and height, our red, blonde, brown manes blowing out behind us. Music was our connection. We enjoyed hours of stoned jam sessions with David adding the B3 to Toby's originals and me attempting to bang out the beat. At the time, Toby was living alone in a converted school bus, struggling to get by while paying child support for two young sons.

A couple of weeks after their business meeting, when their secret had reached the point where they could no longer keep me in the dark, David invited Toby to dinner. This was usually an enjoyable event, as it would include a BBQ and a couple of bottles of decent wine.

Up on deck while relishing after-dinner Vitola de Salidas cigars (Cuba's finest), David began to reveal what the meeting had been about. "Marge. As you know, Toby and I've been working on a business plan. It involves *Sondra* and it will finally bring in some big bucks."

I worked on my cigar, waiting for them to show me more cards.

Assuming the posture of a gangster, arms crossed on his chest and his Cuban cornered in his mouth, "Toby's hooked up with a couple of men who have good connections…" He inhaled, removed the puro, and then let the smoke add weight to the remaining words. "No, they have *great*…drug connections."

Toby shifted his weight to a stretched out slouch too and then nodded and smiled at me.

My mind began to race. *What the fuck is he talking about?* Running drugs was something I had *never* given thought to. He might as well have said we were going to put jet engines on the back of *Sondra*, blast up to Titan, and launch his fishing business in Kraken Mare. Sure, I liked a good doobie, but this crossed a serious line. We had so much to lose. Speechless, I allowed my silence to push them.

"We're going to smuggle some marijuana. Just once. We need to do this in order to raise substantial capital for kick-starting the lobster business I've been talking about." Before I could ask him if he had lost his mind, "It's all set up. You know those Cuban guys that have been coming around the boat?"

"You mean the ones you told me wanted to buy the boat?"

"Yes. But, they didn't really want that. They actually just wanted to rent *Sondra*—and us." How slickly he slid in and out of that lie. "They have connections in Miami who will make the buy in Colombia and figure out all the details for the pick-up."

"In Colombia."

"Yes. Marge, it's simple."

"Stop calling me that."

"Okay... Anyway, we'll just run up to the pier, load up, and then head out towards Cuba. The guys will meet us with a cigboat and pick it up. Just you and me...and Toby."

"Oh great idea. I can just see it. A super-fast ship waving her super-sized foreign flag driven by a super down-and-out Captain into a port full of Colombians with super Cuban connections. Are you listening to yourself? Smuggling? Colombia?"

"I knew you'd react this way." David's reprimands sounded to me like they were Toby's thoughts.

"You *knew*? You *knew?* Of course you *knew*! Because you *also* must've *known* how *asinine* an idea this is!"

David attempted to interrupt, but I was not to be stopped. "We live in paradise on a 112-foot yacht and want for *nothing*, David. And you would sacrifice all of this for a bunch of *lobsters?* And who resorts to smuggling to start up a new business—people who don't give a damn if they live or die! And don't the two of you know what they *do* to people in the jails of Colombia?" I let the questions hang in the air.

"Well, you'd better pack your party panties because *rape* will just be the hors d'oeuvre. You honestly *think* that we're just going to pull up to a Colombian dock in our *inconspicuous warship*, load up the deck with bails of marijuana, and then motor through a coast-guard-free-smuggler-only-zone over to the islands where some other dudes, probably with machine guns, are going to meet us in the middle of nowhere for a fair exchange of grass for cash?! Hey, let's paint *Sondra* pink en route, so they won't miss us! Speaking of *Sondra*, kiss her *goodbye*, now!"

My words curled like the smoke of their forgotten cigars. "No! Hate to use my trump card here but *I, Cook Craig*, am the registered *owner* of this vessel. No to *you*, David Richard Keller and no to *you*, Toby Whatever-The-Fuck-Your-Name-Is! This is *not...going...to...happen*! Do not even talk to me about it again." I turned to Toby and yanked his cigar out of his mouth. *"Go...home!"*

I was disgusted by how recklessly desperate they'd

become. They were behaving as if they had no choice, as though this was a last-ditch effort to survive, with all responsibilities disregarded.

While David drove our zealous guest to the pier, I bunked down in the privacy of the stern for the night. I knew my rant would never stop two men with delusions of suitcases of fast, easy cash. As usual, David needed me to be the catalyst; but when he thought things were in motion, my opinion held no weight. The consequences were both barely imaginable and very real. I knew if we entered that scene, our success would force us to remain there. No one shakes hands with a drug cartel and walks away. My thoughts sped up and overlapped into the night. I didn't sleep at all.

The next day, I decided to take lunch to them at their worksite (my way of accentuating that everything was returning to normal). As they sat down for their break, thinking I was out of earshot, I overheard Toby telling David that the guys in Miami found out that the feds had them under surveillance. I couldn't hear the rest but assumed this would definitely put the finishing touches on my verbal attempt to kybosh their scheme. I was also thinking it would be a darn good time for David and me to get out of Key West for a while and away from Toby. At sunset, we were fishing off the back of the boat when I proposed that we take a vacation over to Nassau, a nice slow trip where we could re-visit all of the places we'd discovered over the past few years. When David agreed to my getaway plan, I knew the plan for smuggling had been abandoned.

"Do you think the two of us can man *Sondra* alone?"

I calmly answered, "Of course." The trip would not involve docking at any piers and was therefore possible with only helmsman and engineer. I knew better than to show how relieved I was that he had said yes.

A month later, shortly after Christmas, we pulled anchor and headed off for what would be the quintessential cruise through the Bahamas. Our first port of call was Bimini. We'd been there enough times for the party to simply pick up where it left off. After a week of pure revelry, we were ready to head out. For the journey, we'd stocked up with Bimini's delicious bread, bushels of fresh tropical fruits, a dozen bottles of Ron Ricardo

Coconut Rum (my favorite) and 25 pounds of smoked swordfish from a trophy catch left sword-less on the dock.

We were ready to leave Bimini, but our main anchor apparently wasn't. I volunteered to put on my mask and snorkel and jumped overboard to free it. Having drift-dived that harbor hundreds of times, I knew there was nothing to fear. When I surfaced, my hair was full of clumps of something with brittle sticks which, upon closer inspection, turned out to be marijuana buds. Looking around, I saw many other sailors in their dinghies, busily scooping up the floating boon with their kitchen sieves. It would prove to be the most marijuana I'd ever see in one place. The harbor was full of it. When "The Authorities" arrived, they began hauling in the intact bales that had begun to drift by on the increasingly-fast incoming tide. Between their bouts of laughter they told us, "Some fool smuggla' ain' carry no gas and mash him plane up bad onna'a reef. An' boy alive still. Mus'a be bless!"

Blessed indeed! Everyone was thrilled at the chance of a free stash. We joined in on the harvest and added a healthy, actually a ridiculously large, bag of weed to our stores. David and I laughed at the irony. We had turned down a role in the trafficking of narcotics only to have them delivered to our water line. It could easily have been us smashed up on a reef.

One morning over coffee, David and I noticed water breaking in the middle of the bay located behind the island where we had anchored for the night. Intrigued, we hopped into the Zodiac to explore it with our snorkel gear. The reef was like a sculpted oasis rising up through 40 feet of clear Bahamian waters, perfect for a free-dive. It looked like the Garden of Eden, lost centuries ago to Mother Ocean who put her salty avatar spin on its exquisite profusion. I toked and snorkeled in and around the forest of coral, a multitude of shapes. My artist's eyes feasted on the colors: schools of silvery pilchard, brilliant red anemones so shy they would retract their flower-like mouths at my approach, lobsters with their come-hither bulging eyes, a multitude of starfish, shellfish, flatfish and the peaceful nurse sharks resting nose to nose. Eventually, David or darkness made me haul my pruney ass out of that paradise.

Next stop was New Providence, a study in contrasts.

One side of the harbor, appropriately named Paradise Island, basked in the sun like an adult Disneyland. The taint of money was reflected everywhere: fixed slot machines, stiffly-priced drinks, haute cuisine and a collective art exhibit by the world's best plastic surgeons. On this small piece of land, people of privilege had transformed the locals into fantasy slaves; the round-helmeted cops looked like British Bobbies, the crisp maids looked French, and the carriage horses adorned in flowered straw hats, Caribbean. From Club Med to Vegas-caliber casinos, everyone waited on you as if you were royalty.

Leaving this mere stone of an island rising up out of thousands of feet of ocean, the costumes and the imperialism fell away, and the culture of the true face of the Bahamas radiated in Nassau. What a face! The pirates and the slave holders had long since lost their power and the descendants of these kidnapped princes and medicine women of all of West Africa have built a culture out of the tragedy of diaspora. Creative and resourceful, the iconic culture is easily recognized in colorful art, exuberant dancing, and the infectious Bahamian Rake 'n Scrape music. Their devout Christianity is peppered with superstitions and myths, such as the four-foot flying leprechaun who was known to steal lunches and children. (When scientists found the evidence of four-foot tall Bahamian owls, things got complicated.) I befriended a few Bahamian women and found myself in backyards surrounded by an abundance of adorable kids co-raised by aunties, grandmas and moms, with everyone poking good fun at each other. Unlike the Silicone Sallys on Paradise Island, these mamas never dreamed of putting bigger boobies or booties on their bucket list.

And, fine dinin' to the Bahamians—raw conch on the dock. The evocative queen conch is actually pictured on the Bahamian flag.

We loved snorkeling for these creatures. On the surface, the water was as warm as a bath. Scanning through my mask across the sand and turtle grass, I recognized the telltale form of a shell. I took a breath through my snorkel and with a kick, dived down to the seafloor, scooped up the shell, and surfaced, tossing dinner into the Zodiac with a satisfying "thump."

David surfaced next to me, clutching his fishing spear in

one hand and a conch in the other. He spit out his snorkel and I saw him grin through his beard. He quoted our favorite Bahamian truism about our catch, "Conch sure puts the lead in your pencil, but you better have something to write on!"

A few free-dives later, we had enough fresh shellfish for dinner, and we headed to the dock to prepare the meat. I climbed from the Zodiac onto the worn wood, hauling up our catch behind me in a cracked bucket. David passed me the hammer and I set to work. Choosing a conch shell at random, I counted three spirals down from the tip and tapped a small hole directly above where the lip opened up into its gorgeous pearly pout. Working a butter knife into the gap, I pried the meat away from the shell. All mollusks, and in particular conch, are incredibly strong. As long as they have an attachment point for their muscles to cling to, it is all but impossible to remove them from their shell. Now that I had separated the conch from its shell, it was easy to grasp the claw and draw out the creature.

A conch looks like a cross between an alien and a cartoon. The body is little more than a single amorphous muscle with two protruding stalks, from which eyes goggle like a shocked accountant. The claw, though as large as a thumb, seems more like a burden for this unlikely creature.

We'd learned that the docks were the best place to prep dinner because the skin of a conch has the most potent mucus imaginable. This viscous, sticky, snotty, messy slime will destroy absolutely anything, and the only antidotes are sand or lime juice. The coating is so tenacious, that it is common to hear an uncooperative person described as being "as stubborn as conch snot." Cleaning up this slop on the boat was all but impossible. On the docks though, we could scrub the conchs with clean Bahamian sand and rinse them with a fresh lime rubdown.

Once de-slimed, the conch was ready for cleaning. Using a sharp knife, I slit up the underside of the meat and rinsed the digestive cavity again with lime, careful to remove the pencil-long spelie. The spelie is considered the penis of the conch, although since I never found a conch without one, I suspect it fulfilled some other function. It was completely translucent and had the consistency of rubber, with a strange ribbing at one end.

It had no taste at all. As David had alluded, conch is considered a potent aphrodisiac, and eating the spelie was a part of the ritual. I held it up to the sun; it was so translucent that I could see the blue ocean through its strange length, and I slurped it down with a swig of David's Kalik (the national beer, brewed on the far side of New Providence).

I cut off the claw, eyes, and small nub known as the "bobby." Then, lifting the citrusy delicacy to my mouth, I ran the incision over my lips to feel the epithelial border between skin and muscle. Working my teeth in, I began to peel the skin back, revealing the smooth whiteness of the fist-sized meat. Skinning the conch is not difficult, but to do so with a soft touch is essential. One false move, and the muscle begins to tear, shuddering and tensing into an unchewable mass. An experienced skinner can pull off the skin in one piece, and the meat will remain relaxed.

There are many ways to prepare conch. For tourists and locals, the fried variety suffices after beating and breading, but the real delicacies of the Caribbean are the ceviche-like conch salad and scorchie. The secret to both is the way one scores the flesh, diagonally, prohibiting the meat from tensing into an unpalatable hunk of tongue-like chunks. Prepared correctly, conch is the sweetest white meat one could hope for in the seasoned ceviche-like mix known as "conch salad." Scorchie is even more traditional, and simpler. Burning hot goat peppers are mixed with vinegar and rubbed over the whole skinned conch. It is marinated and served. Empirical evidence proved that this is truly the aphrodisiac that Bahamians claim it to be. How amusing that it took the Paradise Island crowd so long to discover the intimate joy of eating raw seafood and then to pay such a sinful price for it.

David and I loved hopping a city bus and seeing the back roads of Nassau. It was during these rides that we optimistically discussed the lobster business. After having enough bouncing around over dirt roads, we would hit the closest corner pub out in the burbs. Behind saloon doors, the bar stools would be occupied by men swigging beer and talking soccer, and the tables occupied by the "Dig Outs" (working girls) sucking down Kahlua and Carnation® through tiny red straws. Smokey Robinson's "Crusin" was the hot number on the jukebox. The girls would harmonize beautifully while all eyes flirted with David as they sang the line saying that if he wanted it, he could get it, for a price.

This is where we met Big Betty. I was the size of a purse compared to her. She was all gussied up in a hot pink halter-top and a slightly diaphanous floral-print skirt that drifted even when she was standing still. Her black hair was the opposite—it never moved. Betty's ultra-bright smile bling-blinged while her full lips glimmered with what I later learned was Vaseline.

"Boy. Muddo-sick! Das a scrawny gel yo carry wit yo. C'mon hea 'n sit wit Big Betty." She patted the empty seat beside her and David obeyed. I followed and stood awkwardly on the edge of a cloud of Lily of the Valley. While rubbing David's arm, "Look'a here, gels. Dis be a hard boy! An' dis beard all pumpkin. He be a true boy." They all looked at me with raised eyebrows and affirming chins while chiming, "Um-hmmmm."

David: "Well girls, I'm not in the market today, but we would love to join you. What's everybody drinking?"

All four sang at once, "We be drinkin' Puffs wit K'lua. An' make sure dey no be tots, Honey."

I knew what they were drinking, but had to ask, "What's a tot?"

Betty piped up, "Dat be a drink scrawny like yo. You come down from t' Keys? You some kind'a Conchy Joes?"

"No, I'm Canadian," I said, feeling I had to mention something positive about myself.

"Well, we do live in the Keys on a boat," David jumped in.

"How big yenne's boat?" Betty quickly asked.

"Really big," I quipped.

Next thing I knew, Betty and I were sort of "sharing" my tight galley. She was demonstrating how to prepare the real version of the Bahamian dish, cracked conch, at the same time as she was giving me tips on how to "love yenna's boy 'Bahamian style.'" In between hammering the hell out of a piece of white flesh, "Yenna use coco oil on yo boy Sugar?"

Betty was a whole-hearted being, a gal with the courage

245

to be imperfect. She really was sexy and because she was good to herself, she was able to enjoy being with us despite the tension she sensed. We seemed to need her company more than she needed ours.

The second week that we were in Nassau, my mom and her best friend arrived from Ontario for a holiday. David was always a favorite with my parents and although he was a good host, my Mom commented that he seemed different from the man she had met in Toronto. She described him as being in a constant state of agitation. When our guests offered to treat us to a farewell dinner on Paradise Island at one of the Casinos, David bluntly replied, "I'd rather you just give us the money and Marni will make dinner." After all the cooking I did for that guy, three squares a day, I couldn't believe he was going to deny me the pleasure of a meal out with these two women that I loved. David had a way of letting everyone know that the issue wasn't open for discussion, which was so unfair to our guests and me. All we had was fish and my mom hated fish. She politely ate rice and salad and slipped me 100 bucks. I was humiliated and sad. After sending them off the next morning, I confronted David about his ill-mannered behavior towards my mother.

"Who gave you the right to be the captain of rudeness on this boat? Do you have any idea how much treating us meant to my mother? And you just took that pleasure away from her like it was nothing. Maybe if you ever got around to developing a relationship based on love with someone other than yourself, you would understand."

His retort began forcefully with, "Woman!"

That pushed a familiar button. I turned my back to him and raised my hand to signal "no more," not being the least bit interested in the likely hackneyed fate of any further discussion.

It was into this heavy pall that "the force" swam out of nowhere. Nowhere near shore, nowhere near my plans for the trip back, nowhere even in my thoughts. But there it was. The penis that owned Toby McGregor swam from the pier out to *Sondra* with a knapsack strapped to his head. This arrival seemed menacing to me, but meaningful to David. Based on past experience, I knew an altercation was coming. Once again, as it had back in the beginning in Mahone Bay when we were crewing up, testosterone broke the balance between David and me. I felt the panic pressing my heart against my sternum. Not a single nicety was exchanged as Toby clambered up the boarding ladder. I was neither acknowledged nor beckoned to join the urgent conversation that ensued immediately between the two men.

I heard snippets. "... the Cuban said... purchase... Columbia by end... bank..."

I hadn't uttered a word but my mere presence provoked David. With only a look, I went from First Mate, Navigator, Engineer (and someone whose opinion mattered), to Deckhand, to Galley Slave, to Shut Up. David had become so desperate to be somebody again that he agreed to his friend's harebrained contrivance even before the saltwater had ceased dripping from Toby's profuse hairiness. David ordered me to go below and prepare to start up the engines. The two of them had melded into a wall of resistance and threw the concepts of "chain of command" and "respect for ownership" overboard. I ignored his order. I was frantic. As David scurried about the boat to prepare for departure, I chased after him, repeatedly throwing myself in his way and wrapping my arms around his neck in a desperate attempt to engage him with kisses. I cried shamelessly, begging into his mouth, the only place left where I could find privacy and any hope of bringing him back to reason in the uninvited presence of Toby the Schemer. I pleaded with the urgency and emotion of a child.

"David, please, please! Listen to me! This is insane. *Why* are you choosing to listen to him over me? You're going to *die!* What am I supposed to *do?* What about *us?* What about *Sondra?* Oh god, David, make him go *away!*"

"Enough!" He shoved me out of his face while wiping away my pleadings from his moustache and beard. He took a moment to study the tear-swollen, blotchy mess that I was and, in front of Toby, spoke the eulogy for our love. "I want you out of my way, woman! I want to watch you go running back to your mother" And then those words I abhorred, "I am so sick of being surrounded by a sea of idiots!" He didn't even know that he'd gone too far.

Participating in illegal activities was nothing new to

David. He'd dodged the draft in Canada and the income-tax guys in the US, infringed on copyrights and, according to him, brushed up against the law more than once. Inexplicably, I was the only one that seemed to realize that smuggling was a crime with more risks than T-shirt prints and that the consequences were far beyond fines and lawyer's fees. As I still had not obeyed his commands, he resorted to more verbally-condescending jabs.

Defeated, I retreated to the engine room where I could at least be alone and busy. It was like brigands had overtaken *Sondra*. I'd read about pirates and knew not to fight them. I tried to become inconspicuous and vowed to get off the boat as soon as possible. As I descended down the ladder, a freshening breeze came out of the east and nimbostratus clouds piled low and heavy in the sky. A storm was imminent. Ding-Ding came down the telegraph wire where I stood waiting between the twin diesels, a tolling that echoed in *Sondra's* darkest area where I imagined her memories of past qualms lived. If she could've said her piece, I'm sure that with a curt British accent she'd have spoken in the voice of The Iron Lady, commanding David to abandon his plan.

Within an hour, physical discomfort was added to the excruciating awkwardness already in the air. *Sondra* began to roll in the increasing swells. By the time we reached the Gulf Stream, she was rocking gunnel-to-gunnel. There would be no rest for either my body or my soul. Nobody was talking and, for the first time, no music was playing. Waves pounded, hard rain hit her deck, wind eerily whistled through her searchlight sights, as laboring engines pushed her forward.

Toby had gone from friend to enemy overnight. The betrayal I felt reduced me to dreadful grief. I surrendered to hours of crying, mourning the inevitable. When a boat runs aground, the hull is scraped across the sea floor. Oftentimes the Captain and crew realize this will happen minutes before, but there are no brakes at sea. Then there is the awful grating of earth against hull, the shuddering. Our relationship had run aground. My whole being had foundered. I was a shipwreck. I couldn't throw my life into reverse to save it. Life has no brakes either. The business and lifestyle I had invested years in was beached. There was nothing left to salvage. David had succumbed to fear, fear of not being worthy any more, fear that produced the utter shame of being looked down upon as one big failure. A dreamer, he had impulsively bought *Sondra* without researching his visions and ended up with a disappointing liability that was not designed to cross open water. I knew I was involved with an impractical escapist and my impotent practicality felt like my failure as well.

Afraid of losing what little he had left and not being able to get what he wanted, David had been increasingly trying to numb everything with alcohol. Instead he became numb to the magic of our journey and its sublime uncertainty. I wondered if he felt invisible, a state that would have been totally foreign to him. He was already completely disconnected from his family. He had no crew and he hadn't partaken in the Variety Club for years. Toby was the only person who wasn't criticizing or rejecting him. Surely he must have known from his Crazy David days that the entourage moves on once the blush fades from the rose and yesterday's golden boy becomes today's has-been. Right before my eyes, my partner was succumbing to the greatest trap of all—not success, popularity or power, but self-rejection. I was afraid that contrary to what David thought, his life would further lose meaning and he'd be bereft of any identity whatsoever because he had never realized a reality-based one for himself.

His hope had always been stronger than his fear, which in past endeavors had aided his success, but never had it been so deluded. He'd breezed through early adulthood without learning the skills necessary to embrace his new vulnerability, something that would have given him the kind of power Big Betty possessed. It hurt me immensely to see him sink so low and to ignore me completely at a time when I was literally trying to save his life.

When we finally pulled back into Key West, it was dark and still blowing a gale. Anchors were set and David taxied Toby to shore. Exhausted from the journey, he returned and went straight to bed without a word. I stayed up all night and packed, trying to give meaning to the material things that passed in and out of my hands. I was saddened by the small handful of photos that would represent only a bare outline of all of my adventures onboard. Damn, five years fit into two small duffle bags. After methodically making my last cup of coffee in *Sondra's* galley, I sat down at the captain's table and took in my surroundings with a nostalgia I already felt. This chapter of my life was over and leaving meant altering my whole course. I waited in weary silence for dawn and for David to wake up.

Toby McGregor

29

AN INTERSECTION OF LOSS

Toronto and Montreal
1980 / 81

"Ships that pass in the night, and speak each other in passing,
Only a signal shown and a distant voice in the darkness;
So on the ocean of life we pass and speak one another,
Only a look and a voice, then darkness again and a silence."
-HENRY WADSWORTH LONGFELLOW

THE bus trip to Toronto was dismal. Miserable thoughts diluted my attempt at a positive attitude. I crossed the international border into the land of my birth in dire need of familiar company and some kick-ass merrymaking. After connecting with a group of old friends at Linda and Peter's house and smoking and drinking beer all afternoon, we headed out into the early evening streets of Toronto the Good. By 6 p.m., we were at "After Work," one of the many places to be seen following a hard day at the office. Entering the warmth of the bar, we were greeted by chit-chat, cigar smoke and Kool & The Gang suggesting it was time to "Celebrate." The bar reminded me of Bimini's Compleat Angler with its wood and leather décor, but the featured drink was Canadian Rye Whisky with Canada Dry Ginger Ale. I stared at my very small glass with way too much ice and remembered the warm rum and cold coke in *Sondra's* metal tankards. The Boomers were "power dressed"—females sporting large shoulder-padded suits and males with wide pinstripes, narrow lapels and skinny ties. The androgynous Bee Gee hairstyles made everyone's head look oversized. I had left Toronto in the 70's and returned to the 80's.

Linda was on a mission to set me up. She immediately started flirting by helping herself to others' finger food, sitting on laps, checking ring fingers and getting professions. The guys didn't stand a chance. As a former racing car driver, nerve and speed were something she had an abundance of. She was foxy as hell. Within no time, a neighboring table was dragged over to adjoin ours and I met the next man I would fall in love with.

Within my first few weeks back, I received a phone call from David's new "girlfriend." She called to tell me *Sondra* was taking on water and that the Coast Guard was looking for me, the registered owner of a ship about to sink in a major military harbor. I sought advice from a marine lawyer who took a shelf company and registered *Sondra* in it. Just like that, she was no longer my asset and therefore no longer my liability. This sad state of affairs developed because David had apparently gone on a real drunken binge after he'd put me on the bus. After a month, he surfaced from his rage and stupor, saved *Sondra* and began corresponding with me.

November 11, 1980

Dear Marni,
Hope this note finds you in good health. Thought I'd drop you a line letting you know the boats and I are still in Key West. All is well here. The Sondra II is still anchored off Christmas Tree Island with the Pamie Ann (the boat I bought from the Cuban boatlift), tied off her stern. Over the past couple of months I've been working on the Sondra while working part time painting at the Pier House. It's a great job. I can paint whenever I want and work as many hours as I please. Also, I have a few fish traps out and a small long line, which brings in a little cash and good eating too. I stopped the leaks in the Sondra with tar, which will suffice until I have enough money saved for another bottom job. Probably, that will be pretty soon. So far, I haven't gotten any good offers but I am still advertising discreetly that the boat is for sale. Do you know if the red truck is still at Bradley's place in Maine? Also if it is O.K. If it is, I might take a bus up there and get it. There is no auto inspection in Florida anymore so I can license it here. It would make a great Key West Truck. Let me know if you can find Bradley. Also, I am looking for Russ Quinn if you should see him. That's all for now. Write soon and tell me about your real estate empire.

Love Always,
David

Letter writing was very unusual for David. I made two assumptions. It started because he hoped he could entice me to come back and it stopped because he knew it was too late.

By 1982, my letters were being returned unopened, and though I thought about my past life often (especially during Montreal's wretched winters), my young son and burgeoning film catering business occupied my time, and my mind.

From a romantic perspective, meeting the new man in the bar that first night was like being the "bob" on a big pendulum that oscillated from Key West's crazy men through thousands of miles of possibilities before reaching its counter high point, Toronto's conservative men. I fell victim to the old adage of breaking up with one type and grabbing the extreme opposite as fast as I could. I went for handsome, amorous and employed, but in my haste had blindly misjudged this polished package. One year after my return, I found myself pregnant, unemployed and living in Montreal, *none* of which was my idea and all of which I countered with heels dug in. I hadn't lost my spunk. I'd just ended up with someone who, under a veil of charm, fanatically went about attempting to mold me into something he desired but that wasn't really me.

By 1994, I was becoming restless. I had sold my successful catering business, my son had left the nest for hockey, and my husband had long since flown the coop. For the first time in almost two decades, I had the time and the means to find some closure for my nautical tale. David was unreachable, but I found Russ in the phonebook…

"Dinghy O'Rielly! How are you?"

He laughed that soft chuckle I loved so much. "I'm good Mate Marni, how are you?"

We talked for a long time about all that our lives had shown us since we last saw each other and reminisced about our adventures on the boat. Russ had returned to Toronto and started up a successful framing business. And, of course, David's name came up. There was a strange silence where I thought the connection had been lost. "Russ, are you still there?"

In a totally different tone, "Didn't you hear about what happened to David?"

"No, what happened?"

"He died."

"What do you mean he *died*? When? What did he die from?"

"He was murdered, Marni. A couple of years ago."

"*Murdered*! Who murdered him?"

"Some drug guys did it. Apparently David got into smuggling coke, didn't pay up The Man, so they shot him."

"Who told you this?"

"I was in touch with a guy I knew in Key West who had started a framing business—just to pick his brain a bit. He told me. Said it happened a couple of years ago."

"Oh my god, Russ. Where did this happen? Was he on *Sondra*?"

Russ had no more details and I was too overwhelmed to continue talking anyway. We sadly said our goodbyes, promising to stay in touch. As soon as I hung up, the reality that I would not see David again hit me. I never imagined that he wouldn't always be there for me, that a day might come that I would not be able to return. This filled me with regret that I hadn't kept in touch.

Then strangely, anger began working its way through my grief and I reproached David, "How could you have been so stupid, so greedy, so reckless? How could you do this to *me*? And what about *Sondra*? What did you let happen to her?" An image of how it might have gone down, his last moments, kept coming into my mind. It was horrible. I wondered if they beat him. I couldn't help but try to imagine what he would have been thinking. Was he brave? Was he afraid? Was he alone? And then oddly, I wondered if he still had his long hair and beard when it happened. Finally, in the quiet, cold silence of that winter night with the warmth of tequila in my belly, I gave into my grief and wept convulsively.

For two years, I mourned his death, trying to make sense of it. During that time, I was unable to gather any further information and both David and *Sondra* began to fade into distant memories of another life.

Then, in 1996, while strolling along Yorkville Avenue where David had his first "Head and T-shirt" shop, I bumped into an old friend of ours who owned a small shop there. I was delighted to see him, as he had been one of the regulars at our cottage on Go Home Lake. We decided to have coffee and catch up. So much had happened to both of us since we last partied together some 20 years ago. We talked about businesses that had come and gone, lovers that had done the same, and dreams for our futures.

Not wanting to change the mood of our happy reunion but curious to know if he could shed any light on David's demise, I gently asked, "Did you hear the terrible news about David?"

He looked at me oddly and said without a lot of emotion, "Nooooo, I didn't hear anything. What happened?"

"He died a couple of years ago—murdered in a drug deal or something."

"What!? That's *so* not true!" he said, shaking his head and sort of giggling. "I talked to him *yesterday*. He's living in Saint Croix in the US Virgin Islands, running a tug-boat business."

It took my mind a long time to process what Josh had just said. I held my breath, confused and speechless, afraid that if I breathed, his version of the truth would collapse. I couldn't imagine that what I'd believed and mourned for the past two years could possibly have been simply a rumor. "Are you *sure*, Josh?"

"Of course, I'm sure. Don't be *ridiculous*. Who told you this shit anyway?"

"Well, Russ did. That's why I *believed* it."

"David and I talked about you, Marni. You should call him."

30

A STRANGE KIND OF REUNION

St. Croix, US Virgin Islands
1996

"Time is a brisk wind, for each hour it brings something new …
but who can understand and measure its sharp breath,
its mystery and its design?"
-PARACELSUS

I took my window seat at noon two days after I'd spoken to David. I was about to fly back over our wake of time and *Sondra's* domain of seas. As we climbed through cumulus that rose up like Reddi-Whip, I removed my garnet blanket from its plastic bag and gently laid it over my abdomen, still tender from its recent surgery. Leaning back, I closed my eyes and thought about where I was going and what I was doing. T.S. Elliot's quote came into my mind about how we won't cease to explore and how at the end of all our exploring, we arrive where we started and come to know that place for the first time. Returning to the Caribbean, to David and *Sondra*, would be such a journey.

I don't know what I expected from this visit. I did know that, with my son fully entrenched in hockey and boarded in Ontario, I was ready to hit the gypsy trail again. At the very least, I hoped for closure with David; a chance to say a proper goodbye and leave this time on a celebratory note. Unlike the recurring dreams I'd had over the years where I could see *Sondra* but could never reach her, I wanted to stand on her bow once again, wanted to partner with David and turn over her engines and head into open water. I imagined myself walking up to the bow where I would hang my legs over the edge and dream of where we might go. It seemed like getting back together with David now that he had a bona fide path might be ideal. I had my savings too, so our past limitations would be only a memory and I would be back on the water, a place I always thought I belonged.

As we left the seaboard of the southern states, I asked the stewardess to tell the Captain I was a ship's engineer and would like permission to join him in the cabin for the flight over the islands. Permission granted! I had never seen my old domain from the sky and marveled at the colors and landscapes of beaches sloping down through the reefs and into the sea's depth. As we approached Saint Croix, I could see by the palette below me that the island had multiple ecosystems ranging from desert to lush vegetation. I wasn't sure if it was just the descent or the excitement I felt about this reunion, but the butterflies made me feel like a young girl. Unlike the time I stood at the end of my sidewalk in Toronto waiting for him for the first time so many years ago, I had rehearsed nothing.

David's and my lips left our bodies at the airport gate and met somewhere between leaving and returning. I was too excited to realize that he had actually kissed me! Arm in arm, we headed out, me happily giggling, trying not to smudge my mascara with the tears I couldn't hold back, and him laughing at my sentimentality. Before clambering into his beat-up pickup truck for a guided tour en route to his favorite haunt, I asked him to pose for a photo. Studying him through the camera's lens, I was fascinated by how different he looked without his beard and how non-descript his T-shirt was. For all the time that I knew him, these two things had been his identity, something I didn't think he could ever let go of. He looked…ordinary.

"I guess you won't be chiding me about leaning on your beard anymore."

He smiled his familiar, alluring smile, and I clicked the shutter.

David, US Virgin Islands, 1996

As he helped me into the passenger seat, he hit me with the unoriginal pick up line, "When do you have to be back home?"

I chuckled and answered, "I have to be back home when I feel like being back home, David."

"Come on then. Let's go have a beer and I'll fill you in on all the years you've missed."

The quaint seaside bar, trimmed with an artistic use of driftwood, was filled with locals enjoying Happy Hour. I could see that David took me there to show me off. I was introduced as his "ex-wife" to a dozen friends before we even sat down. They guffawed and teased him, asking which number I was.

I answered, "Seven."

David jumped in with, "But she was the best first mate I ever had."

Over a welcoming shot of Cruzan Rum, icy island beers and a bowl of plantain chips, David began the story. First of all, he told me that he *never* got wrapped up in the madness with Toby.

"After you left, Marni, I lost the plot. I realized that I'd let my ego take the helm. Thought you were expendable, replaceable. God, I was so wrong. Everybody somehow found out about our plan." He snorted ruefully while crunching. "Smuggling! I realized you were right—just too dangerous, too stupid. I took *Sondra* to the Virgin Islands instead and put her to work lobster fishing, like we had always talked about. After only a couple of years, I'd saved up a nest egg. I upgraded the act, and *Sondra* finally became the pleasure yacht you imagined back in Toronto."

He gave me a sly look. He'd known all along about my unspoken dreams of silk scarves and immaculate whites. I could see he was proud, as he described the boutique hotel he'd created with aboveboard staterooms and a chef for the tourists.

"In the eighties, I saw an opportunity to get a piece of the action docking Navy and cruise ships, so I added a tugboat to my 'fleet.' Life was good for me until Hurricane Hugo came into St. Croix's radar in '89." David's brow furrowed as he gazed over my head, just like in the old days when he tried to hide emotion. He looked like he was going to speak, but instead he brought his thumb and forefinger together under his nose and separating them, traced a circle around his mouth, removing the crumbs like I had seen him do a thousand times. Inhaling slowly, he took both of my hands in his. The silence that ensued was becoming the answer to some awful question.

"I lost her, Marni."

"I did everything I could to keep her safe, but I lost her. Hugo was a son of a bitch. I had to choose which of the two boats I would try to save, something that could only be done by confronting the storm head-on out at sea. If I'd chosen *Sondra*, an engineer would have been required and asking this of anyone simply wasn't an option. In the hours leading up to the arrival of Hugo, I gave *Sondra* the best chance I could by anchoring her as far away from shore as possible. Deep down, I knew she wouldn't make it." Tears were rolling down my cheeks and I could tell he was barely holding his back. "You can't imagine what that hurricane was like. There were gusts with vortices like tornados and the winds got up to 140. I saw 22-foot wave sets and storm surges too. Maybe you saw it on TV, but you can't imagine…" He shot back his rum and looked down at our coupled hand. "*Sondra* didn't stand a chance, Marni. The waves lifted her up and pitched her against the shoreline rocks."

I had left David in charge of our girl but he had had no choice but to give her up, a sacrificial boat offered to the wrath of the hurricane.

"And the wreck?" I spoke through my pain.

"Token fragments on the bottom. Splinters."

Sondra was dead.

Compulsively, desperately, we filled the emptiness of loss with more drinks and all the stories of our bygone life aboard that faithful and beautiful ship. Through laughter and more tears, we agreed that the year we spent in Mahone Bay was one of the best of our lives. The Bay of Fundy still topped all adventures to date, and The Bum's Cruise had set the standard for fun.

After finishing our pub-crawl, David thought it would be a good idea to have a special dinner. Over limy ceviche, he told me he had just broken up with a feisty Puerto Rican girl, that he loved his life in the Virgin Islands and enjoyed his work as a tugboat captain. I studied his face as he talked. Could a man have changed more? His cropped hair was still strawberry blond, but would seem correct on any man of his age and lifestyle. That his beard had greyed in fifteen years was no surprise, but I couldn't stop thinking how unremarkable that icon had become. It was little more than a five o'clock shadow, synonymous with any sailor in this port. His wiry frame had filled out, and I realized I'd never seen him so relaxed. Crazy David had become a regular Dave, but the stories we shared closed the gap that time had spread between us. The man I had loved, lost and left, was resurfacing—interesting, lively, confident and attentive. Over dessert with coffee and Drambuie, he began to reveal his feelings about our love, how he felt when I used my Variety Club card, why he let me continue, why he couldn't be the lover I needed. I'd never heard these things from David and had no idea he'd cared so deeply for me. I had come to him looking for catharsis and discovered that he needed closure too. I heard the truth from David, but through the haze of emotion and drink, sadly I forgot it. The heartfelt feelings escaped into the moment. Maybe ultimately it wasn't for me to hear, only for him to say.

After dinner, we went to his modest apartment. The first

thing I noticed was the absence of music—no guitar, no B3. He said he had not played music since I left and that all the instruments were lost with *Sondra*. I thought of those beautiful blue drums, the Leslie's whirling mechanism and the delicate glass valves of the organ. All hands had gone down with the ship.

Sitting on the edge of the bed, I pulled an airplane napkin from my pocket: I had written a poem for him.

UNFINISHED / 5,475 Days

Losing my taste for life,
frantically searching through flesh
of mangoes for tangy mist
of memories.

Patents of the Caribbean.

Five years ago you were murdered
I heard yesterday, that you were alive-
my mourning spent
docu-poetry inaccurate
all energy to communicate
spiritually wasted.

Comical.

I fled you young
in your wake of plans to smuggle drugs,
to convert our converted chaser
into a diesel powered put-on.

You didn't do that either.

A watch would break
before I could rewind fifteen years
and it would be expensive to lift
my face, once more for the sun, and you.
But I will.

Man never thinks new thoughts
day to day, you said,
only reliving the old.

I want to come home.

He took me in his arms and began to make love to me.
He kissed my lips and my neck sweetly as he slowly removed
my sundress. Studying my body as if for the first time, his hands
explored my breasts, putting my nipples into his mouth.
Removing my panties inch by inch, he spread my legs and began
teasing with his fingers and then his tongue. Not a word was
exchanged, only the sounds of my wonder and my pleasure
floated in the air. He had matured, morphed into the perfect
lover. As he entered, I held him with every part of me, hands
grasping his hair, lips his mouth, legs his torso. I wept as he told
me he loved me.

The last thing I remember was both of us screaming out
in pleasure in the knowledge that we had finally shared such
intimacy. Then I blacked out. The final thrust was so deliberate,
so hard, that something deep inside me, related to my surgery,
broke open. I woke up in the recovery room at the local hospital
to David's face looking down at me with concern. Standing
behind him was a woman with a Puerto Rican hand in his. He
introduced her as his girlfriend, Mary Martha.

Four days later, I was released from the hospital. David
and his companion insisted that I stay with them and holiday for
a week before returning to Montreal. They were wonderful hosts
and I became quite fond of Mary Martha, whose feistiness and
sense of humor reminded me of Big Betty. Together, we were
one big vessel moving through the fluid of life.

Mary Martha and I

Early on the morning of my departure, David gently nudged me out of sleep, sat on the edge of the dimly-lit bed and presented me with the last cup of coffee we would share. For the first time, I spoke of my tormented feelings of loss brought on by the false news of his death. And that the only reason I had left him was because I feared my fate would be the same. I wanted him to know I had not stopped loving him, and that I knew we could not go back. We clinked our mugs in a toast to our great adventure, and to *Sondra*. Although we had lost her forever, because of her, we had both found ourselves.

The *Sondra II* – aka Fort Pit, aka ML Q119 of HMCS
1943 – 1989

"You can shed tears that she is gone, or you can
smile because she has lived. You can close your eyes and
pray that she'll come back, or you can open your eyes and
see all she's left. Your heart can be empty because you can't
see her, or you can be full of the love you shared. You can
turn your back on tomorrow and live yesterday, or you can
be happy for tomorrow because of yesterday. You can
remember her only that she is gone, or you can cherish her
memory and let it live on. You can cry and close your mind,
be empty and turn your back. Or you can do what she'd
want: smile, open your eyes, love and go on."

-DAVID HARKINS

ABOUT THE AUTHOR

Marni Craig enjoying life in the mountains of Panama.

MAR / / 2019

WITHDRAWN
Riverhead Free Library
330 Court Street
Riverhead NY 11901

34866498R00157

Made in the USA
Middletown, DE
30 January 2019